DAVID: RISE
A Novel

Mark Buchanan

Book One

The David Trilogy

David: Rise
Book One of The David Trilogy
published by Mark Buchanan, Inc.

All direct Scripture quotations are from the New International Version (Zondervan).

For Information
Mark Buchanan, Inc.
mb@markbuchanan.net

The Library and Archives Canada / Government of Canada
ISBN/ISMN Published Heritage Branch
has catalogued the hardcopy edition of this novel as:

Title: David: Rise
Format: Book
Publisher: M.A. Buchanan Inc.
ISBN: 978-1-7771278-0-0

I dedicate this book
to Nicola
beloved daughter
pixie child
lover of furry things
fixer of mouths
she of quick wit
quirky humor
tender heart

Other Books by Mark Buchanan

Your God is Too Safe

Things Unseen

The Holy Wild

The Rest of God

Hidden in Plain Sight

Spiritual Rhythm

The Four Best Places to Live

Your Church is Too Safe

God Speed

5

Foreword

A novel from one of my favourite authors bringing to life my favourite historical person – David, Israel's ancient singer of songs. Highly recommended!

I love the way works of historical fiction breathe life into people dead and gone. The person may be departed, but often their influence and imprint on our world is not gone. And none more so than David. David's songs are everywhere. Virtually the entire world quotes the 23rd Psalm, words that bring comfort in our darkest valleys. I myself have been making up new tunes to the songs of David for the past 30 years, from "I Lift My Eyes Up" (Psalm 121) in my 20's, to "How Long (Psalm 13)" in my 30's, to the more recent "You Comfort Me" with The SHIYR Poets. David is my favourite songwriter of all time and the human who is the top of *my name a person from any era you would most like to spend a day with list*.

And speaking of lists, Mark Buchanan's books often top my *I need to let all my friends know about this book list*. He's one of my favourite authors. *The Rest of God* is one of the most important books I've ever read. I love the way the way he puts words together that move me sentence by sentence.

I was so excited when I heard that Mark was releasing a novel (finally!), and a novel on the life of David no less! Even though I know the David story from scripture (at least I thought so) I couldn't stop turning these pages—I wanted to know what was going to happen next, and how the characters around David would respond to this passionate and surprising lover of life and God.

A beautiful book packed with insight, humanity and, of course, whispers of divinity. I couldn't recommend a novel more than this. Read it and find a way to sing along with the beloved singer of songs.

Brian Doerksen
Songwriter, Musician, Author

A Personal Note from the Author

I fell in love with David's story, if not always with the man himself, when I first read the Bible at age 21. Since then, I have gone back to his story many times to find my bearings, to figure out both how to live and how not to live, to the point where David's story sometimes feels like a part of my own. Years later, I began to immerse myself in the extensive secondary literature on David and his times (a bibliography of works is included at the back of the book). These secondary sources confirmed, clarified, amplified, and sometimes corrected my growing sense that David represents an historical and literary figure of immense complexity and vitality whose life repays careful study and reflection regardless of one's own personal beliefs.

In 2009, sitting on a sandstone beach on a small island near Victoria, BC, the beginning of this work came to me, unbidden. It came in the form of an almost auditory experience: I "heard" Michal, David's first and later estranged wife, as an old woman thinking back on her life with David. She spoke with bitter, rueful incisiveness. On the spot, I wrote down what I heard.

The novel took another 10 years to complete, with many rabbit trails, false starts, dead ends. In 2018, I decided to break the story into three parts and publish it as a trilogy, beginning with this present book, *David: Rise*, which traces the story from David's "birth narrative" in the story of Ruth to David's coronation in Hebron as king of Judah. In the forthcoming Book II, *David: Reign*, I will trace the story over the seven years of civil war between the House of Judah and the House of Israel through to David's ascension to the throne over Israel at age 37, his establishing of a new capital called Jerusalem, and his expanding and consolidating his rule over Israel. The trilogy will conclude with Book III, *David: Descend*, which will cover the final two decades or so of David's life, beginning with his encounter with Bathsheba and ending with his death. Book II is slated for release in 2021 and Book III in 2022.

This trilogy is a work of fiction. Though I have made every effort to be faithful to the David story as it comes to us in Scripture, particularly in 1 and 2 Samuel, and have drawn widely on academic, popular, and artistic depictions and interpretations of David and his times to ensure biographical and historical accuracy, I have also taken many liberties. The biblical account of David is silent or sparse on many details of character, setting, and chronology, and our historical and archeological knowledge about the man and his times is partial and oftentimes tentative, and so my depictions of any given character – his or her physical appearance, emotional states, deep motivations, inner and often outer dialogue – or any given event – its timing, setting, dynamics - is oftentimes imagined. In some instances, I have wholly invented characters and scenes, though always attempting to be true to the story's cultural, biblical, and narrative context.

One hope I have in publishing this novel, and the two novels that will follow it, is that you, the reader, will go back and read the original story of David.

A Note about Timeline and Narrative Structure

David lived and ruled sometime in the 10th Century BC, during the early part of the Near East's Iron Age; exact historical dates are unknown but are largely determined using King Ahab's participation in the battle of Qarqar in 853 BC as a baseline, and counting back from there to David's reign. Still, much guesswork is involved.

The Bible provides a few internal chronological markers of events in David's life - he was crowned king of Judah at 30, made king of Israel at 37, and died at 70 (2 Samuel 5:4-5). Around these internal markers we can reconstruct his age at various junctures. For instance, he likely was anointed by the prophet Samuel around age 16, killed Goliath around age 17, and married his first wife Michal around age 18. His exile at the hands of King Saul lasted for upwards of 12 years. But all of this is speculative and much debated.

I have arbitrarily chosen 1025 BC as the year of David's anointing by Samuel, 1011 BC as the year of his ascension as king over Judah, and 972 BC as the year of David's death. With dates Before Christ, or B.C. (more typically called now Before the Common Era, or B.C.E.) we count down rather than up.

In the novel's narrative arc, I have broken up this timeline. I tell the main story of David's rise to power, beginning in 1025 BC, in straight chronological order, with occasional flashbacks. But along the way, I insert first-person reminiscences dating from 972 BC, the year of David's death (in Book 1, these reminiscences are from David, from his first wife and Saul's daughter Michal, from his henchman and nephew Joab, and from his personal priest Abiathar; in later volumes, more voices will be added). These two timelines are intended to evoke the varied and conflicting portraits of David that are detectable, if not always readily apparent, in the source material.

Both narrative arcs—the chronological one, the first-person reminiscences—are rendered in present tense, in an attempt to create a cinematic feel, a sense of events happening in real time.

Timeline of Events

1140 BC	Story of Ruth (Great Grandmother)
1125 BC	Birth of Obed (Grandfather)
1100 BC	Birth of Samuel
1090 BC	Birth of Jesse (Father)
1070 BC	Philistines Take the Ark
1041 BC	Birth of David
1043 BC	Saul becomes King
1025 BC	Anointing of David
1024 BC	Exile begins
1011 BC	Death of Saul
1011 BC	David made King of Judah
1004 BC	David made King of Israel
1000 BC	Ark brought to Jerusalem
993 BC	David and Bathsheba
990 BC	Absalom kills Amnom
979 BC	David Forces a Census
976 BC	David Flees Jerusalem
972 BC	Death of David

Saul's Family Tree

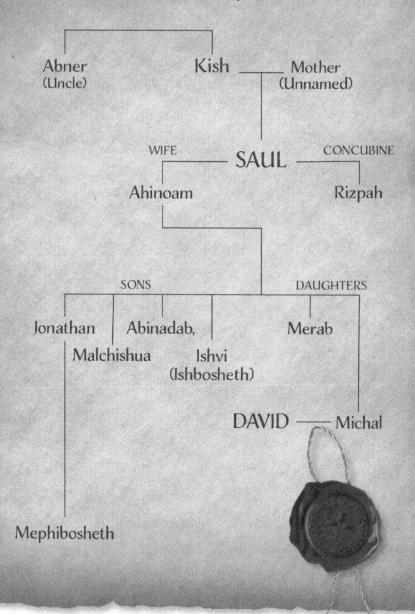

David's Family Tree

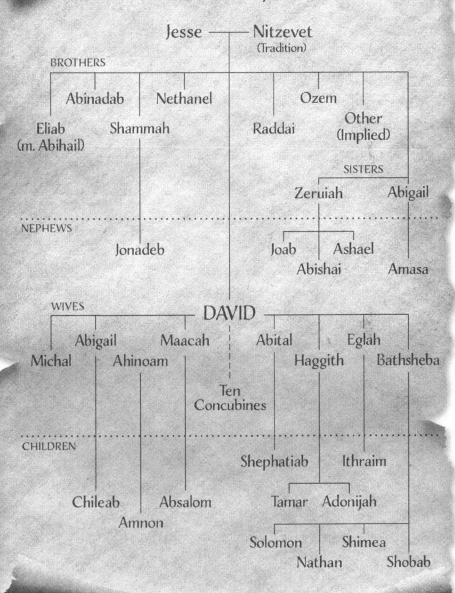

Cast of Characters (Alphabetically)

Abiathar: Priest of David,
descendent of the doomed house of Eli

Abigail: Sister of David, mother of Amasa

Abigail: Third wife of David (formerly wife of Nabal),
mother of Kileab

Abner: Saul's uncle and general

Absalom: Son of David and Maacah

Achish: King of Philistia

Ahijah: Priest of Saul,
descendent of the doomed priestly line of Eli

Ahimelech: Chief priest of the house of Nob

Ahinoam: Mother of Saul (Wife of Kish)

Ahitophel: David's royal advisor, uncle of Bathsheba (tradition)

Amasa: David's short-lived general (David's nephew)

Amnon: Son of David and Ahinoam

Chemosh: Moabite's chief god (also called Moloch)

Dagon: Philistine god

David: King of Judah and Israel

Doeg: Chief shepherd of Saul who massacred
the priests of Nob

Elhanan: Saul's errand boy (son of Jaare-oregim)

Eli: Priest of the house of Shiloh, mentor of Samuel

Eliab: Oldest brother of David (married to Abihail)

Goliath: Philistine giant killed by David

Ishbi-benob: Goliath's nephew (tradition)

Ishvi:	Son of Saul, king of Israel for two years, also referred to as Ishbosheth.
Jesse:	Father of David
Joab:	David's general (David's nephew)
Jonathan:	First son of Saul, father of Mephibosheth
Josheb-Basshebeth:	David's armor-bearer
Merab:	Daughter of Saul
Mesha:	King of Moab
Michal:	First wife of David, Daughter of Saul
Nabal:	Judean farmer, husband of Abigail, later David's third wife
Naomi & Elimelech:	David's great, great grandparents
Nasib:	Philistine commander of archers
Nitzevet:	Mother of David (by tradition)
Ozem:	Sixth brother of David
Raddai:	Fifth brother of David
Ruth & Boaz:	David's great-grandparents
Samuel:	Prophet, judge, king-maker and breaker
Shammah:	Third brother of David and father of Jonadeb
Shimei:	Loyal follower of Saul and later enemy of David
Solomon:	Son of David and Bathsheba
Tamar:	Daughter of David and Maacah
Uriah:	Loyal soldiers of David's, husband of Bathsheba
Witch of En'dor:	Ghostwife consulted by Saul
Zeruiah:	Sister of David, mother of Joab, Abishai & Ashael

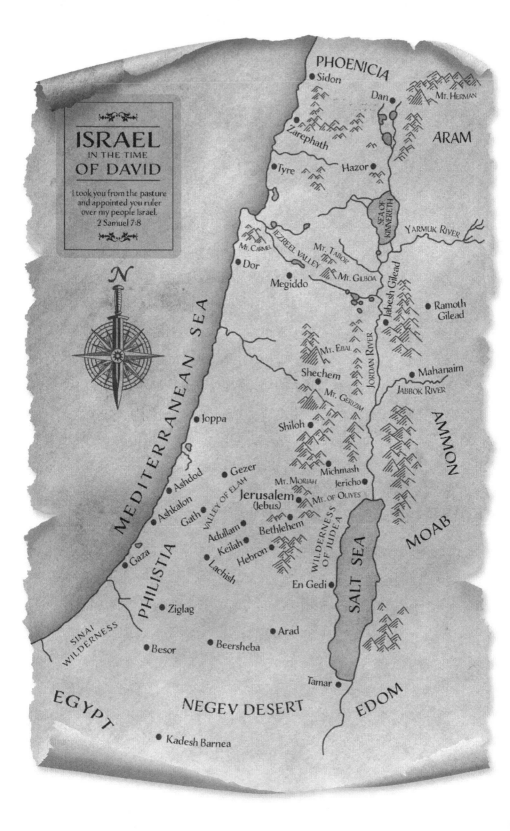

ISRAEL
IN THE TIME
OF DAVID

I took you from the pasture
and appointed you ruler
over my people Israel.
2 Samuel 7:8

PHOENICIA

Sidon

Dan

Mt. Herman

Zarephath

ARAM

Tyre

Hazor

SEA OF KINNERETH

YARMUK RIVER

Mt. Carmel

JEZREEL VALLEY

Mt. Tabor

Dor

Mt. Gilboa

Jabesh Gilead

Megiddo

Ramoth Gilead

JORDAN RIVER

Mt. Ebal

Shechem

Mahanaim

Mt. Gerizim

JABBOK RIVER

AMMON

Shiloh

N

MEDITERRANEAN SEA

Joppa

Michmash

Jericho

Gezer

Mt. Moriah

Jerusalem
(Jebus)

Mt. of Olives

Ashdod

Valley of Elah

MOAB

Ashkelon

Gath

Adullam

Bethlehem

WILDERNESS OF JUDEA

Keilah

Hebron

SALT SEA

Gaza

Lachish

PHILISTIA

En Gedi

Ziglag

SINAI WILDERNESS

Arad

Besor

Beersheba

Tamar

EGYPT

NEGEV DESERT

EDOM

Kadesh Barnea

Glossary of Hebrew Words

Baal: lord

Balagan: chaos

Belial: worthless person; devil

Dybbuk: evil spirit; demon

Elohim: God; gods

Golem: incomplete creation; monster

Hesed: loving-kindness; covenant faithfulness

Meshuga: madman

Mizpah: tower; memorial pillar; a place name

Nabal: fool

Nagid: prince

Nephesh: life; soul

Nephilim: race of giants

Ruach: wind, breath, spirit

Se'er: prophet

Sheol: realm of the shades

Yahweh: The Lord God

Yahweh tardema: deep sleep induced by Yahweh

1023 BC

Fire

Smoke rises in a wide column on the far ridge. Its crown boils white. Its belly churns red. The sun turns blood, the sky black.

Flames scramble up tree boughs, swoop limb to limb. They twist along the treeline. Each tree flares like an angry man in one last doomed act of defiance. David can hear, across the valley, sap whistle, wood pop. He can feel, even from the distance, the heat.

The fire crests the hill, then races downward. Birds burst and rise from grasslands, the rush of their wings like a volley of arrows. Animals in wild panic scatter, the crash of their hooves like many rocks hitting earth.

When he was a boy, he saw a fire like this rage down a hillside, rushing toward him. He was grazing his father's sheep. There was no way to outrun it. So he led his sheep into deep waters. Fire blazed on all sides. The sheep thrashed, they bawled. Several tried to bolt. He had to throw them back in the water, pull them into its saving coolness. The heat was terrible. Afterward, his arms and face swelled with boils, and for many nights his sleeping was torment. Weeks later he was still cracked husks, clipping singed wool from the ends of sheep's coats.

But he saved them all.

It taught him always to know where to find water.

And it taught him to read fires. To think like fire. A fire in wilderness comes blinding fast. But it has a pattern, a way of moving. It is shaped by wind and land and whatever feeds its burning—wood, straw, bramble. A fire in a forest on a hilltop is clumsy, lurching about, whereas a fire in a grassland in a valley is agile and fleet. Some fires linger, take their time, savor destruction. They devour everything with slow, cruel thoroughness. Some rush and scatter, capricious as Ammorite raiders in a drunken spree, lusty, then hungry.

This fire has run out of trees to burn. It will soon run out of grass to consume. It will pour down a gulch of dry sage, burn each bush like a wild beast tearing prey. But the dirt and rock of the gulch will slow it, make it lurch. The wind that has been pushing it will falter among the gulch's bends and turns.

This fire will burn itself out before it reaches him.

So he just watches, watches it burn, watches it spend itself, watches until its last black curls of smoke scrawl a cryptic warning across the horizon.

Tonight, he is safe.

But breathing is like swallowing thorns.

972 BC[*]

Plotting
DAVID

I can hear them talking. Whispering. Murmuring. Arguing. Plotting. They think I can't hear, that my ruined body renders me deaf. That because my flesh is crumpled, my ears have stopped. But it's the opposite. Take something away from a man and all you do is sharpen another part of him. Take his sword, harden his fists. Take his wife, deepen his fidelity. Take his honor, toughen his resolve. Take his freedom, awaken his desperation. Take his might, sharpen his seeing.

And his hearing.

I hear everything: the schemes, the wiles, the judgments, the accusations. Their voices swarming, like locusts. I never did this. I always did that. I was too much here. I was too little there. If we do this and that, he must do thus and such. On and on it goes, day and night.

No one fears me anymore. Many years ago now, maybe twenty, twenty-five, I saw this for the first time, what it was not to be feared anymore. When men lost their alertness and wariness around me.

I was fighting a giant. Not Goliath. His young nephew, Ishbi-benob. Small for a giant. And not the braggart his uncle was, or slow like him. Hard, fast, efficient. We stood face to face on a battlefield. I was already winded,

*Author's Note: I have inserted first-person reminiscences dating from 972 BC, the year of David's death to reflect the varied and conflicting portraits of David that are detectable in the source material.

aching in limb, insides burning. He was just warming up. He circled me like a wolf does when it's run its prey to ground, and now is just enjoying itself, savoring the kill before going in for the kill.

I fell to my knees, dropped my arms, closed my eyes. I confess, not even a prayer was on my lips. I almost welcomed his sword. But nothing happened. And when I opened my eyes again, there was my own nephew, Abishai, panting hard, fresh blood on his hands. Ishbi-benob was sprawled at his feet, his large limbs shaking in death throes.

My men that day ordered me off the battlefield. Like I was an errand boy, there only to bring cheese, fetch water. Of course, they didn't use that kind of tone. They said it with a great display of deference, reverence, flattery—I was too important, my life too precious, I was the light of Israel, and so forth. But I knew: I had become a liability. I was putting myself and everyone else at risk. In truth, I was glad to stop. I had enough blood on my hands.

And I was always thirsty.

No, no one fears me anymore. But this is not my greatest loss. My greatest loss is no one loves me anymore. Not any of my sons. Not any of my daughters. Not any of my wives. Not any of my brothers, or nephews, or nieces. Not any of my mighty men, or priests, or advisers. Not anyone.

And I am so cold.

Jonathan, you loved me. You loved me in ways that only later did I understand, long after you were gone. At the time, I was too young, too desperate, too afraid to understand. Now, I am surrounded always by these people, and yet always alone. You were the brother I never had, though I had seven. You were the father I never had, though I had my own father, Jesse. And I had your father too.

We both had Saul.

I wish I could get him out of me, your father. After all those years fleeing him, he caught me anyhow. I wish you were here to help me with that. To help me once more find my strength in God. To sit with me here in this dying light and sing the songs we used to sing.

972 BC
Small
MICHAL

All anyone wants to hear about is the giant. For those who never knew the man, only his legend, it's all they ever ask. Did he do this? Did he say that? Was he afraid?

Was he beautiful?

Do they not tire of hearing the same thing over and over, again and again, like a dog fetching a stick? Do they think his life narrows down to this one thing, sums up in this single moment? Do they think running toward danger explains him?

Clearly, they never knew him.

So I will tell. I will tell about his smallness. He was not like my father at all. A full head shorter, in fact. When the two walked together, he was no more than my father's shadow, my father's echo, my father's afterthought. My father's diminution. They think, because of the stories, that he was kind and generous and good. But I will tell about his spite, his hardness, his malice.

They think he was big. But he was small.

And he ran from things. Yes, sometimes, he ran to things. But what I know, what I saw, is him running away. From places, from trouble, from danger. From me.

But I will throw them this stick: he was magnificent that day with the giant. I grant him that much. I know it even though I was not there. But there was a time I too could not get my fill of the story, when I too wanted to hear it over and over, again and again. There was a day it explained for me everything about him. I could hear it a hundred times, a thousand, and ache to hear it again.

The stories, of course, they take things out, add things in. He was more afraid than they say. His hands shook when he gathered stones. Joab told me as much. And the words he said to the giant and the words the giant said to him, those were not quite what got written down. And his brothers, I am not sure they hated him. Perhaps they feared for him. Brothers have a way of hiding their true feelings.

And Father, my father, he knew who he was. He knew full well. But he had his reasons for acting otherwise, as you will see in due time.

David loved my father back then. He loved him as a father. And my father loved him as a son, back then. But do not think he is innocent, David, despite what the stories tell you. Do not think he did not conspire to sit where my father once sat, to sit where my brother Jonathan should now sit. Do not think him blameless.

Do not think he is without blood on his hands.

I see him every day now through my window. I've seen him through windows my whole life. He is not the man I first saw, a lifetime ago, fleet and wild and boyish, bright laughter filling his mouth. And he is not the man I saw years back, beautiful and haunted, a desperate fugitive whose dark eyes fell away from me into a long night. And he is not the man I saw, from this very window, years later, when his aging, thickening body glazed up with sweat and he danced the Ark into the city, flailing and reeling like the town drunk.

No, the man I look down on from my window is old and broken and slow. And when up close, a ruin: withering, crumbling. And when near enough to strike, or whisper, or kiss, a devastation of bone and flesh. He walks as though testing the ground, afraid it might give way, might open into bottomless emptiness.

Oh, it pleases me to see him so.

His oldness, I know, only mirrors my own. Every bony dried up part of him, all his tottering paleness—it is echoed in my own flesh, my own bones. We share decrepitude. It is all we share.

His mind is still sharp. I can see that. He is stealthy as a predator. He is wary as prey.

His eyes still pierce. He looks at things far away. Maybe he sees nothing, just vast blankness. Maybe he sees the face of some memory taunting him, the tail of some desire escaping him. Or maybe he sees everything. That was always the thing with him: you never knew what he knew. He saw things no one else did, or could. I will let you decide if this was his strength or his undoing.

His voice, that is still strong.

But he never speaks to me, hasn't in years. A terrible hateful silence has stood between us for decades, though now it is worn almost to nothing. Still, not a word in my direction. Sometimes he seems to smile at me without looking at me. An almost invisible thread pulls taut his wilted skin. Some days the shadow that passes between us is almost affection. But he will not speak to me, nor I to him.

Every day I bear my barrenness. The sorrow of that has not gone away in all this time. Maybe it has grown. Now I must carry it to the grave. And lay it down there. That is my hope, my last and worst consolation.

But even now, too late to cure a thing, and I am a fool for even thinking it, if he called, I would come. I would put my withered body beside his withered body and remember when we were other than this, completely other. He, sleek and swift, quick to laugh or cry, breathtaking. *O Breathtaking*. His muscles were not like most men's, fists roiling in a sack of rough leather; they were open hands moving slow, slow beneath fine silk. I have not forgotten what I felt then. I think one touch from his hand, papery as it now must be, would wake me.

You should have seen me when I was a girl. I too was not hard to look at. Not hard to be with. If we had met then, and then you saw me now, you would stand astonished at what the years can do, the way they bend you, shrink you, hollow you. The dry gourd that life can make of once ripe fruit. Now I avoid mirrors worse than prophets. Both of them, mirrors and prophets, tell you stark and terrible truths about yourself. Prophets tell you, I suppose, with fierce heartbreak, so that it might be otherwise, hard as that may come. But mirrors tell you with cruel indifference, though it can't be otherwise, hard as you may try.

My mirror shows blades that once were curves, jugs that once were breasts. It shows a desert of flesh that was once a well-ordered garden. Hips pointy as harrows. Face ridged and gouged like the landscapes he used to haunt. Everything grey. No ointment can rub this away, no paste can mask it.

But you should have seen me then, when I wore beauty like a crown of field flowers.

My mirror reveals one more thing: I am my father's daughter. When I look into my own eyes, it is my father who looks back at me. His anger. His sadness.

His pride.

His bitterness.

Yes, I am bitter. I won't hide it. The past invades me. It owns me. I cannot tell whether remembering everything, going over and over it again and again, is refuge from my bitterness, or the ground it breeds in.

Maybe both.

There is a dark savoriness to bitterness. A sour pleasantness. It is like the taste of your own blood.

But I will have to take you back there to make you understand.

972 BC
Father
ABIATHAR

He was a father to me, even when he was barely older than me. The night Saul killed my own father, my mother, my brothers, my sisters, my uncles and aunts and nephews and nieces, was the night he held me. He held me in a way my own father never had, nor even my mother. It was the way a shepherd holds a wounded lamb fetched back from a burning wilderness.

He sang over me.

His voice was the voice of God. That sweet, that warm. He sung to music I could not hear. It seemed to come from deep within him, or maybe from far outside him. Both, I think. Our elders say that God sang sky and water and ground and beast into life. And then he made, with his own hands, a man, perfect, flawless, without blemish, within or without. But not alive. So God sang *himself* into that man. Only then did the man's eyes open. Only then did he wake and breathe. Only then did he come to life. When I was a child, I pictured this. I lay on my bed at night and imagined God singing over me, his *ruach* streaming into my mouth, my nostrils, my body. God's breath jolting me to life.

King David did this for me on the night Saul killed my family and burned my town. It was long before anyone called David king. He was no more than I was then, than any of us were, mere boys running from trouble, filled with rage, empty from heartache. Always and forever after, I loved him. I trusted him. I wanted only to serve him.

I have seen him in all seasons. Laughing. Weeping. Dancing. Rejoicing in the birth of sons. Grieving the death of sons. Vigorous and weary. Worshiping, making war, giving mercy, receiving mercy, withholding mercy. Holding pleading hands out to God. Shaking angry fists at God. Hungry. Sated. Wise. Confused. Tender. Brutal. I have seen all, and not once doubted his heart.

Some will tell you he is a cruel man. That he is a hard man. That he reaps what he has not sown. That his god is his own glory. But they are wrong. They do not know him. They are people who wanted something from him and never got it, and ever after held their grudges, sought their vengeance, waited to settle their scores.

The man I knew gave. His giving was like oil poured down on my head until my cup overflowed. He gave me all this—a home, a place, a people, a work. But mostly, he gave me himself. I lay in his arms that first night, before he was king, or *nagid*, or anything, when he was only a frightened man—a boy, really—running from trouble, filled with rage, empty from heartache. And he sang. I drank and drank the shalom of God. Even as his voice lulled me into sleep, it woke me. Even as I walked in the shadow of death, I came to life.

I wish you could hear him sing.

972 BC
Thankless
JOAB

Not all stories end well. I know. I lived long enough. I seen a lot. A lot. I seen beautiful women go ugly. I seen brave men turn coward. There was once a woman, men fought over her, fought like stray dogs. Well, she turned into an old hag. And a nag. Ha, God, could she nag. A real horsefly. First I envied the man who won her; later I pitied him. I seen a man who killed dozens of Philistines, with bare hands. It was like he was killing chickens. Snap, snap, snap. And then something went wrong in him, I don't know what, these things happen, right? Snap. And he started jumping, jumping at his own shadow, see? A loud noise, boom, and he leapt like a cricket. Ha.

No, I seen a lot. So trust me, I know this—nothing lasts.

It's better if you die young. Ha, too bad for me. Look at me. I can barely hold this cup.

Okay, I killed lots of men. That's true. Lots. And one woman. But she had it coming more than any man. So what? We all have blood on our hands. It's just some people—the powerful ones, you know?—they use other people's hands.

When you first spill blood, it shocks you. It's like your mother spilling kettle water on you. You jump back. You howl. You have to teach yourself to hold still. Nobody teaches this to you. You learn it by doing. When I see a man driving a knife between the fifth rib of another man, driving it hard and holding it there, holding it like he's doing no more than steadying a fence post, I know that man's been doing more than just herding sheep. He's killed lots before. Lots.

That was me. Maybe it's hard to believe now—look at me. Look at me try to hold this damn cup. But it was me. Steady. Hard. Never blink.

He thinks I kill 'cause I like to. That's David I'm talking about. He blames me for all the deaths. Abner, Amasa, Absalom, all of them. He probably blames me for Uriah, now he's had time to think it over. But let me tell you, every one of those deaths helped him. Put him where he is, crown, throne, wealth, all. He knows it too. He just can't ever say it. Might tarnish up his hero image, see? But he used my hands for the blood that's all over his.

Sometimes I envy them all, all the dead. Abner, Amasa, Absalom, Uriah. They all died young, or young enough. Abner, he was getting up there. But take Absalom. He was pretty as a show bird. Women went funny around him. Men too. They turned to jabbering fools. He could just smile and wink, and otherwise shrewd people went stupid. I took that boy at his prime, before he had a wrinkle, a grey hair, a bald spot.

Absalom should thank me.

His father should thank me.

Ha. I'm used to doing other people's dirty work and no one thanking me.

And now my grey head will go down bloody to the grave. He'll see to that, David will, and his pup of a son, Solomon. I told you already, he has blood on his hands, all over them. But it's always by—what's the word? Proxy?

It's funny, how nobody knew David for so long. He was a nobody. An errand boy. Now, everybody knows him. I mean, they know who he is. No one really knows him, not deep down. But he got bloody famous. It wasn't like that in the beginning. In the early days, nobody knew him, nobody noticed him. And then, when they did, when he did something brave or important or such—kill a giant, marry a king's daughter, whatever—everyone asked the same thing: "Who is he? Where did he come from? Whose son is that?"

1140 BC

Her Son
RUTH

Naomi watches Elimelech. His back is to her, but she can read him clear as if he's leaning his face into hers. He is distraught. She looks past him, to see what he sees. A vastness of scorched earth. A wasteland of dust. A valley of dry bones. The ground stripped to stones, its only crop thorns.

Far off, high up, vultures turn, and one by one descend, like cold ash falling.

Elimelech turns and walks toward Naomi. His face is blank. He once had a good heft on him, a tidy paunch like a sack of meal tucked under his shirt. He once had a pink roundness to his face. His arms were meaty, and with minimal exertion they lathered up in oily sweat. Now he is all bones. Wattles of loose flesh hang from him. His sweat turns chalky on his skin. His walk, once a stride, a confident bounding, is now a shuffle, a hobble.

And what about her? She was once the prize of Bethlehem, a rare and striking beauty. Many men came, shy or bold, to plead with her father for her hand, each offering a lavish dowry they could ill afford. But her father gave her to Elimelech, ten years her senior, but hearty enough, and wealthy, at least by village standards. A hard worker, well-established. A proven risk. Elimelech seemed astonished with his good fortune, jovial and voluble in a way she'd never seen before, and never since. But he's good and kind, and has provided well.

Until now.

Elimelech can't look her in the eyes. He looks at her chin, at her ear, at her shoulder.

"We must leave," he says.

"But this is our home."

"Our home? Ha. Such a home. It will kill us. It is spewing us out, Naomi. We are not welcome here. The earth rids itself of us."

"Where will we go?"

"Moab."

She recoils at the word, as if he has spat on her. She spits herself, on the ground by his feet.

"Those godless people, no. No and no. They eat their babies."

"That is rumor only."

"No. It is a truth. They make fires to devour them. Their gods are demons."

"What else can we do? Where else can we go? Moab has rain. Things grow there. A seed is more than a stone. A tree is more than firewood."

"Yes, a tree is also wood for an idol. Or firewood for Moloch. And what will become of our sons there?"

"Better to ask, what will become of our sons *here*?"

As though summoned by the mention of them, Mahlon and Kilion emerge over the hill. They are both in their late teens, handsome, with a quickness about them. Though thin with youth and hunger, both have, especially Kilion, a thickness of bone. Naomi smiles to see them, and Elimelech extends his arms like he is welcoming them home from the far country, not just the next village. They smile back and produce what they went for—a small sack of barley grain, ready for grinding, a thin slab of goat cheese.

At the meal, Naomi breaks the news.

"Your father has decided we are moving."

The boys wait.

"To Moab."

The announcement seems not to register, or maybe not to matter. Kilion reaches for the last piece of cheese, and without asking if anyone else wants it, swallows it whole.

* * *

Three weeks after arriving in Moab, Elimelech acquires a thin dry cough. It sounds like the noise a brick layer makes scraping his trowel. Even though they have food now, even meat, he eats little and has yet to regain weight. He sleeps later and later and grows weary quickly. He loses his balance and walks into things, and forgets easily, and grows irritable. He complains of a terrible pain in his stomach. One day, coming in from the fields where he and his sons have hired themselves out, he falls down and can't pick himself back up. His sons pull him to his feet, prop him on their shoulders, drag him home.

Naomi knows he is dying. She admits this to herself but doesn't speak it aloud. Mahlon and Kilion seem not to have noticed. They simply eat the food she prepares for them, and then their father's food when he doesn't touch it. Both boys are gaining strength. Kilion is growing fat.

Elimelech is withering.

One day he doesn't wake. She can feel his body beside her, that the weight in the bed is different, and she knows without looking that he's gone. She gets up and carries him to the table. He is that light. The boys have already gone to the fields. She strips and washes her husband's body and wraps it in clean linen.

They will bury him in the evening, in the back plot. They do not burn his body like the pagans do.

* * *

Mahlon announces that he is going to marry a Moabite woman. Her name is Orpah. Naomi is sick with the news, but silent. She has expected this. It is her worst fear. Soon after the marriage, Kilion announces he will marry Ruth, also a Moabite. Naomi puts on a mask of indifference and endures another Moabite wedding.

But a strange thing happens: she starts to love them, these two Moabite women. They are kind, and wise, and humble. And they revere her. They are helpful in ways she could not imagine any Israelite daughter-in-law being. They are both good cooks. The house has never been cleaner, the household better run. And they are good for her sons, who grow fatter than bulls, even Mahlon.

One day Naomi stands at the window and listens to Ruth, outside, sing a song in her own language. It is sad and beautiful. It reminds Naomi of a song her own father taught her as a young girl, a song of God's mercy and goodness, about God carrying his people on wings, then gathering them beneath the shadow of his wing. She had forgotten the song. She had forgotten the God of the song. But as she listens, the song floods back to her, and then another, and another. She remembers her father singing these songs loudly, his face shining with joy, his eyes cast upward. She sees him twirling his body in firelight, his hands reaching heavenward as though catching windfall. She thinks of their festivals. She sees her father, solemn and bright, holding aloft the shank of a lamb bone, extending it toward her: *Naomi, do you know how long God's arm is? This long! God's arm reached down from heaven and pulled us out of misery. You, Naomi. God did this for you.*

She is pierced with longing.

That night, she tells her sons and daughters-in-law about the God of her fathers. Mahlon and Kilion look impatient, embarrassed. Orpah seems curious. But Ruth seems to wake from a deep sleep. Her eyes are wide and shining. Her skin blotches at her throat. Her mouth is slightly open. Her breathing is shallow and fast.

The next morning, Ruth comes to Naomi and asks her to tell her everything, every story, every song, to leave nothing out. And as Naomi speaks, and sings, and remembers, Ruth falls under the trance of her voice, and her face opens wide.

Naomi can't fill Ruth: her thirst is bottomless.

* * *

Mahlon falls under the wheels of a cart fully loaded. He dies that night, writhing. Orpah is strangely calm. Naomi is grim. A week later, Kilion takes a small cut to his leg. He thinks nothing of it, but the next morning, it is sore and swollen and dark, and by afternoon his jaw locks tight. The next night he dies silently, his eyes wild with terror.

Naomi weeps quietly, Ruth openly. And then Ruth sings, in Hebrew, one of Naomi's songs, low and mournful. The sound sweeps through the house like a soft wind.

* * *

The two women bury both men in the Hebrew way, digging the holes themselves, taking turns. The morning after they bury Kilion, Naomi asks her daughters-in-law to gather. She tells them she is about to give them an order they must obey. Do they understand? Both women just stare at her. She proceeds, speaking alternately with great fire, a voice from the whirlwind, and heartless flatness, a voice from the grave.

"Go back, each of you, to your mother's home. May the Lord show you kindness, as you have shown kindness to your dead husbands and to me. May the Lord grant that each of you will find rest in the home of another husband."

Naomi leans forward and kisses them both goodbye. Orpah and Ruth weep. "No. We will go back with you to your people."

Naomi fixes them both with a dangerous look. Her voice is flint.

"Return home, my daughters. Why would you come with me? Am I going to have any more sons? Can I make you more husbands? Return home, my daughters. I am too old. Even if I thought there was still hope—even if I married tonight and in nine months had twin sons—would you wait? Would you remain unmarried for them? And this—would they want you, old as you would be, if you did wait? No, my daughters, go."

And then, looking down, looking away, Naomi says, "It is more bitter for me than for you. The Lord's hand is against me."

Orpah and Ruth wail for a long time. Naomi stands outside, leaves them to it. After a while Naomi feels a shadow on her shoulder. She looks up. It is Orpah. Her eyes are red. The skin around her nose is raw. Silently, she kisses Naomi and walks away.

Ruth now stands before her.

"Look," Naomi says, "your sister-in-law is going back to her people and to her gods. Go, go back with her."

Ruth flings her arms around Naomi's neck. She is taller than Naomi, and solid, with arms that can shake out a carpet like it's a bedsheet. Naomi cannot move in the strength of her embrace.

"Don't. Don't ask me this. Where you go I will go, and where you stay I will stay. Your people will be my people. Your God my God. Where you die I will die. Where you are buried, I will be buried. May the Lord deal with me, be it ever so severely, if even death separates you and me."

Naomi now finds her own tears coming. She tries to speak. She can't. She shakes her head, but weakly. She trembles inside. When she realizes Ruth will not unlock her embrace, she puts her thin arms around Ruth's ample waist, and holds on.

* * *

Bethlehem is unrecognizable from ten years before. That was a place of desolation. Wind had scoured everything to brittleness. Hunger had carved faces into gulches and ridges, like the land itself. Bethlehem was a haunt. Its land was a ruin of skeletal trees, blighted earth, drooping animals.

But now its earth is a carpet of rich hues: greens, golds, reds. When evening comes, the sky is trellised with blues, purples, pinks. The trees are jeweled with ripe fruit. The animals are sleek, their bones thick-swathed in flesh. Their eyes are great wet, luminous bulbs that hold a perfect reflection of sky and land.

But what Naomi notices first is the laughter. It wings across the air, soaring, swooping, acrobatic as flocks of swallows.

And everywhere is a whirlwind of activity. Harvesters work the edges of towering walls of grain stalks. Others move lithe and quick through orchards, popping their heads inside each tree's dense dome of leaves and emerging with baskets teeming with fruit. Still others dig up root vegetables, ringed and gnarly and huge. The air shimmers with joy. It is as if a harvest festival is already underway even before the harvest is in.

Naomi wants to rejoice but can't. Her heart is a well of poison. All the way home she dreaded arriving. All the way, she recited in her thoughts her complaints against God: his capriciousness, or indifference, or more likely, cruelty. The sheer malice with which God plotted the disaster of her life. The famine. The exile. Life among pagans. Bone-scraping poverty. Death, and death, and death. It's like God is some petty tribal ruler, aloof to the plight of the slaves under him unless he's devising some new way, more wicked than the last, to take from them what little they have. It is like he is a king gone mad. By the time the two women can see the smoke rising from village, Naomi has worked herself into a mood of dark misery.

The arrival of Naomi and Ruth causes a stir—people staring openly, whispering to one another, some shaking their heads in dismay or disbelief. She hears her name, over and over, from the lips of the women she once bantered with, traded with, gossiped with.

"Can this be Naomi?"

"So old. So grey. All her beauty, where is it now?"

"Who is the big woman with her?"

"A pagan, I hear. One of those baby-killers."

"Oh."

Naomi wants to slap them all. It rankles her terribly until at last she stops and turns to face them. A crowd has gathered behind her, staring. Their murmuring is like a swarm of gnats circling their heads. They all fall silent at the sight of Naomi glaring at them, fiery with indignation. Ruth widens her stance, protective of her mother-in-law.

"No," Naomi says to the women. "No, and no, and no. You are wrong. You are all wrong. I am not Naomi. Naomi is dead. That woman is buried back in that godless desert. My name is Mara. The Almighty has made my life very bitter. I went away full, but the Lord has brought me back empty.

No. Not Naomi. Don't call me that, ever. The Lord has afflicted me. The Almighty has brought misfortune upon me.

"And this is my daughter. Her name is Ruth. And she has more of *Yahweh* in her little finger than the whole lot of you have in your great fat carcasses combined."

A gasp of shock flushes from the women. Their faces harden with disdain.

Naomi turns and keeps walking. She can hear the murmuring resume: subdued, but steely, icy, aggrieved. She and Ruth walk to the edge of town and then up the hill to her old farm.

* * *

Naomi looks around at the place, appalled. The land lies in weedy dereliction. The fence is collapsed. The roof's thatch is threadbare. The house's adobe bricks crumble at their base and bristle all over with stubs of straw. Inside, the furniture is scattered, though mostly intact: three thin beds, their straw black with rot, a small table and narrow bench, weathered to grey, two rickety stools, a cracked water jar. There are a few pots and dishes and utensils scattered in disarray. All of it is blanketed in a thick scrim of dust.

The two women set to work. By evening, the place is livable.

But in the morning Naomi's face is pinched hard. Most of their food is gone, just a handful of dried fruit and a mouthful of salted meat left. Maybe she shouldn't have said what she said to those women; she might have to depend on their *hesed*.

Ruth sits down in front of Naomi and clasps her hands. Ruth's hands look massive holding hers, or maybe the other way: her hands in Ruth's hands look small as a child's, but old, withered, veiny. It's like Ruth holds two small shrivelled animals she found dead outside.

"Let me go to the fields and pick up the leftover grain behind anyone in whose eyes I find favor," Ruth says.

It's the only way. They can't get their fields ready by themselves, and even if they did, by the time it took to grow a crop, they'd both be dead. And they can't go begging. And the other alternative is for Ruth to… no, that's unthinkable. Naomi would rather they starve.

"Go ahead, my daughter."

My daughter. That is how Naomi sees her: flesh and blood, as though Ruth once swelled inside her own belly and then grew at her side, mimicking her, learning to speak and walk under her tutelage. Naomi realizes that she would have been more devastated if Ruth had died than either of her own sons. How can this be?

She is living her life now through Ruth. Her fate is bound with hers. It's as if she made the promise to Ruth, *Where you go I will go, and where you stay I will stay, and where you are buried I will be buried*, not the other way around. Her thoughts shadow Ruth's thoughts. In her imagination, she tries to see what Ruth sees, hear what Ruth hears, feel what Ruth feels. Go where Ruth goes.

Ruth is the one reason Naomi doesn't curse God and die.

* * *

Things go well. Ruth finds, first try, a field owned by a man named Boaz, a short man, bald and wide, in his forties. But he is kind and generous. Ruth asks if she can glean his field, and Boaz goes further: he feeds her and has his harvesters strew extra grain for her to gather, and speaks to her with tenderness, almost reverence.

When Ruth tells Naomi, her eyes grow wide with astonishment. "That man is our close relative. He is one of our kinsmen-redeemers."

"Which means…?"

"He is kin. He is obliged to us. It falls to him to make sure we have a future."

"Ah," Ruth says. "A future."

That night, Naomi sings a song from her girlhood. A song of thanks. A song of praise. Ruth listens from her bed and sings quietly along with her.

* * *

Boaz marries Ruth.

He lies with her, and her womb opens, and she gives birth to a child.

A son.

The women who once gossiped about Naomi gather around her. "Praise be to the Lord," they say, "who this day has not left you without a guardian-redeemer. May he become famous throughout Israel! He will renew your life and sustain you in your old age. For your daughter-in-law, who loves you and who is better to you than seven sons, has given him birth."

Naomi smiles. She takes the child in her arms and pulls him close.

"Naomi has a son!" one of the women shouts, and then all with her.

Yes, that's exactly how it feels: a son. *Her* son.

She names him Obed.

Obed becomes the father of Jesse.

Jesse becomes the father of David.

1025 BC

Shepherd

He stands naked before the wind. It pummels him with fists of gusting. It pulls his hair sharply back, tugs hard his flesh. It scours all that is loose in him. He opens his mouth to swallow it. It empties him and fills him. He anchors down his heels against the massive weight of the wind's wild blowing, and pushes himself into it to stay upright.

The sensation is of flying.

Many things come hard for him—speaking with his father, dealing with his brothers, watching his mother's mute anguish—but this comes easy: opening himself wide to the wind, the breath, the *ruach*. Bending himself whole to it. Letting nothing—no cloak, no shield, no armor, not even his tunic—come between him and whatever the *ruach* does in him, however the *ruach* does it.

Here he is in his element. Here all things are clear. Here all things are possible. He is truly, fully, undividedly himself.

He is David.

* * *

This is the best part of the day. The sun is down, but night still waits to spread its cloak. Darkness is only a rumor at the edge of earth. Colors drench the sky. Wind sweeps fields and drives out wilting heat. The white stones that knuckle the hillsides glow. Jasmine releases its perfume. Olive leaves, like handheld mirrors sending cryptic signals, flash silver.

And everything wakes. Birds burst with one last fanfare of song, one last flourish of flight. Insects in grass and sky whirr, and click, and thrum. Animals scuttle, groundlings slither.

The sheep rouse with fresh hunger.

And he rouses too. The languor of midday falls off him in a rush. He is quick and light, keenly watchful.

Which is good. Which is needed. Because the lion rouses too.

He loves this. This alertness in himself. His own sheer aliveness. The deep calling to deep within him, like the roar of a waterfall. The air shimmers bright, as if angels are about to sing. He steadies him, readies himself for come what may.

He rubs the pocket of his slingshot warm and soft, and then cradles in it one of the stones he'd plucked from the stream this morning. It's round and smooth and green. It will be a shame to lose it. But an instinct, sharp and urgent as a thorn, tells him he'll need it, and soon.

He's asked his father, Jesse, three times for a proper weapon. A sword or a javelin. He knows his father keeps a smithy hidden in the hills above their farm. The Philistines have banned all smithies, to keep Israel from arming herself. Farmers who need a hoe or rake or adze made or repaired must travel to Gath or Ashkelon and hire a Philistine blacksmith, who charges double, sometimes triple the price. Then the farmer is checked as he leaves Philistia, to make sure he has paid no bribe to acquire a small sword or dagger. It is one of many reasons the people hate the Philistines. And it is one of many reasons they are starting to resent their own king, Saul: his weakness has reduced them to this thrall, this humiliation, this smallness. In taverns and fields, men whisper to one another a question that has dogged the king his entire reign: "Can Saul save us?"

Jesse has taken matters into his own hands. Every week or so, he goes out at nightfall to his smithy hidden in the hills and works until daybreak. The cover of night hides the smoke trail from his furnace that vents through a crevice of rock. He blocks the cave entrance with thick bramble and foliage to deaden the ring of his hammering on the forge. He comes down in early morning with a bundle on his back wrapped in thick cloth. When he unfolds the cloth, sword blades, spear heads, spikes clank out. He's given weapons to his three oldest sons and trained their hands for war. Now he sells weapons to other farmers.

He's never given one to David.

"You are a shepherd boy. You have a slingshot. You have a knife. What more do you need?"

* * *

The sun-starched land turns blue with shadow. David rises to gather his sheep. As he steps down from his perch, he sees a deeper shadow move swift and furtive between rocks. A lone sheep is just beyond the fastness of those rocks. The sheep's neck is bent to a lush tussock of grass. It is oblivious to danger. David runs down the steep incline, zigzagging, and when he reaches the valley floor, he sprints straight.

The sheep is still grazing. The lion, he guesses, is still crouching behind the rock.

Then the lion, quick as thought, bursts its cover. David is still a hundred paces away. He cannot catch it. His sling hangs ready in his left hand. He begins the rapid switching motion in his wrist that makes the sling's long tethers loop faster and faster. It becomes a transparent whorl of air, a thin sharp whistle of sound. He moves the twirling sling above his head, and then slightly behind it. The lion is so locked in its bloodlust it doesn't hear him coming. The sheep raises its head, suddenly aware of death thundering down. It freezes.

David can see the lion slowing, coiling on its haunches, preparing to lunge. He picks a spot where he reckons it will be in the next few seconds, stretches his right hand to steady his aim, and looses the stone.

The lion crouches full on its hind quarters, and takes air.

He watches the stone pierce the dying light. It hastens like a messenger with news of war. It finds its mark, the back of the lion's skull. The beast lands hard and staggers sideways with the blow. The sheep, snapped from its stupor of terror, bolts.

The lion shakes its head, slow and heavy. It gains its footing and turns toward David. He still runs toward it. The lion stands wavering, confused. It takes a few massive leaps toward the sheep's retreat, then wheels and comes straight at David.

He tucks his sling into his pouch, and still running, unsheathes his knife. The lion regains its strength. It runs at him full-tilt, then shifts into a rearing-up motion, ready to sail at him. David has been counting on this, the animal's precision of reflexes. He runs harder. When he and the lion are almost on each other, the lion leaps. David dives under it, spins on his back. The animal's huge body eclipses the sun. Its shadow swallows him whole. As it flies over him, its taut underbelly almost grazing him, he plunges his knife in its stomach to the hilt. He holds on with both hands. He feels the massive body shudder through his blade. The lion's belly opens like tent flaps. The insides rush out hot. David rolls away just before it spills out on him.

The lion hits the ground on its shoulders, and tumbles, and sprawls. It tries to get up but can't. David walks up to it, laid out in its own lake of blood. The lion turns its head and bares its teeth. No sound comes out. Its yellow eyes grow dim. It flops its great head to earth, panting. David places his hand flat on the warm flank of its heaving chest. He holds his hand there, feels the heart of the animal slow, slow, slow. The lion closes its eyes and stops breathing.

He walks over to where he first hit it. On the ground, his green stone looks up at him like an eye. He picks it up, rolls it in blood-warm hands, and then washes both in the stream.

He gathers his sheep and heads home.

Happy to have his sheep safe. Happy to have his stone back.

* * *

Jesse is angry. Angry at him. At some task poorly performed. Some chore neglected. Something, always something. His anger is never explosive. More a low, steady seething, a frustration that tightens his voice, clips his gestures. Anger compresses the man into a fierce abruptness. He hisses commands through clenched jaw. He puts things down, words and wood and mattocks and adzes, with sharp hardness. It's his way of yelling.

His squatness is a mystery: that from his loins sprang the hulking towering likes of Eliab and Shammah. Even David is taller than his father. But that look that runs like a rumor through all eight brothers, and also in their sisters, Zeruiah and Abigail—strong angular bones, a tumble of dark hair falling in wild curls—is evident enough in their father. When Jesse was younger, before Nitzevet grew sick, he must have been dashingly handsome. But her illness has worn him stumpish and churlish, and aged him faster than the years. His face seems plowed by oxen, in deep furrows, but without the neatness of rows.

"Boy!"

"Father?"

"What is this?"

Jesse stands over a sheep that looks perfectly normal.

"Father?"

"This." Jesse presses a stubby hand into the back of the sheep's coat and spreads his hand wide. It parts the wool so that the skin shows. Just above the sheep's left shoulder, a muddy sore emblazons the flesh. The sore is brownish and reddish and creamy yellow. Bugs spot it like currants. The sheep flinches beneath Jesse's roughness.

"I didn't see that."

"That's what I mean. You didn't see it. You were sitting in your shady oasis composing your little poems, singing your little love songs to the sky, and you didn't see it. Boy, listen: *To see you have to look. Huh?* This is basic. No looking, no seeing. You get that? Look, boy, look. Your head is so far up in the clouds you can't see what is straight in front of you. Ach!"

Jesse tosses his hands up, walks away.

"Take care, boy."

David sits on a rock and gathers the sheep to himself. It trembles. For several minutes he just holds it and whispers in its ear to calm it. With his gourd of wine, he cleans the wound. Then from a vial, he pours oil to soften and protect it.

He knows this sheep well. It was the runt of triplets. It came last, sprawling out doe-eyed and spindle-legged, slickered in a gossamer of blood and mucous. He knew straight away it could not survive, that its siblings would trample it in their rough vitality, their hard, blind rush to their mother's udder, their greedy gulping at her teats. So he did what he had to do: cleaned the lamb and then anointed its shivering gaunt body with the broken womb-water from another ewe, about to birth. She had tried to claim the lambs of two other ewes, so he knew her mothering instinct was potent, overriding all judgment. He nestled the rickety lamb, pungent with the ewe's own smell, into the crook of her neck. The ewe dipped her head toward the lamb, licked the wombstuff off, and then rose so it could totter beneath her, its small mouth pouting toward her teat. The warm milk gorged its mouth. She took the lamb as her own.

And now it is as hardy as any of his rams.

It stings that his father thinks he doesn't care for his sheep.

He settles the flock in the fold and secures the gate. His room is next to this, a low narrow wattle hut, close enough that he can hear any disturbance with the flock. But he doesn't bed down right away. He walks out to the edge of a ridge stretched above a deep valley and sits beneath starlight.

He tries to wrestle away disappointment. He wanted to tell his father about the lion.

* * *

That night he writes a song. It is his longest yet. And the next morning, as the sun leaps up from behind rocks and throws its arms wide across the earth, he sings it aloud to his sheep. They graze unperturbed.

Praise the Lord, O my soul.
O Lord my God, you are very great;
    you are clothed with splendor and majesty.
He wraps himself in light as with a garment;
    he stretches out the heavens like a tent
    and lays the beams of his upper chambers on their waters.
He makes the clouds his chariot
    and rides on the wings of the wind.
He makes winds his messengers,
    flames of fire his servants.
He set the earth on its foundations;
    it can never be moved.

And on and on it goes. The melody sweeps down the hillside like a cooling breeze. A ram and a ewe and a lamb look up. The lamb bleats pleadingly, as if for him to sing again.

But now he is being called. Summoned. One of his father's servants, with imperious urgency, almost bullying him as though David is the lowest servant and not a son, calls for him to come, come now, come quick. A holy man is here. They will not eat until he comes.

972 BC
Save These People
MICHAL

My first remembrance of my father was of his wondrous tallness. Even after I had become a woman, and he was worn by the weight of kingship, he loomed. He was always thin, even when in later years a little sack of stomach, like a smuggled idol, bulged beneath his tunic. But he was never thin in the way some men are, brittle and gangling, ivied with vein, vulnerable to windgust. My father's thinness was a judgment against other men's excess. Against their lack of discipline. His tallness was a vindication.

He was every inch a king.

I recall looking up from the ground upon his great height. Perhaps I was four. Literally, to me, his head was swarmed with sky and thunder, defying heaven. And once in a while he would turn his full attention to me, and it terrified and exhilarated me altogether, as if one of the hill country's legendary giants had deigned to make me its personal doll. He would take me in his lap and move his face so close to mine I felt the rasp of his beard on my cheek. He smelled smoky, like he'd been forging metal. He spoke in a low voice.

"Do you want to know how I became king?"

"Yes, Papa."

"Which story do you want to hear?"

"Any one, Papa."

"Ah, yes. The land was dark. It was overrun by heathen armies, heathen tribes, cruel and stupid, always hungry. Men consulted witches, sought out ghostwives, to try to find some clue to the madness, some path through it. But it only got darker. Israel became like everyone else, senseless, foolish, godless. Priests were wicked. Prophets were solitary. Some were no better than madmen. In those days, the rains rarely came, and the winds refused to rise, or blew like *dybbuks*. Men plowed hard dry ground only to watch seeds die in the sprouting. The house of God lay in ruins. It was like a house after war. It was like a house after slaughter. The shutters were bolted. Inside was no light.

"Those were terrible times, Michal. But then God did what no one expected. He put his hand on a child. On Samuel. He was only about your age, Michal. A little boy. A little boy whose mother, Hannah, dressed him in a fresh linen ephod each year when she visited him at the house of God. The darkness stopped with Samuel. It did not reach him, it could not touch him. He grew tall and strong, and he never wavered in obedience. Eli was like a father to him. And that boy, he eased the sadness in Eli's heart, such terrible sadness. No man should feel sadness like that. But that boy, he lifted it, if just a little.

"And then a night came when the Voice came. 'Samuel,' the Voice said. Samuel leapt from his bed."

At that my father would leap up from where he sat, swooping me in sweeping arcs that made my insides tickle, and I would gasp with both the anticipation and surprise of it. Then he would hold me close to himself. The ground seemed far below.

"'Yes,' Samuel said, running to Eli. 'Here I am.'

"Now Eli was old, Michal. So old. His eyes could only see in strongest daylight, and even then it was like seeing when your head is beneath water. The air itself was a weight on him. He was a good priest, you must know that, Michal. But he held his authority no tighter than he held his cane.

"His sons were desperately wicked. *Belials*. You are too young to hear that tale. But Samuel was eyes and strength to him. Samuel, though no one knew it then, was the *se'er* for all Israel.

"'Here I am,' Samuel said to Eli. 'You called me.'

"No old man likes being awakened, Michal. Remember this. Eli, much as he loved Samuel, was ill-tempered by the intrusion. He sent young Samuel back to bed, and the boy lay there, puzzled."

With that, my father sat down heavy. He fell silent and brooding. He would even close his eyes, feign sleep.

"'Samuel!'" he would shout, and I would leap in his arms, and he would leap from his sitting posture and swoop me again.

This would go on three times.

"Now the third time Samuel stood in Eli's presence," my father said, "this time he did not wake Eli, for Eli was wide awake, thinking thoughts. Yes, my Michal, thinking thoughts: *Could this be what I have waited all my life to hear and never heard?* I want you to imagine that, Michal. The struggle that such a thought would be for an old man, a man who has done his best, his best, who has been faithful, year after year. Whose one and only thought has been to serve God and God's people. And yet the Voice had not come to him. Only silence. And then, when the Voice came, it came to a boy, a mere boy. And the Voice had only blame for that old man.

"What should a man do, Michal? How can man serve a God who feels no affection for him, who will not even speak to him except sideways, through minions? But Eli was a good priest. Faithful. He said to Samuel"—and here my father softened his voice to mimic Eli's voice, its sadness, its weariness, its defeat—"'My son, go back and lie down, and if he calls again, simply say, 'Speak, for your servant listens.'"

My father always fell silent here. I would wait. Sometimes he would end the story here, abrupt and irritable, saying he would tell me the rest later. I knew not to prod him.

But other times he would burst back into the telling with almost a *dybbuk* vigor, his voice mounting with urgency and vehemence, as if he had to press the telling of the tale into a mere sliver of the time it demanded, as if he was telling me all this as we fled an attack, calling back to me, instructing me on what I must do to survive. Samuel heard the Voice again, my father said. He answered in the way Eli said he should. And the Voice told Samuel grave and terrible things, things about Eli's doom. And then the next morning, Eli, who never fell back to sleep, forced young Samuel to tell him the whole truth.

Eli forced the boy to tell him the prophecy of his own priestly dynasty undone, shattered, not one offspring left to tell the tale. The story of the house of Eli's collapse.

After a long silence, my father said, "That, Michal, is how God treats his most loyal servants."

* * *

Samuel was to me like some angry specter bursting forth from the grave, huge and wild and vivid. I'd actually only ever seen the prophet from a distance. But he reckoned in my father's story bigger than one of the *Nephilim*, primordial, massive, dangerous.

Samuel was my father's making and unmaking. And here the stories, which my father never told me but which others were quick to tell, all get muddled. Some say my father was a coward, some say a hero. He was foolishly ambitious, or touchingly modest. He was a man of vengeance. He was a man of mercy. He lusted for the crown. He shunned it. He longed for men's approval. He disdained it. He was Samuel's covenantal friend. He was his oathed enemy. Affection ran like a river through them. Contempt stood like a mountain between them.

I heard all these claims and more.

But this for sure: Samuel one day, when my father was just a boy and Samuel already an old man, poured oil on Father's once black locks. So much oil, it flowed down and damped and slicked his beard. It flowed down and drenched his robe. He has that robe still, kept among his private relics. I have seen it. I have touched it. Even now dark stains are visible on the collar. Even now the fragrance of oil lingers.

It is undeniable proof.

Pouring the oil, Samuel spoke the words that no man should ever have the power to revoke: *You are the king of Israel. Rise and take your place, and save these people.*

1025 BC
Anointed One

W hat is happening?" David asks the servant as they walk toward the farm. The servant is walking so quickly it is hard for David to keep pace.

"The holy man, Samuel, has come. On urgent and secret business. God has sent him to anoint one of the sons of Jesse."

"Anoint him… to do what?"

"He has not said."

"And which son has he chosen?"

"None. He has seen all seven of your brothers and rejected all of them."

"What? Eliab? Abinidab?"

"Yes."

David imagines it—each of his brothers, all of them, one by one, coming forward, being turned back. Eliab would have come first. David pictures him strutting his way forward. Confident. Smug. His head tilted back, ready to receive the blessing that he knows is rightfully his.

Not you, the holy man says. Eliab's face darkens, falls. Words start forming on his lips but never rise. Abinidab steps up next, steps for once out of Eliab's shadow. *No*, the holy man says. *Not you*. Shammah, himself a kind of shadow, slouches forward. *No. Not you*.

Not you, not you, not you, Samuel keeps saying, seven times over.

"You," Samuel says as David steps into the light. "You are the one."

Everyone, including Samuel, looks dismayed.

"Don't just stand there. Come forward," Samuel says, angry.

David looks around to make sure it's actually him Samuel is summoning.

"Now, boy. Come. We are tired. We are hungry. Do not make us wait any longer."

David staggers forward. Samuel almost throws him to the ground. He places his large heavy hand on David's head and pushes him even further down, like he's pushing a sharp stake into soft earth. David looks up at him, this one they call Judge, Prophet, *Se'er*. He has always seemed to David more an *elohim* than a man, like one of the terrible wrathful gods of Moab or Philistia, never pleased, never sated. He makes strong men quail. But David looks at Samuel now and sees he is confused or aggrieved. His lips purse against some eruptive emotion, anger or sorrow or fear.

And now the oil pours down.

The oil on his neck is warm as blood.

He knows the warmth of blood. He has slit the throats of many lambs, lambs he's nurtured from first shivering breath, first tottering step, first mewling bleat. Lambs he's held, firm enough to give them courage, gentle enough to give them peace. He's held them one last time, close against his chest. He's made his voice quiet and soft as still waters. They yield, unsuspecting, to the familiarity of his touch, the gentleness of his speaking. He pulls the blade quick and smooth along the soft flesh just beneath the throat. The lamb's large black eyes shine with wonder, then go dull.

The warmth of each lamb's blood, rushing into his hands, always surprises him. And it saddens him. He always wishes there was some other way: that a lamb did not have to give its life to save his own.

This oil feels similar. It drizzles down the locks of his hair unto his neck, gathering there. An unguent thickness seeps into the collar of his tunic. It is fragrant as ancient trees.

David looks at the seven faces of his brothers. Seven rejected men. Eliab is stiff, Abinidab shaking, Shammah sullen. Only Raddai and Ozem, the ones almost as young as David, appear happy. His father wears a look of terror. He watches until David rises.

Then he walks away, his back as hard and rough as an undressed altar stone.

* * *

"Has our king died?" he asks Jesse that evening, after Samuel has left.

"Don't dare utter such a thing."

"But Father, why did the *se'er* come today? What does he want with us?

With me?"

"Stop. Close your mouth or I will close it for you. It is not for you or any of us to speak of this. Ever. Do you understand?"

"King Saul is alive?"

"Very alive. Do you understand?"

"Yes."

The dampness and fragrance of the oil lingers in David's hair. It stains dark his collar. He touches his hair, and his fingers glide through it and come out with a sheen on their tips. His father falls into his usual foul silence, though his breathing is thick as murmuring.

Only priests and prophets and judges are anointed. And kings. Am I one of these? And if so, which one?

Why will Father not tell me?

* * *

Everything returns as it was. David goes back to tending sheep. To being ignored. His father and brothers never mention what happened that evening when Samuel came, unbidden, unannounced, and left without eating, leaving them all standing in awkward silence, Eliab and Abinidab scowling. But their avoidance of what happened hangs over the household like a long curse, like a prophecy uttered that never seems to come to anything and yet that shapes everything, colors it all, fills each day with unbearable weight.

But the daily rhythms hold. David rises early, calls each sheep by name, counts them, inspects them, and then leads them beside still waters. They toddle along behind him, some jostling to get near him, to press their heads or bodies against his thighs. He laughs, reaches down to scratch their heads.

"You are my kingdom," he says. "The sheep of my pasture."

But it pains him, knowing that this very sheep, vying with the others to get close to him, is the one his father has marked this day for slaughter.

For weeks after the *se'er* has come and gone, he wakes every day, ready to rise to the role chosen for him.

"Here I am," he says, to no one. He tries to imagine what this role will be. He pictures himself a prophet and judge, like Samuel, his words so weighty, so holy, so true, that no one lets a single one fall to the ground: men and women and children run out to the streets to catch each word, hold it, ponder it, like rain after drought.

He pictures himself a priest, dressed only in an ephod, walking in slow solemn steps before the Ark of the covenant, the stones of the Urim and Thummin glowing like planets on his breast, holding aloft entrails of sacrifice, with its blood on his hands.

And sometimes, he dares to picture himself as king. He rides forth from his citadel in a chariot drawn by many horses. Men run on either side of him. Crowds bow before him. His harem stands behind him, awaiting his return.

But even as he sees this, another picture eclipses it: he in his shepherd's tunic, singing over his sheep, making them lie down.

* * *

Three months later, word comes from Gibeah. King Saul has summoned David to the court. He is to bring his harp. He is to play music for the king. The king, the rumor has it, needs distracting.

His father receives the news with the same fearful look that came over him the day Samuel arrived at the house. His oldest brothers wear the same aggrieved looks they wore that day. Raddai and Ozem once again look excited.

"Son," Jesse says, and David almost falls backward from the force of it. Jesse has never once called him his son.

"Father?"

"I need you to take care."

"Father?"

"There are rumors. About Saul. King Saul. That he is afflicted. That his mind is broken. That he is dangerous. I need you to take care."

"Yes, Father."

"And never speak to anyone, ever, about the *se'er*, about the oil. To anyone. Ever."

"Yes, Father."

"And change your tunic. Wear one of Ozem's. He's your size. He has two. Leave yours here."

David cocks his head and looks at his tunic. He wears it every day. Its collar is still rimmed dark with oil.

"You will keep it? You will keep it... safe?"

Jesse says nothing.

* * *

His mother's paleness is all he's ever known, but it freshly startles him this morning. His father, the few times he's talked about her, and only when he's deep in his cups, says she was once a great beauty. The kind of beauty that makes men foolhardy and brave, willing to fight barehanded, or that sets them groaning on their beds in the dark. But his mother now is sorrow made flesh. Her skin is the color of cold ash. She is whittled to bone. Her eyes reflect darkest emptiness. She rarely speaks, and then it is like a ghost whispering in a witch's hut.

He was raised until he was six by his sister Zeruiah, before she married Nathanael and moved to a farm several miles away, and stayed away even after Nathanael died. But until then, she raised David and his brothers, except Eliab and Abinidab and Shammah, who were already men, or nearly so. She lacked even a hair of maternal instinct. Ozem and Raddai remember her brutal sternness—she would whip them for a sideways look. David remembers most her bleakness. She was, she is, like a village swept by plague. An eerie silence attends her ways. Even now, when she comes bringing eggs or collecting wool, the sight of her makes his flesh all cold. He has never been close to his nephews, Joab and Abishai and Ashael, especially not Joab, who is too much like Eliab. But he carries a trace of pity for them. It would be no easy thing to be the sons of Zeruiah. She hits harder than a blacksmith, and more often.

He's always longed for a woman to hold him.

"Mother?"

Silence.

"Mother?"

A groan.

"Mother, I need to tell you something."

She turns her head slowly toward him. Her eyes register nothing.

"Mother, I am leaving."

Silence.

"King Saul has bidden me. I am going to be with the king. He is... not well. I will play for him. I will sing for him. The songs I sing for you."

A murmur.

"I may not return."

With that, a light sparks in her. She raises her head. She looks at him.

"You are going to be king."

"No, Mother. I am going to be with the king. To play for the king. To serve the king."

"Yes. The king."

She falls back into her abyss of darkness.

David notices a thin silver band on her wrist. It has a bright stone embedded in it. The work is delicate, intricate, precise, not at all like the rough-hewn weapons and tools his father smiths and forges and tempers in his cave. But David knows, somehow, that his father made this, and slipped it over her frail hand, unto her thin wrist, maybe as she slept.

David leaves in the morning. His brothers do not come out to see him off. His father—again, surprising him—gives him a gruff embrace, a flinty kiss. There is a redness around his eyes.

"I need you to take care," Jesse says, and turns and walks away.

Before David is over the hilltop, he sees a thick curl of smoke, tipped black, rising up from behind the house.

David knows that Jesse is burning his tunic.

* * *

He has only been to Gibeah once before. His father sent him to trade a donkey there, a rough business of thievish haggling. His father clipped the backside of his head for the price he fetched, though David knew it was good. Gibeah is a steep climb from Bethlehem into a scorched and rocky landscape. Its single virtue is its commanding view of all the land surrounding it. No enemy comes upon Gibeah unawares.

A prostitute stands at the roadside outside the city. She is not much older than him. She is dark with illicit mystery. Her body has the coiled litheness of a panther. Her face is painted with glittery birdlike coloring. She has daubed a paste of thick blackness around her eyes that make them look large and hungry. Her clothing is an artful combination of enticement and concealment, made of tasseled folds that open with the movement of an arm or leg, to a sliver of dusky skin beneath. Her arms are chimes of metal bracelets. A potent fragrance of exotic oils and perfumes wafts from her.

"Come to bed with me."

Emotions rise and clash in him, at the brazenness of this. He wants to run. He wants to seize her, in anger and desire. He swallows hard and keeps walking.

"What are you afraid of, boy? I only bite where it feels good. Come."

He picks up his heels and runs.

The desire in him takes a long time to cool. When it does, one thing remains: sadness. He wishes he could speak of such things with his father, or one of his older brothers. And he touches, lightly, lightly, as if testing a broken bone for healing, a deep wild hope: that Saul will be that man for him. That Saul will be a father.

* * *

But Saul lies curled on the floor. His eyes have the droopy sleepy cunning of an ancient reptile. His spidery arms clutch his spidery legs and hold his knees against his bony chest. He presses his head down into the crook his knees make. A ghostly moan emits from him. His courtiers stand around him. Some look frightened, others agitated. They seem to have given up speaking to him. They all turn to David with the same look of desperation.

The chief official steps toward him.

"Are you the son of Jesse?"

"I am."

"And you play the harp, and sing?"

"I do."

"Play for the king."

David looks around for a stool. A courtier, seeing his need, brings him one and places it a few feet from where Saul lies prostrate.

Saul's spine is like knuckles pressing into the back of his shirt. Every few minutes, a shudder runs through his body. He winches his arms tighter around his knees to keep himself from unraveling. A sharp cry tears from his throat.

David is trembling. He sits on the stool. He keeps shifting to get comfortable, until he realizes the discomfort is within him. He prays. He opens the place inside himself, a hidden inmost place, where the *ruach* moves. It comes from the outside but speaks on the inside, wordless, clearer than words. Words diminish it. He feels the *ruach* as both an aching and a rejoicing, a grieving and a laughing.

The *ruach* says *play*.

He plucks a string. A note shimmers through the room. He plucks another, and another, and another, and the room bursts alive. The sound is fragrance, color, sun, rain, wind. Shadows, stench, heat all fly away. He opens his mouth and sings. His voice is angelic, beautiful and terrible. It is a sword piercing each man's soul. It is worse than doom, finer than hope. It is storm and the end of storm.

Lord, our Lord,
>   how majestic is your name in all the earth!
You have set your glory
>   in the heavens.
Through the praise of children and infants
>   you have established a stronghold against your enemies,
>   to silence the foe and the avenger.
When I consider your heavens,
>   the work of your fingers,
the moon and the stars,
>   which you have set in place,
what is mankind that you are mindful of them,
>   human beings that you care for them?
You have made them a little lower than the angels
>   and crowned them with glory and honor.
You made them rulers over the works of your hands;
>   you put everything under their feet:
all flocks and herds,
>   and the animals of the wild,
the birds in the sky,
>   and the fish in the sea,
>   all that swim the paths of the seas.
Lord, our Lord,
>   how majestic is your name in all the earth!

On and on he sings, until he forgets himself, forgets where he is, forgets who he's with, until he himself is wholly caught up in the spell his music casts.

When he finally stops, there is Saul, seated on his throne, radiant, jubilant, his arms stretched wide in bountiful welcome.

"Ah, my son!" Saul says. "My son. What is your name?"

"I am David."

"Ah, David, the beloved. You will be mine, David. My very own."

David bows, weeping.

972 BC

Oil

DAVID

My Jonathan, we never spoke about the oil the holy man poured over me. It was too dangerous, to speak of it. It was like a writ of death. Like a knife blade held to my throat. Or yours. I was too afraid. Afraid you would tell your father. More afraid—only now I admit this—that it would come between you and me, a wall neither of us could scale. You were, after all, the one I would displace, the prince I would dethrone. You had to become less if I was to become greater. You had to die for me to live.

But you knew. You knew, when? Almost from the start, I think. And still you gave all you had for me to survive—no, to prosper. Not once resenting me, not once betraying me, not even when, for a brief time, I had more affection from your father than ever he showed you.

Why?

I often saw my father Jesse's undisguised love for my brother Eliab: Jesse standing tall, clapping, smiling when Eliab came near, relishing every word and hushing all those around when Eliab spoke. This is my son, he seemed to say. I love him. I'm pleased with him. Listen to him. I will not deny it: I longed to hear my father say, even if only by gesture, just one of those words about me. But never.

But your father, he gave all those things to me, if only fleetingly. It made me dizzy, made me lose my bearings. And then you, you went further. You laid down your life for me. You defied your own flesh and blood for me. You delighted to elevate me, even as you sank.

Why?

After I took the crown and throne, first in Judah, then in Israel, and learned intimately its weight, its loneliness, its bitingness, I wondered many times whether I would wish this for you. You would have made a great king. Your men knew this. You knew this. I think, somewhere inside him, even your father knew this. Was it his own broken love for you that didn't want it for you?

But you gave up all that you had for me to be sitting here.

I am ever thankful to you. But at times, I envy you. And at times, I labor not to resent you.

1025 BC

Jonathan

He goes back and forth, back and forth, Bethlehem to Gibeah, Gibeah to Bethlehem. The journey becomes a kind of trance, a path he walks until he could walk it eyes shut: its bends and dips and rises, its distances between landmarks, its dry places and wet places, all this he knows without looking, and navigates with mindless ease. The prostitute near the entrance of Gibeah solicited and taunted him a few more times in his coming and going, and then ignored him. Now he walks past her without noticing her any more than she does him.

The familiarity of the journey frees him to travel deep inside himself.

His father has returned to himself: angry, distant, brooding. The glimpse David had of something else in his father, some lost tenderness, has gone dark. And his oldest brothers, who kept their distance for several weeks after he entered the service of King Saul, have gone back to bullying him, barking out commands, speaking to him with acidic scorn.

His mother is now utterly mute. Even her moaning has gone silent. He sits with her for long stretches when he is home, and he sings to her the songs he sings for the king. But unlike the king, her darkness never lifts. Her countenance never brightens. Her voice never returns to her.

He tends his sheep, but only when the king does not need him. And the king needs him more and more. Sometimes it is to play his music, until the king slips free his torment the way a man crawls free from a cave's mouth, or comes up after being held under water. Sometimes it is to polish, again, the king's armor that the king rarely uses. And sometimes, it is because the king wants to talk, to confide in him.

"My son," Saul says.

"My king."

"I have been thinking. About these Philistines. Do you know, David, you are the only one I can fully trust with such matters? Even with my own sons I do not share such things."

"My lord, I am humbled."

"These Philistines. They vex me. They are a plague. I think we have put them down, and then I turn around and there are more than ever, everywhere. They are... cockroaches. Vermin. Curs. Or worse: gnats, fleas, ticks. The insect in the skin of the cur. What shall I do, David?"

"My king, I am just a boy. How am I able to advise you on such weighty matters?"

Saul's eyes flash fire. His face twitches. His voice tightens, sharpens.

"Did I not just ask you, son of Jesse, what I should do?"

"Yes, my lord. I am sorry. My lord, you should take the battle to them. My king has been fighting a defensive war. The Philistines strike, and you respond. Which is wise, my lord. Very wise. But what if my king were to do the striking? What if my king were to ride out to battle and throw down the challenge and make these uncircumcised heathens respond? What if my king were to make the uncircumcised fight the battle on our terms?"

"It was not long ago, son of Jesse, when defending ourselves was heroic. When the Philistines controlled all the smithies, and we had barely a weapon between us. We fought them off with rakes. With hoes. You think it is a small matter to mount a war, boy?"

"No, my king. But you have done it before, even before you had swords."

"That was Jonathan," Saul says, snapping each word out like a whip stroke.

It was twelve years ago, but the story never gets old, not to David, not to others in Israel.

Jonathan walks into the camp and all the men turn and smile at him. Each hail him by name. Anything he says makes them laugh or look pensive, as though one moment he's a jester, uproariously funny, and the next a sage, uncannily wise. Men want to be his friend. They want to be seen as his friend. They want to be his confidante. They seek his advice and his approval.

When he speaks to anyone face-to-face, the man leans in, cups his chin in his hand, nods slow and thoughtful, weighs each word like gemstone. But Jonathan's manner is so easy, so friendly, so humble, the man soon relaxes. Even now, with the Philistine army close, bristling with weapons, blustering threats, Jonathan's presence makes each man straighten and walk tall.

They would do anything for him—face a giant bare-handed, steal water from an enemy's well, defy a king.

Jonathan walks to where his father Saul sits beneath a large pomegranate tree. A filigree of shade falls over Saul. The tree's fruit, red as beetroot, hangs down from its branches. Every day, Saul, and only Saul, eats a whole pomegranate in a single sitting. He scalps its top with a short knife and then slices the husk vertically, peeling each inner segment back to reveal a thick cluster of glistening beads. Most days he does this slowly, like a ritual. But today he cuts it in rough haste. He breaks the fruit with the blade. He breaks open each segment of the pomegranate with his long spidery fingers. The seeds fold out from the fruit's creamy inner skin, and he presses his teeth into them. The juice stains his face and hands a darkening crimson. He does not wipe it off until he's devoured it all.

Jonathan stands before him. Saul ignores him.

"Father, we must speak."

"I am dreadfully busy."

"Father, I know you suffer. I know the prophet has left you undone."

Saul does not answer this. Two days ago, Samuel—old now, but not reduced, still dreadful to look upon, still able to make even his silence thunder—entered the camp and said words to Saul that left him pale and shaking. No one but Saul heard those words. But afterward, Saul was paralyzed. His army mostly deserted him. It dwindled to a mere six hundred men, with barely a weapon among them.

"Father, it is time to strike. Our delay only emboldens our enemy and terrifies our own men. They can be rallied to battle, I know they can, few as they are. They are strong, and determined. They are brave. They are Gideon's army. We can take the enemy by surprise and be done with their yoke on our necks."

A smirk flits across the fat face of Ahijah, Saul's personal priest. The prophecies say this man will not live to see 30, and Jonathan thinks for a moment of hastening that prediction. Why his father indulges this self-regarding fool is a mystery to him. Ahijah is the great-grandson of Eli, the grandson of Eli's wicked son Phineas. That whole priestly house is under a curse. Samuel no more acknowledges Ahijah's existence than he would a gnat's. Jonathan wishes his father would cut the man off, cast him out, stop listening to his wheedling flattery and slippery lies.

"And what?" Saul says, singsong. The pomegranate had turned his lips and teeth a garish red, as if he'd been eating an animal raw. "Send them out with farm tools? With rakes and pruning shears? What do you propose, dear son? That they hoe the Philistine like soft soil, pull up their innards like root vegetables? Boil them in a pot? Hmm?"

Jonathan speaks with cold calm. "You don't know your men. One of your men could kill more Philistines with a winnowing fork than ten Philistines could kill us with a broad sword. Try them."

Saul's face ticks with anger. "You don't know your place, boy. These men would fold like bedsheets at the sight of one Philistine sheep-herd with a slingshot. They would break and bleed. You dare speak to me, your king and father, like I'm your dog? You insolent little viper. You son of a rebellious woman."

And then, with regal finality: "I've heard your counsel, and I've weighed it carefully, and I find it reckless and foolish. It is the whim of an idler. It is the idealistic pomp of a young whelp whose dreams exceed his skills. I reject it. Good day, little princeling."

Jonathan walks away and summons his armor-bearer, who is barely more than a boy: smooth-cheeked, delicately boned. But he's blurringly quick. He's felled men twice his size by some maneuver no one saw coming. Jonathan speaks something to him, and his armor-bearer looks straight at him and says, loud enough for anyone to hear, "So be it, my lord."

No one sees them the rest of the day.

* * *

Heat off the cliff walls boils the air. Jonathan shades his eyes against the sky's searing brightness and looks up at the underside of the cliff to the north. His eyes chart a course up its side. The cliff is a lizard's hide of horns and ridges. Jonathan sees they can go almost straight up, crab-walk slightly west, then veer sharply east, half leaping to secure purchase, and then bolt straight up again, up and over the top.

"Come, let's go over to the outpost of those uncircumcised men. Perhaps the Lord will act on our behalf. Nothing can hinder the Lord from saving, whether by many or by few."

"Go ahead," his armor-bearer says. "I am with you heart and soul. Do all that you have in mind."

"Let's move to where the guards can see us."

The armor-bearer nods.

Jonathan closes his eyes as though listening. Then he says, "If the guards say to us, 'Wait there until we come to you,' we will stay where we are and not go up to them. But if they say, 'Come up to us,' we will climb up. That will be our sign that the Lord has given them into our hands."

"Do all you have in mind."

The Philistine guard on lookout sees them and cries to the others, "Ha! Look! The Hebrews are crawling out of their hidey holes." All the Philistine guards, a good number, run to the cliff edge and look down. They laugh, they gesture rudely. "Come up to us and we'll teach you a lesson."

"Climb up after me," Jonathan says to his armor-bearer. "The Lord has given them into the hand of Israel." They both move up the cliff sure and swift, agile as geckos. The men above whoop and holler and taunt.

"Are you ready?" Jonathan says, just before cresting.

"As you are, my lord."

Both men pull themselves up, and the Philistines—twenty of them— step back to give them momentary room. The Philistines stand in a semicircle, swords drawn, one slowly spinning a spiked mace, another with spear cocked above his shoulder. Jonathan smiles at his armor-bearer, who smiles back.

And Jonathan's gone, rolling on his shoulder and leaping up like a cobra in front of the spearman, sliding his sword slantwise under the man's protruding belly, and then spinning to use the guard's own spear to skewer the neck of the guard beside him. His armor-bearer is a shadow on his flank. They drop their blades into chests and guts like they're merely sounding water. The fight widens out. The Philistine guards back off, rush in, spin round, get confused, afraid, enraged, sloppy. And all the time they are falling, falling, falling, until the ground is a blanket of corpses.

An astonishing thing happens next: a frenzy of terror rollicks through the nearby Philistine outpost, and then the next, and then all of them. It swoops down on the war camp itself. Brave men yelp, bleat, sob. They run every which way, frantic, unruly with panic. Rumors mount and batter hearts until every warrior's courage melts away. When they can't flee, when in the madness of their stampede they lose all direction and run into the wall of each other, they hack and flail their way through with bludgeons and swords. They fight against themselves.

Only then does Saul, seeing what is happening, muster his army and command them to finish the job.

Saul's eyes are as narrow as two knife cuts.

"It was Jonathan who took the battle to the Philistines."

"Because he is a man after your own heart, my king. He has your courage. You gave that to him. All Israel knows of the thousands you have killed. All Israel remembers your victory at Jabesh-Gilead all those years ago. We all sing your mighty deeds, my king."

David closes his eyes, turns his face upward. In a voice luxurious and sweet, he sings, "swifter than an eagle, stronger than a lion, our King rides forth."

A tight smile pinches Saul's face. He turns toward the shadows. He makes a low sound that could be humming. When he turns back, his smile is dazzling.

"I am pleased that I have sought your advice, David, my son. It is good advice. It is like the voice of *Yahweh*. I will do as you say. I will take the battle to those uncircumcised whore-mongers. I will teach them a lesson."

"*Yahweh* will be your buckler and sword, my king."

"And my spear?" Saul asks. "Or is that all in my hand?"

972 BC
Rescuer
MICHAL

My father told me his stories by firelight. I watched the shadow of flames play across his face, and this held me as much as the stories did. The hiss and crack of pine logs, fragrant with sap, played like timbrels to accompany my father's voice. Many times I asked him to tell me of his childhood. He rarely did. He told me instead stories of our people, the Benjamites.

"Our father Jacob—our father Israel—he loved Benjamin, his youngest, almost as much as he loved Joseph. Benjamin was his only other son from the womb of Rachel, and O, how he loved Rachel. When you are older, my dear, I will tell you that story. But it is not for delicate ears.

"But in my time, all had forgotten Benjamin. They forgot what we meant to Israel. They forgot Israel's affection for Benjamin. For us. By then, we were no one's favorite. We were small. Despised. Rejected. When I was chosen as Israel's king—chosen by God, Michal, by God himself, and anointed by God's own prophet—everyone was surprised. Some mocked. Many doubted. 'Who chooses the rejected?' they said."

"Father, how did you prove yourself as king?" I knew this story, but it was my part to urge him along, to keep pulling from him each detail as though it were a confession.

"Nahash the Ammonite king besieged Jabesh-Gilead. He demanded blood tribute—the right eye of each man. Some men are cruel that way:

they want their payment in flesh, in a man's vitality and dignity, his own lifeblood. A man's wealth—take it. It can be replaced. A man's land—he can find more. But a man's vision, never. Take that, and all is lost. Some men are cruel, Michal. They use their power to take from you what can never be given back.

"The people of Jabesh-Gilead—how would they respond to such a cruel demand? They asked for time. And then they dispatched a messenger—to me. To me, their king. Their anointed one. I was plowing my father's field, just over there," and he gestured toward the south, now steeped in night's blackness. "I was pulling behind a pair of oxen when the messenger reached me.

"Now, Michal, when Samuel anointed me, and no one but he and I and God knew, the Spirit fell upon me in the way a great wind sometimes comes down from the sky. The *ruach* entered me. It filled me—my legs, my arms, my heart. It all rushed in at once. It threw me to the ground. Strange words came from me. It changed me. Things I feared, things I doubted, worries I carried—it all vanished. I could see deep and far. I had vision. And when I stood up again, I was a new man. I was Samson, Gideon, Jephthah. I was all, and more. I could do anything. I would do anything.

"This same thing, the *ruach* falling on me, it happened when that messenger came to me with news of Jabesh-Gilead. Samson's strength came on me. Gideon's courage endowed me. Jephthah's resolve bolstered me. I was ready to slay. I could see. I had vision, and I knew that no man should take another man's vision.

"But I knew, even so, I could not do this alone. And I knew this was the moment all Israel would gather under my kingship.

"I remembered the Levite and his concubine. That is a story too terrible and dark, my sweet, for your tender ears. Let me say, his concubine was sore abused in this very town, in Gibeah, by men whose children and grandchildren walk among us to this very day. Their fathers and grandfathers did things that should not be mentioned by decent men. They wanted to abuse the Levite. But instead they abused his concubine. It was the death of her. The Levite found her in the morning. He took her dead body, and—now, Michal, I will say this quickly, because it is so grim—he took the body and carved it into twelve pieces, and he sent a piece each to the twelve tribes of Israel, and they rose as one man against us, against

Gibeah, against Benjamin. And they slaughtered and slaughtered, until we were almost no more.

"I remembered this miserable tale. And I knew what I must do. I took one of the oxen, and I killed it, and I carved it into twelve pieces, and I sent a piece to each of the twelve tribes. The tribal elders would know its meaning. They would arise again as one man. And I knew another thing, Michal. I knew that this would be the final undoing of what the men of Gibeah, the men of Benjamin, had done. I knew that the other tribes of Israel would forget our shame at last.

"And this is just what happened. We rose as one. We rescued Jabesh-Gilead. And no one doubted me after that. No one mocked me. No one rejected me. All saw me as I was, Israel's king. Everyone. Men who despised me now hailed me. They sang of me. Saul has killed his thousands, they said. Thousands, Michal. Thousands."

Father would gradually sit taller through the telling of this. His face would thrust out toward the firelight and glow like metal pulled from the coals for hammering. He laughed.

I rarely saw my father laugh.

"Father, tell me about your enemy."

"Which one?" my father said.

"The one who wanted to be king."

"Ah, yes. That wicked man. He doubted me most. He mocked me openly. He plotted against me. He gathered others, a ragtag of evildoers and scoffers just like himself, and he fed their contempt with his own. And worse, he was from my own people. A Benjamite.

"When I returned from battle, with all the men of Israel now loyal to me, he approached me like a frightened lamb. My oathmen wanted to kill him and kill all the cowards that followed him. But my enemy came to me whimpering. On hands and knees. A whipped dog. A flea. Michal, it is not right for any man, even a king, to desire the humiliation of another man. To take away his dignity. But this, this was right. To see my enemy on his knees. To see him put his face in the dust. To have him beg me. His voice shaking like tamarisk leaves. Knowing I had the power in my hands, these hands"—and Father would open his large hands wide—"to give or to take life. There he was, prostrate, confessing. Begging. Grovelling. Yes, it was as it should be.

"I showed him mercy. It is the glory of a king to be merciful, Michal.

Always remember that."

"And now your enemy is your friend, Father?"

"No, Michal. Not my friend. My subject. Now Shimei is my subject. Now he bends the knee to me."

1025 BC

Giant

Saul summons the armies of Israel in the valley of Elah. It lies between Israel and Philistine territory. There are cavernous mountains toward the east, pastureland toward the west. The valley is long and wide. A bright shallow brook sings down its north edge. The hills on either side of the valley rise in chalky treeless slopes, steep at one end, easy at the other.

The Philistines gather on the south slope, Israel on the north. Israel's armaments are still sparse from the days when the Philistines had power enough to control their production. But now most Hebrew men have a weapon in hand, if only a spiked club. They are eager to fight. They speak confidently.

"I will cover myself in my enemy's blood today. My cup will run over," Eliab says.

Shammah laughs. "I will plunder their foreskins until I have too many to carry."

A clank and hiss and din rises from both camps: blades honed on pumice, metal hammered on metal, the loud talk of men. Both sides assemble, raggedly at first, then gradually rank on rank, the spear men in the front, slingers and archers behind them, sword men last. Behind that, but only on the Philistine side, are horsemen and charioteers. Saul's bowmen and slingers have been instructed to take out as many riders and drivers and animals as they can.

The smell of sweat is sharp and rank. Silence falls. All stiffen for combat. Saul, the only mounted Israelite, rides down from his tent high up on the crown of the northern hillside to survey the troops, to rally them. He is beautiful. His armor glows. His silver locks banner out. His trimmed beard glistens with oil. His shoulders are squared. He holds his head erect. The Israelites break out in raucous cheers, and then in song:

> Saul has slain his thousands.
>   Saul breaks out like mighty waters.
> Remember, O proud Nahash,
>   how your gloating turned to mourning
> When our king rose up
>   to scatter *you.*

But as Saul descends, a gap opens in the middle phalanx of the Philistine troops. A man with black armor steps forth. Every Israelite strains to see him, the impossibility of him. The sheer mountainous bigness of him. He is as tall and as wide as two men. His arms are as thick as most men's waists, his head as large as most men's chests. The Israelites fall silent, while the Philistines clap and howl with lusty joy. They shake their weapons, stomp the ground, gibber and shriek.

The giant walks slowly toward the midway point in the valley. Then he speaks. The sound of his voice, its deepness, is more terrifying than the sight of him. That night, men will compare it to the worst the earth can do: ground splitting, mountains falling, waves crashing, wind hammering. News of your child's death.

"Bring me a man," the giant says. Each word is a massive boulder hurled toward the Israelite line. "If he defeats me, we become your slaves. But if I defeat him, you become our slaves."

With that, the Philistines break afresh into howling and gibbering. It is a clamor of bloodthirsty jubilation. They scream taunts. They mimic acts of savagery and obscenity.

The smell of urine pierces the air around the Israelites. Saul turns pale. He reigns his horse into dead stillness. Then he kicks sharp its haunches and rides hard up the hill. He does not appear before the troops again that day. He sits in his tent, unseen.

Every day, the giant comes and does his show all over again. At night, the Israelite men sit around fires and mock the giant, and make brave, and speak boldly.

"Tomorrow, I plan to end this."

"You do? And how? One of the poisoned thunderclaps from your arse?"

"Shut up! I haven't seen you do anything but piss yourself."

Sometimes they speak in low tones about Saul.

"Is he not our champion? Where is the liberator of Jabesh-Gilead? What of the thousands he has killed? Can he not kill one man? Or Jonathan— where is he, and that armor bearer of his? Could he who slayed so many uncircumcised not slay this oaf?"

And each morning, the troops assemble again, and the giant comes forth, and any courage Saul's men felt the night before turns to water.

For forty days.

* * *

Saul's war keeps David homebound. The king has no need of him. His older brothers are with Saul, at war with Philistia, and so David is left alone with his father and the servants and younger siblings.

It is a relief not to suffer his older brothers' constant reviling. But Jesse makes up for it by piling on the work and doubling up on his churlishness. He makes David slave away and criticizes his every act. But there are times, and they come more often and stay much longer, when Jesse is walled up in dark misery, trapped in wordless sorrow. He avoids everyone. He walks as though in the shadow of death.

David doesn't know which he prefers, his father's anger or his sorrow.

Today, Jesse is angry.

"Damn you, boy. Must I do everything?" Jesse points to a task half done, a fence repair David began but hasn't finished. But next, David knows, it will be something else—a languid animal, a misplaced tool, a cracked water jar, a fraying rope. Or—more likely—it will be something amiss in him— the way he speaks, or moves, or looks. "Wipe that stupid grin off your face. What the hell right do you have to be happy?"

David tends sheep in the mornings. A servant replaces him midday, and David returns to the household to help with sundry things, some of it the work of womenfolk. But he secretly savors it all. He is learning how everything works, how everything interrelates, the connections between livestock and feed and hides and fleece, between crops and mills and ovens and markets. He is learning how each thing weaves together like the reeds of a basket.

It's the sheep, though, that he loves most and best, more than all these other things. He arises early each day and stands at the gate and calls each one by name. "Tamar," he says, and a doe-eyed ewe bleats, shy. "Tabitha," he says, and another bleats, bold, and pushes its head against his leg. "Absalom," he calls, and the surliest ram scuffs the earth, swaggers about, bullies its way forward. David saw this instinct from the start and named the ram "father of peace," as a jest, as a wish.

One by one they come, and then off they go, out the gate and up the ridge and down the narrow path toward pastures they have not grazed recently, where grass has sprung up verdant and lush. The sheep jostle to get near him, except some of the rams, who push toward the front. As they wend their way, David often stoops to pick up and carry a young timid lamb or an old tottery ewe that can't navigate some steep narrow twist of the path. He breaks up fights between rams, and always he urges his flock on when they stop to graze a patch of grassland undergrown with noxious weeds or too near a nest of vipers.

Today, he travels many hard miles to reach the place he has in mind. It is an expanse of green pasture. A grove of leafy trees casts a lacework of shade. Here the land levels. The brook they have followed as it rushes white and loud down the hillside, pools here, deepens, darkens, stills. A bend in its flow makes a gentle grassy bank. The sheep can easily wade in and lap up water. At first the sheep eat and drink greedily, and then they slow and ruminate lazily. And then they lie down and sleep.

David watches. He listens.

The *ruach* is soft as his own breathing. It moves like breath. It is wordless. His mother, in her rare spells of alertness, sometimes spoke to him of Ruth and Boaz, his ancient kin. She told him that Boaz would hold Ruth in the night and spread his arm like a wing over her. He would sing to her a song until she fell asleep.

"Mother, what were the words of the song?"

"There were no words."

"How did he sing a song with no words?"

"Those are the best songs, my beloved. Words cannot always say all we need to say. Or all we need to hear. The song Boaz sang to Ruth was a song like that. His love for her was too deep for words."

The *ruach* is a song like that. David hears it, its wordless beauty, and it so fills him and calms him, he falls asleep with his sheep. When he awakes, nothing has come to harm them.

* * *

When he returns that afternoon, the household is deathly still. David fears that his mother has slipped into the realm of the shades. But Jesse waits for him, and David sees from his face that it's something else. His father's perennial look of weary disgust has been replaced by a look of fear.

"I need you, son."

"Here I am."

"The king has summoned provisions. I must send them straight away. You will take them to the valley of Elah. Eleazar has laden two donkeys with grain and wine and cheese and salted meat. All is ready. Go now, straight away. You must be there by dawn tomorrow."

"Do the armies of the Lord prevail against the uncircumcised?" David asks.

Jesse is silent.

"Is our king well?"

"He might need you," Jesse says. "He might need you more than before."

* * *

Not far outside Bethlehem, the hills fold up into mountains, and the mountains rise toward the citadel of Jebus. His father has always warned him to give this place wide berth. The Jebusites, they say, are wicked people, barely human, thieves, whores, miscreants. They have savage tempers, filthy lusts. They practice black arts. They eat their own children. They eat pigs. They are a haunt for witches. They tattoo their bodies, even their faces, and pierce their flesh with hooks.

But he knows that passing close to Jebus is the quickest path to the canyons beyond, and that these open out into the Valley of Elah. So he goes near, passing under the citadel's shadow. All the while he looks up at the city's massive fortifications. Atop its thick high walls of stone dance a band of hideous marionettes, effigies of every disfigured scrap of humanity, rigged by some dark magic to writhe and flail and gibber. It is a dance of menace and vileness. The sight of it strikes cold fear into him.

"If I were king," he says aloud to himself. "I would tear that place down."

He presses on. Soon the walls of Jebus are behind him. He starts the steep descent into the treacherous canyons to the south. Beyond there, he knows, lies Judah's desert, stretching into wild barren places. Places, his father says, even God doesn't go.

* * *

"What will be done for the man who kills this Philistine?"

David's voice is sweet as a pan flute. But there is also a sharpness to it, a whistle of urgency. The men around him seem to snap out of a trance at the sound of his speaking.

He moves with agility, almost dancing, and passes a small barley loaf and a slab of goat cheese to his brothers and cousins, a few others, as he works his way down the ranks. They take the food with hands dark with grime, thrust it into their mouths, gnaw it hard. Crumbs pepper their beards. The men all smell of slow rot: piss and sweat and fear and boredom.

"What will be given for the man who removes this disgrace from Israel?" Every time David asks this, he looks toward Goliath, and the eyes of whomever he's speaking with look that way as well. The giant appears strangely small from this distance, a little man all alone. And he looks tethered to the ground, stuck there. He's maybe large as an ox, David thinks, but likely just as slow.

One man finally answers him. "The king will give great wealth to the man who kills the giant. He will also give him his daughter in marriage and will exempt his family from taxes in Israel."

"That's all you've got to say, boy? That's all you care about? What's in it for you? What the king will give you? I should have known as much. You are such a little princeling."

David turns. It is Abinidab, his brother. The second oldest. His name means father of fathers, but Abinidab is childless. His wife carries her barrenness with sour grimness. Abinidab carries it with fierce resentment. He has turned into a quickness with his fists, a shortness of temper, a thirst for strong drink. Most of the other men avoid him for fear of him. His lips shine with grease from the meat he's just devoured.

And then Eliab, David's oldest brother, is there too. His name means God is my father, but he struts and boasts as though it's the other way around. His face is scorched bright red from sun. His anger turns the red several shades deeper. The cords in his neck pull taut, like over-tightened lyre strings, and vibrate as if some brusque hand plucks them.

"Why are you here? Who's looking after those few sheep? You just left them in the wilderness to fend for themselves, didn't you? You are so arrogant and lazy. Your heart is so wicked. You're just here to watch the battle. To watch real men fight so little boys like you can go on playing."

David's breath dries up. He sputters a reply, but it comes out thin and shrill. He takes a breath and tries again. "What? What have I done? Can I not even speak?"

"Apparently not," Eliab says.

David finds his voice again: "I'd like that. I'd like to see some real men fight."

David turns and almost runs into a third brother, Shammah. Shammah rarely speaks and doesn't now. He looks at David in a way that might be derision, might be apathy, might be mild pity. His name means desert, and David always thought his was the truest name among his siblings: a parched and haunted expanse where nothing grows, where wild things wander, where all things wither.

David steps around him and walks several paces down the ranks of men before resuming his question. Those who answer him—most stare at him in sullen wordlessness—always answer in the same way: great wealth, the hand of the king's daughter, exemption from taxation.

He feels a hand on his shoulder. He turns. It's Ashael, smiling as always. Ashael is here like he is, running errands for Israel's army, and to bring news back from the front, where his brothers Joab and Abishai fight.

"Uncle!" Ashael says.

"Ashael."

"This is exciting."

"No, Ashael. This is embarrassing. None of these men have a spine. They smell like latrines. They rot in their own fear. They cower. They shame Israel. They shame *Yahweh*. They bring disrepute on the living God. And great reward awaits the man, any man—you, me, even one of my craven brothers—who kills this uncircumcised fool."

"Why do you care so much, uncle? Have you seen the king's daughter? She's a female version of that uncircumcised Philistine you're itching to kill. You'd have to be as blind as I think that giant is to want her."

David is taken aback. He hasn't considered that Merab might be the daughter Saul intends to give in exchange for the giant's head. *Isn't Michal the intended?* David has seen Michal several times when he's played music for the king, though she seems never to have noticed him. Her beauty distracts him powerfully and haunts him afterward. He has written many songs about her, so maudlin, so keening, so swollen with longing and self-pity, he doesn't even let his sheep hear them.

Her aloofness, almost haughtiness, adds to her beauty in his eyes. He thinks about her constantly, especially at night, in ways that fill him with shame and elation in equal measure. In his mind he has lain with her many times and imagined every curve and dip of her body, his hand tracing out slow, slow her skin's lithe geography. Sometimes his desire is a deep melancholy, an ache in the bones, almost satisfying in itself. Other times it is hunger that spins toward violence, grows horns, grows fangs. He wants to take her down like a wolf takes a ewe lamb.

"Shut up, Ashael. You talk too much. Run, run, do your errands. Do what you're good at. Run." David speaks with the same harshness that Eliab has spoken to him. But then he regrets it instantly.

"Ashael, I am sorry. I speak as a fool."

Ashael laughs, and it is like a fistful of coins tossed in the air, chiming as they fall. He seems incapable of holding anything for very long—a grudge, a thought, a shekel. His innocence is a fast, clear brook that hides nothing.

But he runs anyhow. His running is magnificent, swift and agile as a gazelle. His feet a blur, his body floating. A thin bright blade slicing wind, and a spear shaft turning in it.

David looks at him and loves him. *O, Ashael. May harm stay far from your dwellings.*

* * *

"Are you the one wanting the reward?"

David turns. A thin man with broken teeth, showing through his sneer like a string of tiny skulls, stands before him.

"Who are you?"

"Who am I? Who are you, insolent little whelp? I am Shimei, royal official of the mighty King Saul."

"Yes, I am the one."

"You? You think you can do anything? With your little child's hands that have never seen blood, let alone work? You are just a boy."

"I am the one."

"Come with me. Stupid boy."

Shimei leads David through a knot of men and up a steep, narrow trail to the top of the ridge above the valley. A tent of goatskins is set among dry scrub under a pomegranate tree. Hanging from a pole at its entrance is the king's crest: a hawk, midflight, seizing a rabbit in its talons.

"Wait here." Shimei parts the flaps of the tent and steps inside. David hears voices: one hesitant, stammering, apologetic; the other reedy, rapid-fire, lacerating. David knows this second voice well. It is Saul.

The tent flaps open and Shimei summons David to enter.

"A boy? You brought me a blood boy?" Saul says. Shimei looks down.

"My lord, you asked me to..."

"You worthless servant."

"My lord." David speaks directly to Saul. "It is me. Do you not know me?" Saul fixes him with a puzzled gaze.

"You are a scrawny boy. And short. Did you lose your way, child? Did your daddy send you to look for stray sheep, and you wandered too far?"

"My lord, I..."

"What's that? Speak up. I can't understand baby talk."

"My lord, I have come to tell you that I will fight this uncircumcised Philistine."

"You will do what? Oh, my. How brave! What a brave little lad." Saul looks around. His attendants shake their heads, let out cough-like laughs. But Shimei flings his head back, barks with laughter, hits his own chest to make it louder.

"But with what will you fight him, little child? Will you subdue him with babble?" Then loud, to all those around him: "Will the mouth of this infant silence the avenger?"

David does not answer.

Saul looks toward the shadows, starts to hum one of the songs David has sung for him many times.

Then he takes several quick steps toward David and leans into his face and whispers: "Have you seen this giant?"

"Yes, my lord."

"You have? And the sight of him does not make you... hmm, how shall we say, *your bladder ticklish?* Even my bravest warriors, even Joab and Amasa, lack—what is the word?—*manhood* when they see him. They lack *chutzpah.*" Saul underscored the word with a gesture as though clutching testicles. "This giant, so ugly. So foul. Such a stench. Such a mountain. *A mountain.*" With each word he gets louder, and on the word *mountain* he roars, his arms shooting skyward. "And you, you are a... a boy. A pretty little unshorn boy. Like one of my maidens. Like one of my minstrels. And you smell of sheep. This giant is no sheep. He smells of rotting entrails. He is a lion. He is a bear."

David shakes, but not with fear. With indignation. With anger toward all this cowardice. He thinks of his brother Eliab, sees his proud ruddy face, hears his loud boastful talk, and knows that, in the pinch, it all means nothing. He looks at Saul and wonders why he will not do what is expected of a king.

"A lion? A bear? When a lion or a bear come against *my sheep*, I kill it. I will do the same with this uncircumcised Philistine."

"Ho! I like you, boy. You have pluck, yes. That's refreshing. How a king needs a man or two with pluck. My kingdom for just one such man. But you are no man. You are a boy."

And then Saul leans his face close again to David's and whispers, "Do I know you?"

David starts to answer, but Saul holds up a hand for silence. He stares off in the distance. He grabs his angular cheeks with his long fingers, pulls his crepe-like skin toward his jawbone. It looks like he's peeling off his face. He starts humming again. His eyes roll up to the whites. His body goes rigid. It's as if he's left the scene but left a decoy of himself. His attendants hover close.

Saul shivers from his trance, keenly alert. He looks quick and sharp at David. "Yes. You want to fight, you shall fight. Shimei, bring my armor."

A look of contempt twists Shimei's lips. He balks. "Now."

He leaves the tent and soon returns, bearing mounds of fighting gear. David knows every piece of it intimately, so often has he caressed it with oil, buffed it to a bright sheen. And he knows it won't fit, not a scrap of it. All the same, Shimei, with haughty officiousness, smirking all the while, strips David and suits him up. David's head looks severed and plattered in the armor. The sleeves of the mail drape his knuckles. The sword makes his arm droop. The shield tilts him lopsided.

"Can you walk?" Saul asks.

David moves with an awkward mix of waddle and lunge, like some overfed fowl and fat sheep all bundled together, trying to negotiate some craggy peril.

"Sir, these are yours. I am not used to them."

Saul laughs. "I see. Indeed. You are a boy, after all. Not a king. Not me. Nothing at all like me. No king here," he says, and elicits more laughter from his attendants, a loud bark from Shimei.

"I could only hope, my lord, to be even half as brave and skillful as you.

But my lord, let me go as I am."

"As you are?"

"In my shepherd's tunic. With my slingshot."

"You know the stakes of this little game, boy? This is not some child's war, where after a little sweat and maybe a small cut, a tiny bruise, you go home to suckle your mother's breast, and wake the morrow with no shadow on your path. This is real war. This is you impaled and gibbeted and left for the birds to pluck your eyes. This is your sweet childish blood soaking the thirsty earth. This is every man and woman in Israel enslaved. This is your father in a Philistine yoke, grinding barley like blind Samson. This is your mother and sisters humped by pig-eating heathen."

"Sir, let me fight."

"Perhaps you are crazy." Then to everyone, loud, "Did Shimei bring me the village idiot?"

Laughter, but not from Shimei.

Then to David, in a whisper, "A spirit of madness inhabits you, yes? You speak plain, you don't gibber and drool, claw the ground, but you are not right in the head, are you?"

David is silent.

Then louder: "Or do you think me crazy, boy? You have me for a madman? Is that it?"

"My lord."

Then a whisper again, barely audible: "What do you want with me? Have you come to torment me?"

"My king, do you believe there is a God in Israel?"

Saul leaps up, shouting. "You best be mad, if now you dare question my faith."

"My king, I know you believe. I have seen it. You are like Abraham. You are like Jacob. You are a father to all Israel. This giant has come against *Yahweh. Our God.* And the armies of the Lord. And you. He has come against you. He raises his hand against you, the Lord's anointed. Our God will not allow this. He will be with me. Let me fight."

Astonishment blazes through Saul.

David has the armor off. He is back in his tunic, and a pose of ease loops down through his body.

"I feel I know you, boy."

"Yes, my king."

"Who is your father?"

"Jesse, of Bethlehem."

"Jesse. Hmm. The weapon-maker."

"A farmer, my lord. He is a farmer."

"Ah, of course. An innocent farmer. Honest worker of soil. Toiler of fields. Milker of cows. Shearer of sheep. It must be good to live without secrets. How deep and unshaken must be Jesse's sleep."

"Yes, my lord."

"And you, boy, son of an honest farmer—you wish to fight a giant? With what, one of your father's pruning hooks?"

"My king, I wish to fight him just as I am."

Saul removes his crown. He holds it in a thread of light falling through a gash in the tent's roof. He turns it slowly in his long hands.

"Do you know the weight of this?"

"Six hundred shekels?"

"Do not pretend with me, boy. You know exactly what I mean."

"No, my lord. I do not know the weight of it."

"Crushing. I can barely stand beneath it. Yet I remove it and feel no relief. When it is on, my bones break. When it is off, I am like chaff. A windgust could blow me away. A pebble could fell me."

Saul puts the crown back on. He pushes it down until he winces.

"Crushing," he says.

"My Lord, I am thankful you bear its weight for all of us. For Israel. For me."

Saul closes his eyes. His face is plowed empty. His lips move silently. When he speaks, it's as if he is speaking only to himself.

"Son of Jesse, be careful what you wish for."

* * *

When he was five, a black desert snake bit him. It had burrowed in the loose rock and soil his father had dug for fence posts. He was playing near the post hole, throwing stones into it, six or seven at a time, from further and further distances, with greater and greater force. Then he would lie on his belly, reach down the hole, and fetch each stone. He'd move back a few paces and try tossing them in again. It was something he'd watched Eliab do.

But once, on his belly, he kicked the pile of rock and dirt and a snake coiled out and latched hard on his thigh. He felt only a slight prick, no more than if he'd brushed a thorn. When he looked down, he saw the snake's dark glossy body, its skin a braid of black diamonds, slither away into scrub brush, and he saw four puncture wounds, perfectly symmetrical, in his leg. His father had told him what to do if he was ever bitten by a viper: stand up so the wound was beneath his heart. Move slow. Let the wound bleed free.

He had stood and taken no more than ten steps when he fell face down.

He awoke, burning with fever. He was in his father's arms. He awoke a second time, hazy with sickness. His father was rubbing oil on his wound. The oil was cool, and his father's hand warm, moving in slow gentle circles. His father sang quietly. David had never heard him sing. His voice was gritty, flat, dry, but strangely melodic.

When David woke again, he was lucid and hungry. Many days had passed. The room was empty, but a delicate light played on the walls, and a breeze, sweet with the scent of orange blossoms, spun into the corners. And there was something else, just a hint: the red-earth smell of his father.

This is the memory he draws from, the deep well he lowers his dry bucket into, whenever he needs courage: waking hungry, fully alive, to the lingering scent of his father's vigil, the hovering note of his father's song.

He draws on that memory now as he walks into the Valley of Elah.

The giant is still far away. But David can measure his outrageous size against the dead tree the giant stands beside. Goliath is nearly that tree's equal in burl and girth and height. Even at this distance, the giant's voice comes to him clear.

"Today I defy the armies of Israel. Give me a man and let us fight each other."

David steps out from the creek bed with five stones in his hand. They are perfect. Each is round and smooth and hard, almost translucent. He puts four in his pouch and puts another in the pocket of his sling. He has already rubbed the pocket warm and soft.

He walks toward the giant.

Goliath cocks his head and squints. He seems to be trying to make sense of what he sees. Then his face turns crimson.

"A boy?" Goliath roars with anger. "I demand a man. Give me a man. Give me a king. Give me a prince. Give me a warrior. Am I a dog that you come at me with sticks? May Dagon squat on your heads and expel his stinking bowels."

David keeps walking toward him.

"Come here, little lamb. I will carve you up and give your flesh to vultures and jackals."

David starts to jog. He looks to his left: the armies of Israel look down on him from the hillside. To a man, their faces are blank. Above and behind the army stands Saul. He has pulled himself up to his full height. He has one hand on his hip and the other holds a spear, its shaft planted firm on the ground. He wears his crown. Sunlight flashes from it.

Jonathan stands beside his father. David has only seen Jonathan one time before. He sat in the shadows once when David played music for Saul. He entered the room after David started playing and left before he finished. He listened with his eyes shut, his head tilted back in a kind of rapture.

One of the soldiers, this morning, told David that Jonathan had offered, many times, to fight Goliath. Saul refused, in anger. "And what next?" the soldier had heard Saul say to Jonathan. "My throne? My crown? You son of a rebellious woman."

Then David sees Jesse. His father. His father's face moves in and out from behind a rank of soldiers. It must be him: the disheveled thinning hair, the thatch of whiskers crawling up his cheeks, migrating down his neck. David tries to make sure, but the face disappears entirely.

* * *

He remembers almost nothing else. Only, faintly, the deepening pull on his shoulder as the sling gains speed. Faintly, the lightness of everything—the air, his body, his heart—as the stone unpockets from the sling. Faintly, the giant standing stock still, then teetering, then falling headlong, his taunts stopping mid-air. Faintly, the weight of the giant's sword, pulling him backward as he lifts it above his head, driving him earthward as he swings it down.

And then Saul is there, embracing him, lifting him into his arms. His face shining upon him.

"Ah, my son, David, my son, my son. I knew you were the man of God's own choosing. I knew the moment I first saw you. Such great reward awaits you."

But David keeps looking for his father. He can't see him anywhere. And later, when he asks several soldiers, even his nephew Abishai, even his brother Abinidab, they all say, "What are you talking about? He was never here."

972 BC
Dead Eye
JOAB

I was there. Fighting for Saul. For Israel. But mostly, for myself. I hate Philistines right good, even after some's become friends. See, a Philistine killed my father when I was just a boy, right there in front of me. Laughed while he did it. No, not laughed. It was more the sound a pig makes eating. I wanted nothing so much as to spend my entire life bathing my hands in the blood of them uncircumcised swine. Ha, obviously I was there.

It's hard now for me to get it all right-side-up, what with the legend that's become of it and all. At the time I thought we were done for. Everyone did, though they all said afterward that they knew in their gut that my uncle was destined to win, you could see it in his eyes or the way he moved, and more nonsense like that. Ha. Really? Nobody knew for nothing. Except maybe him. He never seemed to doubt himself for even a blink, walking around like he was some kind of prince. And Saul. Saul knew for sure. For all that man's craziness, he saw things. It was like he had a ghostwife whispering in his ear.

But really? I saw that skinny boy of an uncle of mine, dressed in his dirty tunic, walk down from the king's tent with not a stitch of armor on, not a weapon in sight, and at first I breathed relief. We all knew why the king invited him into the tent. My uncle had been strutting around the camp making no secret of what he'd do if he were in charge, how he'd march straight up to Goliath like that giant was no more than a simple-minded cowherd, and knock him dead. And the king promised a lot to whoever shut that big oaf's mouth. My uncle seemed pretty interested in all them prizes.

He amused me, my Uncle David, talking all like that. But his brothers—they're all uncles of mine too—it made them all angry as hyenas after a lion chases off their kill. Eliab, he was sort of my friend, if uncles are friends, if any kin is. We kinda grew up together. He told me David had always been swaggery and braggy, pretty much from birth, and for no good reason. Nobody liked him. Rumor had it he wasn't even real kin. A bastard. Who knows? I, me, I never much noticed the kid. Until that day.

When old King Saul first called for my uncle, the whole lot of us were terrified by it. And bitter too, more than we already were. We all knew the king was the one supposed to fight Goliath. It was his job, fighting the Lord's battles. There were one or two of us who might have done it, fought that slow, stupid oaf, but what kept us back—well, okay, we were scared, that's true—but what also kept us back was how old Saul would see it. He'd think we were setting ourselves up as rivals. He was pretty touchy about that anyhow. He'd see our bravery as betrayal, not loyalty. Going out like that to do his job for him, well, ha. It was like saying you wanted to be king, not serve the king, see?

More than a few of us figured Saul still had it in him. When he rescued Jabesh-Gilead from Nahash, he slew hordes with his own hands. He was a *dybbuk*. With a spear, he was like Samson with his ass's jawbone. There was even a song about it, him killing all those men, almost a thousand. That's how most of us knew the story, since most of us, except for some real old-timers, were too young to have been there. Until that battle, people didn't want Saul to be king. "Can Saul save us?" they used to ask. Well, Saul answered that, didn't he? Ha!

But now he was funny in the head, Saul was. He saw things that made him shout and sob. Rumor had it that he was awake half the night, and we saw for ourselves that he'd fall asleep standing on his feet. And he'd sleep like the dead.

And he threw things. You had to watch yourself. You'd be minding your own business, cleaning your armor or such, and a bone or stick or rock would come flying at you. You'd look up, and there was Saul, flinging something at you like the village madman tossing his own waste.

He did things altogether, more and more frequent, that didn't add up. No man could make head or tail out of him half the time. So when my uncle, after all his bragging about how he was gonna kill the giant, gets himself invited into Saul's tent, we all stood quiet and still like we were trying not to be noticed by a wolf. No one spoke. I think we feared we'd jinx the thing if we said a word. And then we saw Shimei, that little weasel, go out and come back lugging the king's gear. It was a bad sign.

So when I seen my uncle come out of that tent like he'd gone in, dressed as the farmhand he is, it was a good sign. I clapped and laughed out loud. All the men started talking all happy and relieved, joking and such. The king, see, he's in his right mind after all. We're all so happy, it's like we've won the battle, not avoided it.

But then Saul steps out of his tent, and it's then I knew we're done for. You study to read a man who's above you; you have to or else it will be the ruin of you. You learn the smallest things, see? I guess it's like sailors know wind or hunters know tracks. You watch, real close, how squared or slouched the man's shoulders are, how quick or slow his hands move, whether his feet tread light or not, if his body is all loose like a hand or tight like a fist. You learn to read his face from far distances, to know whether he's feeling this or that.

What I seen, it turns me cold. Saul, he's going to let that boy fight.

Now even back then, I'd been fighting a while. One arm, it's cut up everywhere. I'll show you. See? I'd almost lost an eye once—I got this nasty scar up my forehead, down my cheek, see? I'd killed seven men at that point in my life—okay, one I just mangled. Three I killed with bare hands. I'm saying, I knew what's involved, fighting that giant. Even if you win, you lose. Yeah, he's slow. We all know that. Probably can't see more than ten feet in front of his own fat toes. But within that ten feet, he's like the walls of Jebus. There's no getting past him. Even the meanest man among us is like a baby to him.

But that boy almost saunters. That's how sure he is. I'm embarrassed to be his kin. He walks, not first to the battle line, but to the river at the edge of the valley. I think—oh, maybe he's lost his nerve, he's veering home. But he starts pulling up stones from the creek like he's fetching up fish.

The Philistines, they know something's going on. Total silence. They watch, not the way people watch when they get nervous, but like they watch when they get curious. It's not like that on our side. We watch too, but pissing ourselves. We're all thinking about our wives, our children. We're thinking about our mothers and fathers, and all that. They're all gonna be slaves soon. It might have taught my mother a lesson, okay, but I didn't want my brother Ashael wearing some ox's yoke, grinding grain. Or even Abishai, for that matter. Though it might do him some good, for a spell.

My uncle starts moving quick. The Philistines must have thought we were sending a messenger boy to surrender. But he starts running fast, straight at Goliath. The giant looks confused at first. He can't bring himself to get battle ready. I could read that, any fighter could—his contempt. He refuses to take this seriously. He stands careless and wide, like a bully baiting a yapping dog. He shouts insults, makes rude gestures. Ha, it'd all be funny if it wasn't.

The boy just keeps running. His slingshot is out, swinging and swinging. Old Goliath is still blathering away, but otherwise all of us, both sides, are quiet as the grave. We're so quiet, we can hear the slingshot. I once heard an army of locusts coming at me. This was like that. At last the giant—he's still standing wide—pulls a knife from his belt. It's longer than most men's swords. It's all I guess he'll waste on the boy. He starts moving too. A bull all riled up. I almost look away, okay? He is my uncle, after all. I know what's about to happen. Goliath is gonna gut him like a lamb. A lamb to the slaughter. He won't even step back to avoid the blood.

But it's not what happens.

There is only one place in all that giant's armor that can do him any harm. A tiny little patch of soft bone, small as a shekel, right here, right between the eyes. You have to have the hand of God to hit that spot straight.

David hits it. Deadeye.

It is a sound no more alarming than a woodpecker knocking a tree. *That will anger him*, I think. Goliath just stands, doesn't move. Then the big oaf's arms go limp, like this. His knife drops. He sways. He buckles. He drops straight down, a big tree falling. His face hits the ground so hard it doesn't even bounce back.

My uncle cuts his head off with the giant's own sword. It takes him five hard whacks. Then he picks up that head in one hand—that surprises me, his arms seem so thin—and holds it high.

The Philistines, they go crazy. Every one of them starts running for cover. We go after them.

But not me. And not the man beside me. We both stand there, doing nothin'. The man asks my name.

"Joab," I tell him.

"This boy, this giant-slayer—you know him? You know whose son he is?"

"He's my uncle. His father is Jesse of Bethlehem."

"This is truth? He's your uncle. He's… so young? A boy. You're a man."

"I'm the firstborn of his family's firstborn."

"Does he have a name, this uncle of yours?"

"David."

"I will follow this David," the man says. "Anywhere. Anywhere he goes, I will go. Anything he asks, I will do."

The man runs down the hill to join the rest.

But me, I just stand there.

972 BC
Dowry
MICHAL

I never liked my sister, Merab. She bossed me. She resented me. She was born with a mulish stubbornness and no beauty—maybe the lack of the one made for the abundance of the other—and I was born with much beauty and sheepish pliability, a readiness to become whatever any man asked.

Once, when we were girls—she was maybe eight, I four—she had a moment of kindness toward me. Our mother often raged terribly at one or both of us. I think now, now that I know of such things, that she was bitter all through. But one day her rage reached a new pitch, and she took a stick and hit me hard all over—my legs, my buttocks, my back, my neck, my head, over and over, and afterward she would not console me though I crumpled to the ground and wailed loud.

Merab picked me up. She stroked my wounds. She spoke soft words to me, the only time I remember her doing such. She told me to pay no mind, that Mother had many worries troubling her, that she never meant to hurt me. Mother never hit me again, not with a stick, and Merab never consoled me again. But I had seen that side of my sister, though ever after she hid it well. For that, I did not hate her.

But when my father offered her in marriage to David, for that I did.

The first time I saw David was the day he became champion of Israel, the day he killed the giant, and from that moment I never wanted anything so badly. I heard his song before I saw him. It rose from the valley like a mass of swallows dancing on air. It flew from town to town on the wings of lutes and harps and tambourines, and it was carried by the glad voices of wives and daughters, sisters and mothers. It tilted and whirled toward me. Boys ran along the edge of the procession. Men joined in. They laughed, they clapped. They gulped strong drink. Some men even bellowed the song themselves.

By the time the song reached Gibeah, it was an anthem. The women danced as they sang:

Saul has slain his thousands,
and David his tens of thousands.

His name smote me. I could hardly breathe. I knew of the victory hours before—the news came to us by a swift-footed messenger. But that news was a wind that kept gathering, a wave that kept mounting. It must have started in the village of Socoh as barely a whisper, a simple song of thanks, but by the time it reached my ears, it was loud, fierce, defiant.

Then a cheer went up, so loud it drowned the song. The crowds in the streets below surged forward. I watched from my window. I caught a glint of spear tips pricking over the hilltop. They seemed to spin in sunlight. Then I saw the ranks of soldiers, at first obscured by the crowd, but the crowd kept parting to let them through. Then a break in the ranks. A large space opened. In it, pretty maidens spun. They shook timbrels and sang over and over, faster and faster:

Saul has slain his thousands,
and David his tens of thousands.

The refrain built until it almost exploded. Then it stopped full. And then it began anew, slow and rhythmic at first, but building. Over and over, faster and faster.

And then there he was. I saw him through the window of my father's house. Even from the distance, I gasped at his beauty. The girls singing in the street pricked me with jealousy. I wanted to be among them, in the swelter and the dust, to join my voice to the voices of milkmaids, scullery maids, washerwomen. I would have stripped my royal gown clean off and become as undignified as a servant girl to sing for him, to dance before him.

His hair was black and fell in rings to his shoulders. His skin was ruddy. His step was light. Everything in him flowed like water. Everything about him was effortless. His face at first wore a solemn expression, but then something made him laugh and everyone laughed with him. His eyes, his dark eyes, were brighter than stars. How the champion of Israel distinguished himself that day.

I loved him from that moment.

David and my father stood together amid the throng. Everyone cheering. The song rising. I tried to read my father's face, to divine what he was feeling. But his eyes were hidden in shadow.

They came, David and my father, into his throne room. And then they were alone. I watched from behind the lattice. David bowed before my father, and my father did something I had never before and never since seen him do: he bowed in turn.

"You won a great battle today, David, my son. The people salute you. They sing for you. They say you killed ten thousand! One man was all I counted, but the people say ten thousand. Well, that is quite a feat. How indebted we all are to you."

"*Yahweh* gave me strength."

"Ah, yes. Indeed. Indeed. What would the champion of Israel wish from his king?"

David hesitated.

"Sir, I feel… Wasn't there… for the man who killed Goliath, weren't there certain things promised?"

"Certain things?" my father said. "What things? Did I promise you anything?"

"No, my king. It's nothing. I mean, I want nothing. It is enough for me to serve you."

"To serve me. Yes. This can be arranged."

"Thank you, my king."

"But you also want to be my son?"

"My king?"

"My son-in-law, I mean. You want to marry my daughter, do you not?"

"My king, I would not ask such a thing. I am a lowly shepherd. I am unworthy."

"Yes, of course. But you asked me for what is promised. Should I not give you what you deserve?"

And I knew then, because I had learned from an early age to read every tone and every texture of my father's voice, that he was going to offer him Merab. Ugly obstinate Merab. Merab to be his wife, Merab to share his bed.

Hate welled in me, for all of them.

1025 BC

Train My Hands for War

We must train you properly. Train you for war. A boy running around in his shepherd's costume slinging stones, this will not do. Brave as you are, my son."

"I am honored, my king. Since I was a boy, I have dreamed of someone training my hands for war."

"Ah, yes. Since you were a boy. Hmm. I'm sure you have, out there with your sheep, playing with sticks and stones. Well, this will be different. Let me introduce you to Abner. My uncle. The best fighter in Israel. He can leave a hundred Philistines bereft of their foreskins before even one knows it's missing. I have asked him personally to undertake your training, to leave no stone unturned. Or unslung."

David laughs. Neither Saul nor Abner do.

Abner is short, wide, brutal-looking. His face is a wild terrain of pocks and scars and seams, a Judean wilderness left to the elements. His features are blunt. The bridge of his nose twists one way, then the other. He is expressionless. He doesn't smile or frown. When he speaks, his mouth barely moves. All the same, David senses he's deeply unhappy about this assignment.

"No little prince crap from you, understood?" Abner says.

"Understood."

"I see you swagger or brag even once, I'll cut you down myself. I'll do what Goliath threatened but was too stupid to do, too slow to make happen. And unlike that old doddering windbag, I got eyes that see.

And I'm damn fast."

David wants to say, *Then why didn't you fight him?* But says instead, "Yes, my *ba'al*."

"Enough talk. Grab that sword. Let's see what you got."

Abner's shield bearer holds out a sword, and David takes it. He's only held a real sword twice. The first was three years ago when he snuck into a stash of his father's weapons, forged in his secret smithy, to be sold that week in the black market, and spent an early morning wheeling it, slicing air with it, thrusting it into the belly of a hay bale. He returned it to its bundle only minutes before his father walked in the shed where he hid the stash.

"What are you doing here?"

"Nothing."

"I don't want you here. Ever."

"I'm sorry."

The second time was when he raised Goliath's sword and brought it down, again and again, on the giant's thick stump of neck, hacking away like he was hoeing hard earth. The blood from each blow spattered on his tunic until the hem was red and dripping, warm then cold. When he ran afterward, he had to will himself to ignore its wet stickiness slapping against his knees.

He twirls the sword now in his hand, to surprise and impress Abner with his skill. Abner looks at him with blank expression. David grips the sword's handle, acts as if he's about to leap one way, spins, and comes at Abner sideways. Abner, hardly moving, slashes the sword from David's hand, then places the tip edge against David's neck.

"Next time, I won't spare you. Now stop the games. Not all Philistines are big and blind and stupid like the giant. They are lizards. They can catch a pretty little damsel fly like you without blinking."

For the next week, Abner is brutish with him. He bullies him. Mocks him. Mostly, he shakes his head silently, with slow disgust. He makes David repeat movements—thrusts and feints and parries, lunges and rolls, techniques with his shield, using his spear in close fighting. He pushes and pushes David until his body is spent but must keep going, until the instinct for killing is all that's left.

"This is what real battle is like," Abner says. "Running at a big wide target like that giant, that's nothing. Your dainty little body didn't even break a sweat. Real battle, your mind shuts down, your body feels nothing even when everything howls with pain. You keep going anyhow. The sword and your arm, they become one. Sometimes, you can't let go after. Your mates have to peel back your fingers for you."

At least once a day, Abner puts David on the ground, just to show he can. He presses his face into the earth until David tastes it, its grit and salt, until his mouth fills with dirt, and after, when Abner leaves him to pick himself up, he has to spit it out and slap it off. His cheeks are bruised and abraded from Abner's harshness. Mostly, when Abner puts him down and holds him there, he says nothing. David can feel the man's strength, the wrenching coiling power in him, the way he can concentrate his strength into a pinpoint of lethal force.

But sometimes, Abner puts his mouth close to David's ear and whispers. "You're so pretty, but I'll fix that." Or, "I don't have a clue why Saul likes you. You bring nothing to his kingdom."

These moments pull up David's memories of Eliab, of Eliab's cruelty. Once a week, often more, he'd find David alone and would hurt him in some way, physically and verbally.

"You are not one of us, you know? You're a bastard. That's why my father can't stand you. You remind him of his mistake. That's why my mother lives in shadows. It's her heartbreak." And then Eliab would kick or punch him, lay him out, and then hold his face in the dirt, just like Abner.

One day Abner pushes his mouth so close to David's ear that he can feel the cracked dryness of his lips, like a shed snakeskin, against his lobe.

"Don't think I don't know what you're up to, little boy. Don't think I haven't known your game from the beginning. I know you lust after Saul's crown. Saul's throne. Saul's kingdom. I'm watching you. And I am telling you, never. It will never happen. I will make sure of that."

David never answers him. But he thinks, "One day, I will get you."

972 BC
Closer Than a Brother
DAVID

Ah, my dear Jonathan. No one speaks your name any longer. Of course, that is my doing. When at long last I took your father's throne, I forbade the mention of your father's name, and my orders were heeded over much: not only him, but his wife, his sons, his daughters, your wives, your children, and you—these names never passed another's lips again, not at least in my hearing. I did not even know your poor maimed son Mephibosheth was in my kingdom until I tracked him down like a fugitive. And, I confess, his fear of me had turned him into such.

But your name is on my lips, always. Do you remember, my brother, that first day we met? It was the day I killed the giant, the very same. Or was it after that? All those days, all that happened years ago, is now a reverie to me. I was in awe of you then. All those stories, even then they were only whispered as rumors are whispered, to keep your father's jealousy from flaring and running like grass fire. But the stories were told anyway, of your bravery, your skill, your beauty.

What surprised me was your humility. I thought I'd meet a proud man, but I met you: kind, gentle, funny. And willing to become nothing, for what? So that I would become great. What did you see in me that no one else did? My father barely saw me, and what he saw he didn't like. My brothers saw me, yes, and hated me. My mother, my dear mother, Nitzevet, she saw me and loved me, but her seeing was from a great distance that I could not cross.

But you, when I had nothing, when I was nothing, you stood up close to me and saw me. You saw I had something, that I was something. But what I cannot forget is that you loved me with or without these things. You would have loved me even if I was nothing and had nothing. You did love me that way, in my nothingness.

You taught me how to find strength in God. It wasn't any prayer you prayed, not any words you spoke. It was you. Whenever you drew near, the Lord was my shepherd, and all my wanting quieted. Whenever you drew near, my heart grew still.

How I wish you were here with me now, in this dying light, where I have become trapped in the cave of decrepitude, this terrible withering of body but alertness of mind.

And I am so thirsty and cannot remember where the water is.

1025 BC
Friend

Jonathan stands there, tall as his father, as thin too. But not with his father's eyes, heavy-lidded, wary: Jonathan's are bright like sun cresting hilltops, but they fall to great depths.

"You are David." It is a statement, not a question. "I saw you kill the giant. A valiant deed. Heroic. It saved us all. I thought you might be older." This last observation is not a taunt, perhaps a compliment.

"I am just a boy, as everyone keeps reminding me."

"Yesterday I watched my father's uncle train you. Impressive."

"Impressive? What was impressive about it?"

"You."

"Ha. Funny. That's not how Abner sees it."

"Oh, he's an ass. Don't mind him. He does that with everyone, tries to break them. He did that with me. What he won't tell you, I will. You were born to fight. You were born for the battlefield."

"Really?"

"I've watched Abner train a hundred men, starting with me. Most men he succeeds in breaking. And even those who survive him, they don't have what you do."

"Which is?"

"Vision. You see things before they happen."

"Hasn't helped me best Abner."

"But he fears it. He fears you. He fears what you have. Trust me."

David is shorter than Jonathan by several inches, though Jonathan is slighter of build. David's shoulders jut out a hand's breadth on either side of Jonathan's. Jonathan puts both hands on those shoulders and smiles at him.

"Anyhow, as I said, thank you. For your heroic deed."

"What about you? You have done enough heroic deeds for all of us."

Jonathan laughs. "Right. Have you heard the one about me killing two thousand Philistines with a cony's bone for a knife? Or slaying them with your foul breath. Seems old Samson pales beside my exploits."

"It's not true?" David says. "I am crushed with disappointment."

"It was only twelve hundred. And my sister helped."

"But you did take out an entire Philistine phalanx, did you not? Just you and your armor-bearer?"

Jonathan looks away. "I try to forget that."

"Why? We all remember it. We can't get enough of it."

"No," Jonathan says. "You remember only part of it."

"There's more?"

"I will tell you. For your ears only."

* * *

"Cursed," Saul says, "is any man who eats before I have avenged myself on my enemies."

And then he sends his six hundred fighting men, freshly emboldened, to join Jonathan and his armor-bearer in their rout of the Philistines.

The air turns misty with blood, the ground muddy with it.

But a remnant of Philistines escapes. Saul's army tries to catch them. But they droop and lag with hunger. Killing is like digging a ditch. It is a long strain on the limbs. It makes the men's own flesh a dead weight. They need food.

They enter a wooded area. The cool of its shade revives them slightly. They pick up the pace. But then they slow. Beside the trail something moves on the ground, a viscous mound of amber liquid that brims and oozes into a wide puddle. Each man looks at it with desperate longing. Their arms impulsively stretch toward it, their hands opening like a plea. Then they jerk back as though stung.

Jonathan pauses when he sees it. He plunges the end of his staff into the sticky pulsating mass. He turns the staff slowly and then lifts the tip out. It is honey. It comes up in a golden translucent ribbon. With each turn of the staff, the honey wraps itself around its tip into a tight glimmering ball. Jonathan carefully turns the staff around, end to end, and swallows the honey in one gulp. His eyes flash with astonishment. His body straightens.

A sound of shock and envy ripples through the ranks.

"Your father bound the army under a strict oath," Abner says to Jonathan. "'Cursed be any man who eats today!' That is why the men are faint."

Jonathan turns on Abner with a swiftness and force that makes the older man step backward.

"My father," Jonathan says, and the words themselves are spoken as curse—final, terrible, irrevocable—"is a *nabal*."

Abner recoils. It is as though Jonathan has spat on him.

"Who calls their own father a fool? Who calls their king this?"

Jonathan raises his body to its full height. He dwarfs Abner. His mouth curls in scorn as he speaks: "My father has made trouble for the country. See how my eyes brightened when I tasted a little of this honey. How much better it would have been if we had eaten today some of the plunder we took from their enemy. Would not the slaughter of the Philistines have been even greater?"

Jonathan's defiance looses something primal in the rest of the men, and in camp that evening they hack the necks of the plundered livestock. While the animals lie athwart the ground, still panting in their death throes, they excavate the flesh, pulling sodden slabs of it off the bone with bare hands. They devour it uncooked.

Saul is sickened. He commands it stop. He takes a Philistine cart captured in battle, hews it with an axe, and piles its splintered pieces in a towering mound. He takes fire and lights it. It blazes hotly. The flames leap high and the wood pops loud. Fistfuls of sparks burst into the black night.

"She's pourin' down sulfur on us, boys," a soldier calls out, "just like Sodom."

But no one laughs. Saul steps close to the firelight. His body is a flame itself, a slithering braid of blackness and redness. "This," he says, in a voice both aggrieved and imperious, his long arms sweeping over the fire, "is an altar to the Lord."

The men are silent. Then, one by one, and then many at a time, they cook their meat over the fire's white and powdery coals. When the meat is done, they eat it with slow, stiff dignity, as though they are different men from those who earlier gulped raw flesh. Now they are men who stand apart from that, who sit in judgment on that, who would never stoop to that.

When they are sated, Saul stands up again.

"Let us set out again. We will go after the Philistines by night and plunder them until daylight. Let us not leave one of them alive."

"Do whatever seems best to you," the men answer.

Saul is about to issue the next command when he senses someone standing behind him. He turns. The bald head of the priest Ahijah shines in the firelight. His face is sheeted with oily sweat.

"Ahijah?"

"My lord, let us first inquire of God."

Saul is puzzled. Ahijah is capable of, even prone to, great shows of haughty piety, but he seems to have no more true feeling for God than a Philistine whore does. He's compliant, yes. He's unintimidating. He does what Saul asks and agrees with everything Saul suggests. He's not the least like Samuel. And many of the men, Saul included, have spells of religious fervor. When some tragic misfortune seems to demand strange rituals to assuage divine anger, or secure divine favor, they turn to Ahijah. The priest rises to these occasions with stern solemnity: grand elaborate gestures, darkly intoned incantations, the brandishing of hieratic authority.

He has his uses.

But to initiate something, and so plain a thing as inquiring of the Lord—this is new.

Saul looks at him quizzically. He catches a flicker of movement in Ahijah's eyes: the priest is looking elsewhere, with that smirk he often wears. Saul turns to follow the line of his gaze but can't see past the shadows of the fire. He can't see who or what Ahijah is looking at.

"Alright," Saul says, his voice weary. "Shall I go down after the Philistines? Will the Lord give them into Israel's hands?"

Ahijah holds a bowl of sheep fat. He flings the fat onto the fire. It flares and hisses spectacularly. The priest closes his eyes, murmurs what sounds like a foreign tongue. He intones a prayer in a voice breaking at the edge of shrillness. He waits. The fire banks down to a throbbing glow. The night is vast. The silence huge.

Ahijah looks gravely at Saul.

"God will not answer."

All the men know what this means: there is sin in the camp, and God is silent with anger. A knot of dread tightens in Saul's chest. He is suddenly on wide alert, bristling with imperial command.

"Come here, all you who are leaders of the army," he orders. "Let us find what sin has been committed today. As surely as the Lord lives, even if it lies with my son Jonathan, he must die."

Ahijah touches Saul's shoulder, and Saul leans his ear to the man's mouth. He whispers something that makes Saul's face darken.

"You stand over there," Saul says to the leaders of the army, pointing to one side of the dying fire. "Jonathan, come. My son, stand with me."

The leaders rise and move to their place. Saul strains his eyes into the darkness, looking for Jonathan. Then his son appears, walking slowly toward him. His mouth is a straight line. His eyes are hard. He has come from the direction where Ahijah had averted his gaze. Saul turns to read the expression on the priest's face. Ahijah is looking at the ground as though praying. The knot of dread in Saul's chest tightens.

Ahijah goes through an elaborate ritual of casting lots, shaking painted stones in a clay jar and drawing them out, pronouncing on their meaning. One by one, Israel's leaders are eliminated.

It is down to Saul and Jonathan.

Saul gives the next command loudly, but the tightness in his chest is now in his throat. The words come out thin, taut, sharp: "Cast the lot between me and Jonathan, my son."

The fat priest wears a look of piteous reverence. He places his painted stones in the jar and prays, "O God, reveal thy will in this matter. Speak, O Lord, and make clear the one on whom your guilt rests."

He shakes the jar with ponderous motion. The stones clatter in the jar's hard belly. He holds it against his own belly to still it and waits until he hears the last clack of the stones. Then he waits a moment longer. He reaches into the mouth of the jar, pulls out his fist. When he opens it, the red stone sits on the flat of his palm. "Saul," he says, "our great king has been found innocent. The lot falls to Jonathan."

"Tell me what you have done," Saul says to Jonathan, barely audible.

"I merely tasted a little honey with the end of my staff. Must I die for this?"

Saul is shaking now. "May God deal with me, be it ever so severely, if you do not die, Jonathan."

All at once, the other men erupt in a melee of shouting. They surge forward, engulfing Saul, the priest, Jonathan. They pull Jonathan further into the throng of themselves. They openly shout defiance at Saul. The king is bewildered, then enraged. And then he walks away. The night shuts on him like a door.

At dawn, the men break camp, wordless. On the far hill, the remnant of the Philistines watch. They shout something. It is no more intelligible than branches rattling together.

Only later do they realize that Ahijah has disappeared like smoke.

And with him, even Saul's pretense of hearing God disappears as well.

* * *

"Would your father have… carried through with his vow?"

"With killing me?" Jonathan says. "Maybe. Who's to say?"

"Jonathan, I'm curious about something else. If you don't mind."

"Ask. Ask anything."

David hesitates.

"Ask me, David. Withhold nothing from me. I will do the same with you."

"It's also about your father."

David feels like he is about to pass something very valuable, very fragile, very dangerous to Jonathan, something he fears dropping.

"Go on."

"I served your father for many months before I fought Goliath."

"In what way?"

"I was one of his armor-bearers. In fact, when he had his armor brought for me on the day of battle, I knew every piece of it, its exact weight and color and design—all of it. The greaves. The helmet. The breastplate. Everything. I had seen it and polished it and hung it a dozen times or more. I also knew it would not fit me."

"And so?" A slight impatience enters Jonathan's voice. David takes a breath and continues.

"I was his musician too. I sang, I played the harp. It made your father…" David stops, seems to search the space in front of him for the right word. "It made him calm."

"Ah," Jonathan says. "That was you?"

"That was me."

"I should have paid more attention. I confess I never noticed you until you killed the champion of Gath. Our family—and nation—owes you a greater debt than first I thought. You have brought my father much peace. But you said you were curious about something."

"Yes." Again David hesitates, looks away. "He didn't know me, Jonathan.

That day I fought Goliath. Your father looked straight at me and had not the least idea who I was. Before, he called me by name. He asked after my father and my brothers, and even once my mother. He spoke about what great warriors Eliab and Abinidab and Shammah were, how thankful he was for all of us, and sometimes…" David pauses again, but then charges on. "Sometimes, he confided in me. He spoke his heart to me. He called me his… he said kind words to me."

"He called you his son."

"Yes."

"And so?" Jonathan says.

"Well, that day I stood before your father in the valley of Elah, it was as if he had never seen me before, not once, not ever."

David sees the moment clearly now, Saul leaning toward him, his eyes keenly inquisitive, making judgments with quicksilver speed. There was not even a hint of the dull glaze or cold terror that David had often seen in the king's eyes. Yet Saul's quick bright eyes, looking straight at him, were devoid of the tiniest flicker of recognition. At first, David thought Saul might be doing this on purpose—a game, a ploy. But as David made his case about why he should fight, as he talked of lions and bears, as he stumbled and lurched around in the king's armor, as he strode out to meet the giant, he realized it was no game, no ploy.

Saul never knew him.

"Is there more?" Jonathan asks.

"Yes. He didn't recognize me. But in a way, he did. In a way, he knew exactly who I was. And somehow that made it worse. I know I am making no sense. I'm sorry."

Jonathan looks away. The silence widens between them.

When Jonathan turns back to David, his eyes are wet and red.

"My father is not well," he says. His voice is a whisper, and unsteady. "You know this."

"Yes."

"There is more to it than you think."

"Oh," David says.

"He fears…" Jonathan's voice trails off.

"He fears what?"

"You know, he never wanted to be king. Not at first. He was searching for his father's stray asses and ran into Samuel. Samuel—did you ever meet him? Such a grim, sour old man. I never liked him. He was always in a hurry, always angry. Well, Father—just a boy then—gets lost, can't find even a lump of those asses' dung, and he runs into old Samuel. Samuel pulls out a horn of oil and anoints him right there. Just like that. The Lord's anointed. He makes Father king, and not a single person, save the old prophet himself, is there to witness it or vouch for it. Then Samuel gathers all Israel, to pick their king. But really, it's to confirm God's choice. Or maybe Samuel's. The people come together. Samuel makes a speech. Tells everyone how bad kings are. They take and take, he says. But the people say they want one. So Samuel has them draw lots. And the lot narrows and narrows until only my father is left standing. Except he's not standing. He's hiding. He's crawled under a pile of saddles and packs. He's scared witless. Running from the whole thing. When I think of it, I want to weep."

"I didn't know this."

"It's not something one boasts about, a king hiding like a thief. Any more than one boasts about a father trying to kill a son just for eating honey. But what I'm saying is that my father came to the kingship reluctant. No part of him wanted it. He was dragged into it. So it's surprising."

"What's surprising?"

"How much it means to him now. How much he clings to it. How much he fears losing it."

Both are silent.

"There is another thing," Jonathan says. "Another shameful thing. Why am I telling you all this?"

"We withhold nothing from each other."

"Yes. But these things are for your ears only."

"Yes."

"It was the last time Samuel visited my father. Father had won yet another great battle—there were so many in those early days. He was unstoppable. This victory was against the Amalekites. Israel's oldest enemy, from the days of Moses in the desert. Father routed them thoroughly. Crushed them. But he kept alive their king, Agag. And the best of their livestock. He thought Samuel would be pleased, but the *se'er* was furious. He hewed Agag to pieces himself, right in front of my father. And he told my father a terrible thing."

David waits.

"I should not be telling you this."

"You need not."

"I can trust you, David? Trust you never to betray me? Or my father? Or my family?"

"I give you my oath. I will make a covenant of loyalty with you."

"My father is often harsh with me. He treats me like a bastard son. But understand this: I would die for him. I would kill for him."

There is an iciness in Jonathan's tone. A darkness in his eyes.

"As you should."

"David, listen. Samuel tore the kingdom from my father. For not killing Agag. For keeping a bunch of damned sheep. For that. And he told my father that he was giving the kingdom to another—to a neighbor, to a man after God's own heart."

David can hardly breathe.

"Don't you see, David?"

"Pardon?"

"Don't you see—why my father is so afraid?"

"Yes."

"And don't you see, who this man is?"

David's heart thunders. It is so loud in his own ears—a war drum, a mountain falling, a giant roaring—he fears Jonathan can hear it too.

"I, no. Um, no. I don't see. I don't see who it is."

"Don't be foolish, David. Everyone knows who this man is."

"Everyone knows?" David's voice is thin, tight.

"Yes, everyone."

"They do?"

"Don't play coy, David. You know too."

"I do?"

"David," and Jonathan puts a firm hand on David's shoulder, looks at him eye to eye. "I am the man. That is why my father sometimes hates me. It's why he wants me dead. It's why he would have carried through in killing me. It's why he's not right in the head."

1024 BC

Bride Price

King Saul offers David his daughter Merab for killing Goliath. David is amazed. And reluctant. She is a princess. He is nobody from nowhere. Not long ago he was a mere shepherd boy and errand boy, a mule with two legs, running here, running there.

But he hesitates for another reason: she is homely as a goat. Her arms and legs are stumpy posts, and the whole of her is thickset as an ox, and she's ruddy like a man should be. Her voice grates. Her hair is a roof of thatch. It migrates down her cheeks. There is stubble on her chin. When Saul offers her, David demurs.

"I am unworthy to be the king's son-in-law."

Saul nods, with grim clarity.

But Michal, Saul's youngest daughter, she is another story. She is everything Merab is not: delicate, radiant, soft-voiced, creamy-skinned. She has a body firm and curved as lathed wood, though to touch it, he thinks, would be like peeling fruit. Her hair is lustrous dark, moonlight on river.

And she seems smitten by him. Merab looks at him with something between hidden lust and open loathing, but Michal blushes when he's about, whispers to her attendant. And then, most disarming of all, she stares at him with unconcealed desire, her dark eyes a private chamber she's beckoning him to enter. He gets tongue-tied around her. Words skew on his lips. Or he talks too much, too quickly. Words rush wild and panicky from his mouth faster than he can shepherd them. He speaks of his exploits in battle, trying to play them down and play them up at the same time. In her presence David feels stained and burdened with his own ordinariness. He sees himself as he is, or recently was, no more than a minion picking twigs and burrs from sheep's coats, bundling barley loaves and cheese slabs to his boorish warrior brothers. And she is every inch, in every movement and word, the king's daughter.

Soon after, one of Saul's servants asks for a private word with David. "Look, the king is pleased with you. We all like you. Become his son-in-law."

David knows that Saul has given Merab to another man. He's out of danger there. The thought that now Michal is being offered to him makes his throat dry. But he knows enough to again protest his unworthiness. "Do you think it is no small matter to become the king's son-in-law? I am only a poor man, and little known."

He knows this is no longer true. His fame spreads. He sees how the young women, and even some of the older ones, look at him. He sees how the young men flock to him, pressing hands to his shoulders in camaraderie, pleased at all he says. He sees how the old warriors at first resented him, but more and more give him grudging respect. His nephew Joab the other day stood athwart him in the armory. David thought it was a challenge. But then Joab put his hand behind David's neck, pulled him close, and kissed him on the cheek. And Saul's attendants at first held aloof from him, but now hail him, seek him, savor his every word. Almost fawn over him. It's as though he's the king's son already.

And last week, he bested Abner. Abner, at Saul's insistence, had kept training David. But his attacks on David, his acts of personal humiliation, were becoming harder and harder to inflict. He tried, one last time: came at David to trip him, hurl him to the ground, whisper his taunt. David anticipated every move. It was as if Abner was slowed to quarter speed and was announcing all of his movements before he made any. David waited, and when Abner made his final move, stepped aside, tripped him, flung him down, and put his mouth to his ear.

"You are yesterday's man. If you touch me again, I will kill you."

* * *

"I am unworthy to marry the princess Michal," David says, but he doesn't feel unworthy.

David watches the servant return to bear the news to Saul. Regret shafts through him like a spear. He almost calls him back. But the servant returns soon enough anyhow. This time, other servants huddle around.

"The king wants no other bride price," the servant says, "than a hundred Philistine foreskins to take revenge on his enemies. You have five days to accomplish this."

David lowers his head to hide his pleasure. He imagines Michal's dress falling off her thin shoulders. He imagines her naked body glowing.

"Tell the king," he says, "tell him I am humbled. That I am honored. Tell him I am pleased to become his son-in-law. Tell him yes. Oh yes."

* * *

David musters his men and they leave that day. He plans to start at the Philistine outpost near Micmash, where Jonathan and his armor-bearer once routed a whole phalanx of Philistines. David went there one day on a scouting expedition and studied the landscape. He'd spied then a difficult path, treacherous and precarious, probably the one Jonathan took, that crisscrosses up the cliff face.

He and three of his men climb it now. It will give them the virtue of surprise. The plan is that, as he and his three warriors climb, his other men will come up the easy way. Together they will wipe out whoever is there. Maybe twenty foreskins. Then once they take this outpost, they will all wait until night and ride in on Micmash itself. Raid it while the town sleeps. By morning they should have their hundred foreskins.

It all goes so well, David gets an idea.

And so it is that, two days before Saul's deadline, David returns to court and hands a bulging leather pouch to the servant who sent him. When the foreskins are counted, one after the bloody next, they total two hundred.

The servant walks into Saul's throne room. The king is staring, transfixed, at something on his robe.

"My lord, your servant David has returned from battle."

"My servant who?"

"David, my lord."

"What battle?"

"You sent him to fetch the dowry price for your daughter Michal. One hundred Philistine foreskins."

The news appears to mean nothing to Saul. Or to puzzle him. He cocks his head, arches his eyebrows, purses his lips. "I asked for foreskins? A hundred?"

"Yes, my lord. David has brought them back. But not one hundred. Two hundred!"

"Two hundred? Foreskins?"

"Yes, my lord. For Michal."

"She will be… thrilled," Saul says. "And the son of Jesse, is he… well?"

"Very well, my lord."

"Oh."

"The foreskins, my lord. They have been counted twice, to make certain. Two hundred. Would you like to see them?"

A look of revulsion convulses Saul's face. "No," he says. "I believe you. And you are certain that the son of Jesse is well?"

"He is hearty, my Lord. We all are in great awe of him. He is a valiant warrior, and…"

"I do not ask your opinion of him."

"Forgive me, my lord."

"Call him. I shall see him now, alone."

The servant leaves and David enters. David bows, head bent.

"Yes, yes," Saul says. "Stand. Stand up. Be a man."

David's ruddiness glows in the dim light of the room. His eyes are bright with laughter. He smiles at the king, and it is as if sunlight blazes in from some long-shut window suddenly flung wide.

"I applaud you, son of Jesse," Saul says. His voice is measured and calm, with a hint of singsong. "My servants tell me they are in awe of you. *Great* awe, to be exact. Well done. Well done."

"I merely want to serve my king and my God."

"Ah, yes. And nothing more, I'm sure. Well, you will serve us both, your God and your king, by becoming my son-in-law."

"It is my great honor to accept, my lord."

David notices that Saul's right hand grips the shaft of his spear. The hand trembles like a fly freshly trapped in a web, trying to get loose, but its frantic efforts to escape only trap it deeper.

* * *

David marries Michal. They are rapturous. They cannot stop looking at each other. Touching each other. He smiles like a fool. She twirls like a dancing maid, laughing. Jonathan claps and sings and laughs and dances, as though he's the one getting married.

Saul looks on. He doesn't smile. He doesn't laugh. His bony fingers fret the edge of his robe. His eyes flash anger and then go dark, over and over. His lips twitch like he's talking to the dead. Ahinoam, Saul's wife, hovers between her husband's gloom and her children's gladness.

That night, Michal enters the marriage chamber. David sits, nervous, at the edge of the bed. Her eyes are hooded with shyness. She wears a simple cotton smock that merely hints at the outline of her body. But then she stands with the lamplight behind her. The cotton becomes diaphanous. Her naked body glows beneath. Desire rises fiercely in him, and he stands up and takes her. They plunge down and down. It is like falling into a swift wild river. They are fish returning to the place they were born.

"I love you, David. You are my beloved," she says.

Her voice is a hummingbird shimmering on air.

He feels so many things—joy, desire, shame, fear—he can find no words. And this word *love*. He has only ever spoken it to God. Never to another person.

Michal waits for him to speak. He sees giddiness in her eyes, and then, after a few moments of his silence, a fearful wanting.

"I…" he says.

"Yes?"

"I am thankful you are mine."

But what is unspoken casts a shadow over them like the ragged wings of a crow.

* * *

David is summoned to Saul's chambers, to play for him. He finds the room empty. His harp and stool sit ready before the throne, set there by a courtier exactly ten paces from the throne's footstool, according to Saul's orders. But the throne is vacant. Saul has a slightly acrid smell, not unpleasant but sharp, and he masks this with a heavy musky spikenard. David can usually tell if he is nearby. He sniffs the air and smells nothing. Saul has not been here all day. He sits, tunes his harp, watches triangles of light move across the floor, climb the wall. He plucks a few notes. Then, tentative, as though tasting each word, he sings a few lines from a song he's been working on.

The king rejoices in your strength, Lord.
    How great is his joy in the victories you give!
You have granted him his heart's desire
    and have not withheld the request of his lips.
You came to greet him with rich blessings
    and placed a crown of pure gold on his head.

Then he sees it: Saul's crown of pure gold. It rests on a narrow stand just behind the throne. Even in shadow it glows. He is surprised he didn't see it when he entered. He gets up. He puts his harp down. He looks around. He walks toward the crown, stands over it. Looks around again. And then, carefully, slowly, he takes it up in trembling hands.

He puts it down.

He takes it up again.

And then, knowing full well the folly of this, he puts it on his own head. He keeps his hands on its band, to keep it from falling, to feel its girth.

"It suits you."

He turns fast, so fast the crown almost falls from him. He starts to remove it.

"Oh no, don't. Please. Leave it. It looks… magnificent. Your dark curls, your ruddy skin. You were born to wear it, my son. If I put my robe on you, who could tell us apart? Who would not say you are the rightful king?"

"I was only playing."

"Of course, playing. Pretending."

Saul comes over, reaches up with both hands, adjusts the crown on David's head.

"You see now how heavy it is, yes? You were right: six hundred shekels. Just like Goliath's spear tip."

David feels his face burning.

"Ah, perhaps it doesn't quite fit. Pity. It's too big. Your head too small. You're still just a boy."

"Yes, my lord."

David takes it off, hands it to Saul. Saul is about to place it back on its stand but then puts it on his own head.

His voice goes low, hissing. "You want this, don't you, son of Jesse?"

"My lord, no. You yourself see, it fits me not."

"Yes, I see. But a man's head, no matter how small, tends to grow into such a thing."

Saul sits heavy on his throne, locks into brooding silence. He seems to be gathering his next words: David fears he will speak banishment, casting him away forever.

But when he speaks, it's cheerful. "Play for me, son of Jesse. I am not quite myself this morning. Play me one of your songs. Play me the song I heard you sing earlier, about the king and his victories."

David plays. He curls his body over his harp like it's an injured lamb he's sheltering and starts pulling from it mournful sounds. The music rises and plunges. It weighs and lifts.

"Not that!" Saul says, standing again, shrill with fury. "Play me the king's victories. I told you that."

"O my king, this is that song. It begins this way."

"Not that song!"

David plays again, a song he improvises: happy, jaunty, lilting. His voice is sweet and high. He sings of the king ruling in peace, ruling with justice, ruling with mercy, God watching over, approving.

Saul sits, leans back, closes his eyes, smiles thinly.

David feels the lingering, ghostly weight of the crown on his temples, aching like an old injury.

972 BC
Your Father's Spear
DAVID

O Jonathan, before your father was ever a terror to me, he was pure mystery. We both wanted something from the other. I knew that even then. But what? I was so young, and everything unfamiliar to me—armies, women, friends, the minds and ways of kings, the minds and ways of any man—but there was a moment, only once, when I glimpsed the something inside your father. It was fear. Fear down to his roots. I knew it, because I had often felt such fear myself. That lurking, hovering, stalking dread that whatever follows you and whatever awaits you is a terror you cannot shake and cannot avoid.

I learned a prayer that day. I have prayed it most my life since: *Surely goodness and mercy will follow me all my days, and I will dwell in the house of the Lord forever.* I spoke it, I speak it now, over and over, against my own fear, my desire to run, to hide, to quit, to rage. I put that prayer in one of the songs I sang for your father, and for a time it helped him, pulled him out of his valley of death into a place of feasting. His face, only moments before stained with his agony, would brighten, open.

But he kept slipping away on me, further and further. And after a while, no song could reach him, no melody could summon him back. I was shouting against a plundering wind. It took all my words, scattered them, shattered them.

Do you remember the time we stole your father's spear? His rod and staff, that spear. It was rash of us. But in our youthful frivolity, our naivete, we thought it amusing to hide it from him. Did you take it? Did I? Whose idea was it? All I recall now is us running through the forest laughing, the spear in your hand, or maybe mine. I must have held it at some point: I remember its surprising weight. And the warmth of its shaft, as though we had just pried it from your father's clutches, not found it leaning, orphaned, against the wall in a corner of his throne chamber. But you held it too. I see you raising it aloft, twirling it on the tips of your fingers, its tip blazing in sunlight. We tossed it a few times. It flew sure and straight, a winged thing, and easily found its target.

Your father was not angry, not at first. That came later. No, he was bereft. He grieved it as though for a slain son. I have only a few times seen a man so stricken, so utterly lost and empty. And then came his wrath. It was terrible. But not so terrible as his grief.

We never confessed to him. We dreaded the consequences. He once, we all know, tried to kill you for eating honey. What would he demand for this transgression? Ten thousand rivers of oil could not atone. So I snuck it back into his throne chambers late that night, and not one word was ever said of it.

But he never let it out of his sight again.

Our Story

Jonathan and David are rarely apart. They drink together and talk late into the night. They compare strategies for killing Philistines and borrow freely from each other's tactics. They sing together the songs David composes:

Ascribe to the Lord, you heavenly beings,
  ascribe to the Lord glory and strength.
Ascribe to the Lord the glory due his name;
  worship the Lord in the splendor of his holiness.

They swagger like happy drunks, kick the air like horses in springtime, laugh at their own silliness, clap their hands to applaud themselves. They turn themselves dizzy, round and round, and fall into each other's arms, and laugh harder.

"You sound like a braying donkey when you sing."

"You sound like a squawking stork."

"You… you sing like a… a…"

"Like what, O poet?"

"A hyena. You're ruining my song with your terrible whooping."

"You both sing like sons of God."

They stop dead. It is Saul, entombed in shadow. How long has he been there, watching, listening?

"Father?"

"Don't stop on my account."

"We're done, my lord," David says. "I have things to attend to."

"Hmm. Yes, I suppose. But it's a shame to stop such a gladsome celebration. Such revelry. You almost made me believe for a moment we aren't at war. That no Philistine prowls outside, likely in earshot, thinking of ways to kill us all in our sleep, to slake his dark lusts on our women, to humiliate our old men, to enslave our sons. What a gift. What a debt I owe you, both of you, to help me forget that."

Neither man responds.

"My daughter must be ill? I know she loves to dance. How sad she must miss these festivities."

"Father, stop," Jonathan says.

"You dare issue me a command, you arrogant whelp?"

"I dare to spare you your own humiliation."

"Out!" Saul says, but not loud: slow, quiet, steely, sharp, a knife slipped beneath the fifth rib, a spear thrown with deadly precision.

Both men leave.

* * *

"You have changed?"

"I hope so."

"It's not a good change."

Michal stands by the window, in a wedge of shadow by its edge. He can only see her outline dimly.

"Do I displease you?" she says.

"I don't know how you could please me more."

"In bed, yes. I mean besides that. You seem bored with me."

He walks over, touches her back lightly. She stiffens, pulls away.

"I have taken great risks for you, David."

"As I have for you."

"I would die for you."

"I have killed for you."

"Those are not the same things."

"I don't see how they're different."

"Sometimes I think my father is right about you. You're just a boy."

* * *

At first, she waits up for him when he carouses or confides late into the night with her brother. She brims with silent accusation when he comes in, sets things down with crisp violence. Sometimes they argue, but mostly she is wordless. More and more, she goes to bed before he returns. He comes into the room furtive as a cat, undresses like he's laying ambush. But when he beds down next to her, he can tell she is awake, rigid and icy. He speaks her name aloud, but she doesn't answer. He touches her back, softly. It is like touching a graven image.

But then she will surprise him. She's playful, almost giddy. The girl he met. She looks at him adoringly. When he sings, she closes her eyes in delight. Sometimes, she reaches out her hand and twirls the ends of his lock. She is hungry in bed.

He cannot tell one day from the next, one hour from the next, which wife will be waiting for him.

But more and more, it is the graven image, stony and mute.

More and more, he leaves her waiting.

* * *

"I'm sorry about that," Jonathan says.

"About what?"

"What happened yesterday, with my father."

"No need for apology. He was right. We live in dangerous times."

"But it's my father's ways that embarrass me. His unwillingness to speak straight. His trickery with words. He always leaves what he's actually thinking unsaid."

"Fathers are difficult."

"You have not told me much about yours."

"Jesse. He's... difficult."

"But differently from my father?"

"Yes. Differently."

"How so?"

David looks away. A rush of emotion tightens his throat, thins his words.

"He's... he doesn't say much. He closes in on himself. Like your father. But for different reasons. Your father, because a darkness falls on him. My father, because a darkness lives in him."

"Meaning?"

"My mother has been dying since she brought me into the world. My father blames me."

"But your mother, she still lives?"

"Yes, in shadows. But also, in light. It's as though she sees the world beyond the world. Sometimes, sitting with her, I can almost see it myself. The green pastures. The still waters. The Lord with me."

"Your father loves you, I'm sure, in the way fathers do."

"I don't know. I wish. I hope. I don't think so. I think he hates me. Eliab says I am a bastard. The son of a maid my father slept with and then cast away."

"Do you believe him?"

"I would, but my mother, she loves me as a son. Her son. An only son. More than all her other sons. Why would she love me that way, or at all, if I was a bastard?"

"I sometimes think my father doesn't love me. But he would do anything to protect me. To let no harm come to me. That's a kind of love. But a father's love is not straightforward like a mother's love."

David thinks of the look on Jesse's face when the *se'er* anointed him, and then again when Saul summoned him. The expression of dark startlement, the flush of wild panic, like he was watching a spear flying straight at David and was poised to leap, to catch the tip in his own breast.

"Yes," David says. "It's not straightforward at all."

* * *

"You hate me."

Michal has waited up for him and now comes in cold fury toward him. "What?"

"How can you say love me when you treat me like this? Ah, that's it: you never do. You never say you love me."

"Treat you like what?"

"Like I am your chattel. A prize you took from a battlefield and dallied with until something shinier caught your eye."

"There is no one else."

"How quickly you deny what no one's accused you of. But now that you bring it up, I see how women look at you. And you at them."

"Well if I had some warmth and kindness from you…"

"From me? You who find every reason to avoid me?"

"Maybe I avoid you because you are like a stone."

Michal starts throwing things at him, clay things, wood things, metal things. He leaves, angry.

Later that night, when he comes to bed, she is asleep. Deeply. But her pillow is drenched.

* * *

In battle David's vision is like a soothsayer's. He sees things before they happen. He knows precisely what to do, where to go, when to strike, when to circle back, when to withdraw and then surprise the enemy with a flanking or pinching maneuver. Each movement is almost scripted for him. Watching a battle is like watching a memory, an event he's already lived through and knows the exact outcome of. When other commanders ask him his secret, he tells them that the Lord is a shield around him. But he never tells them that the Lord unfurls each plan as stark and sudden as a burning bush. Only to Jonathan does he disclose the whole matter.

Every campaign he leads meets with resounding victory. Saul and Amasa and Abner and Joab and Eliab—all have killed their thousands. But David has killed his tens of thousands.

He wears armor now. His shepherd's tunic, his slingshot, the sandals he wore, the five stones he collected in the stream bed in the valley of Elah, including the one that felled Goliath, are all enshrined at Nob, where pilgrims travel to behold them, and some claim a healing from touching them. But he rides out now in bronze greaves and breastplate, with helmet and shield, an iron-tipped javelin on his back, an iron sword on his belt, a dagger on his thigh. He has learned the art of war. It is as if he has been a fighting man since his youth. He is unconquerable.

It seems that no one anymore remembers Jonathan's exploits, or Saul's. But they celebrate David like he's one of the judges of old, Samson or Jephthah or Gideon, a man of single-handed prowess who destroys enemies without hardly trying. Sometimes he worries that all this renown will spoil his friendship with Jonathan, but Jonathan seems variously oblivious to it or swept up in it himself. Jonathan now looks at him the way he once looked at Jonathan, awed and cowed, as smitten as a villager, as wooed as a maiden, quick to do his bidding.

Then one day, Saul throws a spear at him, and everything changes.

* * *

"David"

"My king?"

"Do you know our story?"

"Our story?"

"Of Israel."

"Some of it, my king."

"Do you know the saddest part?"

David thinks it is when the men of Gibeah, of Benjamin, of Saul's tribe, raped the Levite's concubine, and the Levite then cut her up into pieces. But he knows better than to say this. And, anyhow, he is learning to distinguish between times Saul wants him to answer and times when he doesn't. This is a time, he senses, when Saul doesn't.

"No, my lord."

"The brothers, the twin brothers. The brothers who shared a womb and then shared nothing else after that."

"Jacob and Esau?"

"Or Esau and Jacob," Saul says. "That is the proper order."

"Yes, my lord."

"That is the saddest story of all. Do you know why?"

"Because… they were brothers but not friends?"

"No. That's common business. That is the way of most brothers. Most see each other as rivals. Surely you know something of this, son of Jesse? No, what makes the story so sad, so tragic, is that Jacob stole Esau's most precious thing. He stole the father's blessing. Jacob took it from Esau almost right under his nose."

"Yes, I know this story, now that you speak it."

"The part that breaks my heart, every time, is when Esau comes in from the field. He has been hunting for his father, for wild game—his father loves wild game. The smell of it. The taste of it. The effort in finding and killing it. Esau is out in the wilderness, being faithful to his father, and he comes in and finds that his little lying, smooth-skinned brother has duped him. Conspired against him. He has tricked the old man, tricked him in his blindness. Isaac can't see a thing even if it's in front of him. Jacob, and his mother, they exploit this. Jacob steals the one thing that matters most. He steals the father's blessing. And it is a beautiful blessing. Full of promise. 'Let peoples serve you,' Isaac prophesies. 'Let nations bow down to you.' Jacob gets all of it. Every last bit. All by deceit."

David waits. He is short of breath more and more in Saul's presence.

"And Esau, do you remember, son of Jesse, what he gets?"

"Yes, my lord."

"Tell me then. Tell me, since you know, son of Jesse."

"Esau gets… nothing."

"Oh, it's worse than that. It's less than nothing. Esau gets exile. Deprivation. Shame. Servitude."

"I see what you mean, my lord. It is a terrible story."

"I said it was tragic."

"Yes, tragic."

"But that is still not the most tragic part. The worst part is when Esau discovers what has happened, that his father has given his blessing to the deceiver, the thief, the little heel grabber. Esau weeps. Terrible bitter tears. And this, this is what breaks my heart. Esau begs his father for one little drop of blessing, one word of kindness, one little glimmer of promise. 'Bless me too, father, bless me too,' he says. But the father doesn't. The father can't. The blessing is all gone. All gone. Poof! Vanished!"

Both men are silent for several minutes. David tries to quiet his own heart. He thinks this ancient story through, turns over each detail in his imagination. The saddest part, he thinks, is not Jacob stealing Esau's blessing. It is that the stolen blessing is still not enough for Jacob. He keeps wanting more.

Saul, suddenly cheery, speaks again. "Do you know my servant Shimei?"

"I do, my Lord."

"He is a faithful servant. Loyal. Loyal like a dog. You toss him a stick, he runs for it. You whistle for him, he runs to you. He is eager for approval. He is happy if you simply scratch him behind the ears. A good loyal dog."

David waits. He hates Shimei. He is not a dog; he is a jackal.

"But you, David. You are like a son."

David still waits. Saul searches David's face. He wears an expression David has seen before, when Saul studies a map or a battle plan, or listens to a letter read to him from a pagan king: his features tighten, darken, skew. He looks shrewd and puzzled all at once.

"I love Jonathan very much," Saul says. "Very much. He is such a fine boy. A good boy. But is he a leader? Is he… a king? Does he have what I have? Or what *you* have? I see, I know: men love him. They follow him. But you, you're different. Aren't you? Men—ah, and women, yes, so many women, not just my Michal—they, well, it's different with you. Isn't it? You are… a *ba'al*. A lord. A god. People follow Jonathan. But they worship you. They throw themselves at you. They would do anything for you. You pull them to yourself like the ark pulls a milch cow. Such power, son of Jesse. Such power. It must be... intoxicating. It could be... misused. Misunderstood. Especially, especially if it doesn't work the other way, if men, if women, have no hold on you, no pull on you."

David's sweat is like oil on his neck.

"Now, my Jonathan, he is brave. We all know this. But not always... hmm, prudent. Son of Jesse, one day you will be a father. You will father many sons with my beautiful Michal. And then you will know what I know: how you long for your sons with a terrible longing. It goes deep. It hurts. You want them to be more than you are. If you are a shepherd, you want them to be a great shepherd. If you are a warrior, you want them to be a champion. If you are a king, you want them to be king of kings. Do you see? So I want Jonathan to be a king after my own heart. To surpass me in every way. Do you see?"

"Yes, my king."

"But," and here Saul leans close, "he is *not a king*. He is not a man after my own heart. It is hard to give my blessing to that. But you, you're different, aren't you?"

Saul clears his throat and begins speaking in his sing-song voice.

"When I was a boy, my father sent me on an errand down south. Have you been there?"

"The wilderness of Judah?"

"No, toward Elah."

"Yes."

Saul always seems to forget this, the battlefield where David first won his fame. Or he remembers and pretends to forget.

"Then you know: the route there is a maze of canyons, forests, gorges. Easy to lose your way, yes? Maybe not for you, son of Jesse. For you, everything comes easy. You are too clever to lose your way. Too good. Too favored. But I lost my way. It was terrible. I kept telling myself not to worry, that somehow it would work out—some servant or prophet would happen along and sort me out. Night was coming fast. That place is alive after dark. A thousand hungry things wake and prowl and want nothing more than to eat you. I would not survive in the open. And just then, as though thinking the thought made it real, I saw a cave. The mouth of a cave. It was narrow, so narrow I would never have seen it were I not standing right where I was. Another foot backward or forward, that opening would have appeared only a seam in the rock. But there it was, like a mouth grinning at me sideways. You see how thin I am? Even I had to force my way through.

"Inside was utter darkness. But I could tell the cave opened wide. I felt it, the emptiness just beyond me. I knew I was alone in there. I could smell that. There was nothing living or dying in that cave. I felt my way along, down and down, until I found a sandy flat ledge between large boulders. I curled up there. I slept. I slept like Adam must have slept when God opened his side. *Yahweh tardema*. The deep sleep of God.

"I woke in the night. I forgot where I was. Have you ever known fear, my son? Fear that stops your breath? That makes all your skin tighten? I had fear like that. I have sometimes woken in terror with thoughts of being captured by the uncircumcised. Thoughts of the slow, intimate, almost loving way a Philistine would torture a Hebrew king. This was worse fear than that. I cried out. I'm not ashamed to say it. Sometimes it's all we have, my son. It's all we have, to cry out.

"It was answered, that cry. Someone was calling me. For a moment, I thought it was God answering me."

David looks at him, inquisitive.

Saul laughs.

"It was not God. God does not talk to me, son of Jesse. Does he now? It was one of my father's servants. My father had sent him to look for me. That servant heard my cry. The minute I realized who it was, the minute I saw the light of his torch, I came to my senses. I rose and walked out.

"And that's why I love you, my son. To me you are that voice. You are that light."

Saul's eyes are wet. His irises are huge and dark, dark as the cave he describes.

"Tell me about the Voice," Saul says.

"My king?"

"The Voice you hear. I know you do. I see it. Sometimes, I almost hear it speaking to you. It's how you know things, isn't it, son of Jesse? I have heard the Voice myself, when I was a young king. It's why I'm different. It's why you are different. Why we are different. Why Jonathan is nothing like us. It's our power, isn't it, son of Jesse?"

A hoarseness has entered Saul's voice.

"I don't..." David says.

"Don't what?"

"It's not something I can describe. It's... I see it sometimes. Other times I feel it. It's there." David points vaguely toward the ceiling. "And it's here."

He puts an index finger just below his breast bone. "There are seldom words. But it's clear."

Saul has stopped listening. He has disappeared inside himself. His eyes are lightless and locked on some infinite distance. His body is rigid. David wants to touch him, to stir him, but refrains. Saul's mouth moves without opening. He moans, low and sad.

David picks up his harp and plays.

He hears the spear before he sees it, its shaft whistling the air. The spear narrowly misses him. He feels the wind of it fan his neck. It hits the stone wall and clatters to the floor.

Saul is blinding quick. He rushes forward and grabs it, and this time crouches to charge him. David has seen Saul in battle many times. He is a cagey fighter, fast and strong and devious. He knows how to decoy his moves, shift weight and clench muscle to fake his next thrust. But David knows this. Saul feints a flanking move but comes straight at him. David anticipates it and steps aside. Saul drives his spear hard into the wall, so hard the spear tip sinks into the mortar. Saul's body hurtles after it. The bone of his skull hits the wall. He reels back, dazed. David starts to reach out a hand to steady him, to not let the Lord's anointed fall to the ground. But then he throws down his harp and runs.

Saul is pleading: "David, my son, please. I'm sorry. Come back."

And then, screaming: "Son of Jesse, I order you, come back!"

David runs until his soles burn.

Even in his fear, he feels free. Free of everything.

972 BC
I Love You
MICHAL

Not once did my father ever tell me he loved me. But he did. I know he did. He loved me in all the thousand small ways that there are no words for, not in our tongue, not, I doubt, in the tongue of any people. Is there a word for waking startled from sleep, hours before dawn, in cold fear that something terrible has happened to someone dear to you? But is this also not love? Or is there a word for the murderousness that rises in your heart when someone by your side is imperiled by another? Or for wanting someone to stay exactly as they are, always? But these things too are love, no?

I love you. My father's lips never spoke those words, but his whole life was a continuous enacting of them, one long single gesture toward them.

I see now that he was protecting me from him, from David. At the time, in the moment, my father's rages and cunning only angered me. And frightened me. But later I saw that he did all that he did for love, love for me, for Jonathan, even for Ishvi. Did my father know that David was anointed to replace him? The rumor was that his madness was the torment of not knowing, the torment of endless suspicion. But I think otherwise. I think my father knew better than anyone, better than David himself, better than even old Samuel. He knew that David was a hand raised against him, the Lord's anointed. And I think my father's journeys in the netherworld, when his body locked in the rigor of death and his eyes rolled with terror, confirmed all that he'd guessed. He saw there, more real than anything he could touch, David enthroned, ruling with an iron scepter, making us kiss him lest he become angry, and he saw himself, and Jonathan, and me reduced to vagrancy and begging. His vassals.

So he tried as best he could to prevent that. To protect us.

David, he too never told me he loved me. But there were no thousand small ways he showed it either. No single gesture toward it, unless you count desire, which faded fast enough anyhow. I would hear him sing his songs to his God each morning, pouring out his heart. He told his god, over and over, in words more vibrant and alive than birds aflight, *I love you, love you, love you.*

And I waited, at first with joy, and then with dread, and then with bitterness, for him to come bursting through the door, filled full with all the love he felt for *Yahweh*, ready to spill some on me. To give me even one crust of that bread.

The door never opened.

1024 BC

Fugitive

David runs to the house of God. David runs to Nob. He dispatches a young boy to find Ahimelech, the chief priest, and waits in the outer court. He notices a tall gaunt man standing in blades of shadow. The man seems partly made of shadow. His bones are blades beneath his flesh, his face a terrain of broken and austere flats and ridges.

David knows this man, by reputation. His name is Doeg. He is an Edomite, Israel's ancient enemy. But this Edomite is Saul's chief shepherd, though he is no lover of sheep. David once saw him hit a ewe like he was hitting a mule or a dog. He once saw him show a boy how to shear a sheep. He pulled its ears back hard so its head yanked up vertical, and he took the shears to its trembling body like he was scaling a fish. The sheep collapsed in a dead faint from fright. Doeg yarded up its slumped body and finished the shearing.

David hated him from that day.

Doeg's movements are so slow they seem entranced. David surmises he's on pilgrimage, on a journey of atonement or consecration, deep immersed in his own need, oblivious to all else. Ahimelech appears, and David gestures for the priest to huddle with him in the far corner of the house. The priest is thick with flesh. His forehead sweats from exertion and nerves. It gives his skin an oily sheen. David can smell the man, the mingling of ointments and incense and bread and garlic and sweat.

"Why are you here?" the priest asks. "Why are you alone?"

David speaks low and emphatic. "Priest, can I trust you?"

"David, you have come to me many times before. Why now do you ask me this?"

"The urgency and secrecy of my business."

"That is why you are alone?"

"Yes. My men will meet me. The king has sent us on a mission. Urgent, and very secret. No one must know. I—we—must make haste. I need bread, for me and my men. And anything else you can find."

At first Ahimelech doesn't answer. He looks at the stone floor with eyes so heavy-lidded they appear closed. His large body shakes so hard his robe flutters. He is like a startled sheep, David thinks, like the sheep Doeg sheared. David is about to repeat himself when the priest speaks in a voice brittle and staccato. His breathing is gulping.

"I have no ordinary bread. Only shewbread, the bread of the Presence. Consecrated bread. Holy bread."

"I will take it."

"It's... holy. Only for priests. Not even a king can eat the shew bread. Not even Saul."

"Give it to me." The edge of David's voice is serrated with threat.

"Not even a king..."

"Priest, please. Give it to me."

Ahimelech's breath is shallow, tortured.

"Your men must be pure," he says. "Your men, and you, have you kept yourselves from women?"

"There are no women on this mission. And purity—this is the way we do it. I demand this of all my men. Even when our mission is unholy, we keep ourselves holy. How much more so today?"

David is spinning this tale on his feet. Its mix of truth and untruth gives him a strange boldness. Each word works on him like strong drink. Each seems to work on the priest like a knife pressed to his throat.

"Yes, my lord."

Ahimelech bustles off. His roundish body moves between shadow and light. David glimpses Doeg again, his gaunt frame inscribed against the back wall. The man stands in utter stillness. He sees, just beyond Doeg, the thick door to the room where, he knows, the Ark of the Covenant is kept. *What I might do with that*, he thinks.

Ahimelech returns. He holds a bulging cloth bundling the food: bread, cheese, a gourd of wine. He hands this to David. The bread is cool inside the cloth, and surprisingly heavy. The cheese gives off a sharp smell.

"And a weapon?" David says. "Have you a spear? A sword? The king's business is urgent. I had no time to prepare."

Not a lie. The king's business is urgent. He had no time to prepare.

David left Gibeah two days ago, in wild haste. In his last glimpse of Saul's house, the lights shone from the windows. Inside, he knew, the king presided over a feast he'd prepared for David's burial.

* * *

Saul sits amidst a blaze of torches. He turns his spear in his hand, back and forth. His eyes move with the spinning of the spear, back and forth, searching the room.

"Jonathan!"

"Father?"

"Where is the son of Jesse? This is the second day of the feast that he has missed. I thought when I did not see him yesterday that he had made himself unclean. Perhaps he's been out killing. Perhaps, I thought, he has blood on his hands. But he is not here this evening. Where is this son of Jesse?"

"Ah, David," Jonathan says. "Yes. I'm sorry. I forgot to mention: his oldest brother ordered him to return home. An urgent family matter."

"An urgent family matter?"

"His family is offering a sacrifice in their hometown."

Saul leaps toward Jonathan. "You son of a perverse and rebellious woman! Don't I know that you have sided with the son of Jesse to your own shame and to the shame of the mother who bore you? Now, before it is too late, bring him to me. The son of Jesse must die!"

Jonathan takes several steps back

"Father, why? What has he done?"

And now Saul's voice is almost piteous. "Jonathan, do you not see? As long as the son of Jesse lives on this earth, neither you nor your kingdom will be established. He has returned home to be made king. Can you not see that? He will ride in on a chariot, with servants running before him and an army at his back, and he will overthrow my kingdom. Your kingdom. *Our* kingdom."

"Then I will have him as my king. I will give my oath of loyalty to him."

Saul wheels and hurls his spear at Jonathan. It grazes his side. Jonathan picks it up. He is about to break its shaft over his knee. Instead, he throws it width-wise on the ground and leaves in anger.

The next morning, David waits in the coolness of dawn, crouching in the hollow of a large field stone. The sun, just up but not yet warm, glazes him red. He hears Jonathan speak, indistinct, and a voice as peeping and indecipherable as a bird's answers back. Then the twang and whoosh of an arrow, and the thud of it hitting the ground. Then the thump of feet running, stopping mere feet from where he hides.

Jonathan's voice rings out on the chilled air, half pleading, half angry: "Isn't the arrow beyond you, boy? Hurry! Go quickly! Don't stop!"

David, from his crouching and hiding position, sees the boy pluck the arrow from the ground and turn to run back to Jonathan. Jonathan says something to him. And then there is silence.

David stands. Jonathan is alone at the edge of the field. The sun splays behind his back like a pool of blood. David walks toward him, bowing. When he stops, his tears fall so hard they turn the dust at his feet to mud.

"You are the man," Jonathan says. "You have always been the man. It was never me."

"Jonathan?"

"You are the one Samuel spoke about. The man after God's own heart. He anointed you, didn't he? Samuel did. He poured the oil on your head. Don't lie to me, David."

"Yes."

"You must leave," Jonathan says. "My father intends you great harm. You must flee and not look back."

"For how long?"

"You can never return. Not while my father yet lives."

"I will do as you say."

"And you must promise me one thing."

"Anything."

"That when you come into your kingdom, I will sit at your right hand."

"Yes."

"Now go."

David runs. But he knows he has made a promise he cannot keep. He knows one of them will die first.

Knowing this is a like sword piercing his heart.

* * *

"I have Goliath's sword."

"Huh?"

"You asked for a weapon. I have the sword of Goliath, the Philistine," Ahimelech says. "The giant you killed in the valley of Elah. That's here. It's wrapped in a cloth behind the ephod. It's all I have, but it's yours if you want it."

Ahimelech has regained some composure. His voice has lost its quaver. It's almost picked up a hint of churlishness. Clearly, he wants David gone.

"There's no sword like it," David says. "Give it to me." Ahimelech walks toward the ephod and David follows him. He cannot see Doeg, and it fills him with both relief and fear. Ahimelech lifts up a long rigid shape swaddled in coarse grey cloth. A rough cord binds it top and bottom and middle. Ahimelech's nervousness returns, and his hands fumble on the cords. David wonders if he should offer to unveil the weapon himself, but only waits. Finally, Ahimelech lifts the sword out of the folds of the cloth and holds it flat across his palms, offering it to David like a newborn child.

David has not seen or held it since that day in the valley of Elah. He is freshly surprised at its length and girth. The handle is thick and long, made to fit two burl-like fists. The blade is the height of an ordinary man. David, even before he takes it, remembers its weight, its surprising urgent downward pull on the shoulders and arms. He braces himself for this. But taking it, he finds it light.

"There's no sword like it," he says again.

He straps it to his back and ties the bundle of food to his back as well.

"Remember," he says to Ahimelech. "The king's business is secret. No one must know. No one."

David leaves and does not look back, but he knows Ahimelech watches him. He sees himself through Ahimelech's eyes: his fugitive haste, his ragged aloneness. The priest will wonder where the companions he spoke about are. He will wonder why he takes an uncut trail. He will watch him, wondering, until David shrinks in the distance, until he becomes a smudge on the horizon, until he shivers into invisibility.

Until the priest is sure he's gone.

972 BC
Brother
MICHAL

I always loved my brother Jonathan. He was the most kingly man I ever knew. Every inch of him was noble, and yet every part humble. My brother Ishvi—that man strutted before he walked. He was grasping after power in the womb. But he had no more capacity for rulership than a quail has for thinking. It is a terrible combination, power and folly. But my Jonathan, he could have led Israel with integrity of heart and skillful hands. He could have led us to a greatness to rival Edom or Moab, even Egypt. But now I think he didn't have it in him, that his hands were too open, his heart too wide. He was too trusting. He was too good for the throne. He was too good for this world.

I cannot recall him without laughing. I see the wide brightness of his smile, hear the music of his laughter, remember the ease he had with everyone, children and old men and hardened soldiers, and kings. And me. He could draw me out of my moods when no one else could, when all the world seemed my enemy. There he was, smiling his smile, bidding me take his hand. It was easy to enter his joy.

I always loved him.

Only David loved him more. Or more than he loved me. His loyalty, his affection, his willingness to give himself, entrust himself, risk himself: David gave all this and more to my brother in a way he never gave any of it to me. Nothing was too much for Jonathan. And this was true for Jonathan toward David. He would have given David his very life. And, yes, the rumor is true—his robe, his tunic, his sword, his bow, his belt—all the symbols of his coming kingship, of his right to rule Israel, all his regalia, Jonathan handed to David as if they were no more than old rags he'd outgrown, no more than an aged slave he had used up. It humiliates me now. If I had thought even a moment about it, I would have been humiliated then—my own brother, the prince, the king in waiting, acting toward the son of Jesse like some cowering vassal, some kowtowing minion, swearing oaths of covenant, begging for kindness when David had no power to give or withhold anything. When David should have been the one begging.

I began to hate David then.

And I saw something. I saw that the more I hated David, the more my father loved me. I could, like a sluice does a water course, turn my father's affections toward or away from me by the simplest of choices. A hint of disdain toward my husband, calling him son of Jesse, walking out of a room he walked into—these small gestures pleased my father immensely. And the opposite: saying his name, showing him any hint of affection, touching him with my fingertips— all such things galled my father terribly. It was an easy thing, I saw, to be my father's daughter.

I betrayed my father once to protect David. That was when I still thought that risking everything for him would make him love me in return.

So I played a trick on the guards my father sent. They were to lay in wait for David outside my room. But I helped him escape from my window, and I told the assassins he was ill. When they finally forced their way in—my father had actually ordered him brought down, bed and all, to kill him— they discovered my ruse: I'd dressed an idol in David's clothes, put a scruff of goat's hair on its head, mounded the idol beneath bed covers.

Father was furious. His anger frightened me. He could hate me, I saw. He could kill me.

So I told my father David had threatened me. I said he had taken my hair in his fist and pulled my head back and pressed his knife to my throat. I said that he told me he would kill me if I didn't help him. Father accepted this. It seemed to please him, even.

And maybe it was true. It's hard to remember now. Maybe David did all this, pressed his knife to my throat. Balled my hair in his fist. Leaned his face to my ear, hissing, warning, threatening.

It's hard to remember exactly.

But I do remember that after he fled, I waited. I waited for him to come back. Or even just to send word. I visited the place, for weeks, where sometimes we had stolen away to make love. But he never came. He met with Jonathan several times, I knew that. He even for a brief spell, through my brother's persuasion, came under my father's graces again.

But he never came back for me.

I wanted to forget him. But every day, and every moment of every day, I thought of him. And every thought turned me into what you look upon now.

1024 BC

Thirsty

David ran all day as a boy. He ran more than he walked. His feet were swift as winged things, moving for the sheer love of it, the utter joy of carving air, tasting wind. Earth skimmed beneath him. His father would send him on an errand, and he would run all the way, his body growing lighter with each step. He would arrive exhilarated, anointed with golden sweat no heavier than mist, his breathing barely altered. He itched to do his business, turn around, and run back.

But now when he runs, he feels his body grow denser with every step. His feet are heavy and clumsy. Blisters on his heels and soles make every step a fiery trial. He worries he'll trip and injure himself. He worries that if he stops and sits, he will never rise and set out again.

He's sure shadows stalk him, crows watch him, the wind carries rumors of him. The shadows, the rumors, the birds: each and all spread their dark ragged wings, flap upward, and fly fast to Saul. Everything is ripe with betrayal. Even docile creatures are skittish around him, as though they've been warned about him. Every cave is a trap that Saul has laid. Every wadi is a maze in which Saul lies in ambush.

Finally he collapses. But the burning in him only worsens. His blisters erupt. His muscles stiffen. His bones ache. He once saw an old man from the next village rot from the inside. His last days were spent twisting and howling, clutching his bed as though clinging to thin roots on a cliff edge. Whatever that man suffered, he thinks, has wormed its way into him.

The bread is gone. He is empty all the way down.

He failed, at Nob, to get a gourd of water, and his mouth is dry as a potsherd. He feels a surge of anger toward that fat priest for not thinking of it. And then he feels pity. That priest was wracked with terror. It turned his sweat rancid. It made him shake like he was impaled. David ponders this, the way fear can make a man pant or weep, make his mind an army in rout. He himself felt no fear at Nob—he had deep calm and searing clarity, the kind *se'ers* are rumored to have. But he feels fear now, feels it trace a cold bony finger down his spine, feels it curl and uncurl its hand around his throat.

Am I dying?

The old men in his village used to talk frankly about death. They spoke about death's patience. The way it bides its time. It's in no hurry to take what belongs to it. But one day, you feel its shadow fall across you. And you just know. Those old men walked in the shadow of death, in the grave's steep and narrow deepness, and he never paid them any mind: theirs was the gloomy musings of dotards who'd forgotten how to take hold of life with both hands, if ever they had.

But it all comes back to him now. He sees what they saw. Death comes to all. It can't be fought or bribed or tricked. It may seem coy at first, but that's just the false modesty of the tyrant, whose power is absolute, whose whims are decrees, who can skewer you at will. It can afford not to raise its voice. Modesty is a pose it strikes to lull you into thinking you're safe. But just to unnerve you, it brushes you now and again, to let you know it can strike anywhere, any way, any time.

His mother's been falling toward the grave his whole life, so long that he stopped yearning for her to be well, though in younger years it was his constant prayer—to see her dance, to hear her laugh, to have her scoop him up in her strong arms and hold him. But she is a vapor. And he is to blame. His father has always let him know this without ever saying it aloud: that the cost of his flourishing is her dwindling. Death plucked her like a midwife into darkness even as the midwife pulled him into daylight. How intimate she has been with death all these years. Each day it holds her head in its hands, almost lovingly.

But if he is dying, here, now, why is he still so hungry? And why is he so thirsty, so thirsty he'd be willing to break into a Philistine camp and steal water just to slake it?

* * *

He wakes in darkness.

My God, my God. Why have you forsaken me?

He wonders if he is on *Sheol*? The pain in his feet brings him to himself. And it is cold, and *Sheol* is constant burning. The desert in daytime weaves fire into stone and air, but at night it laces ice into everything. The iciness jerks him into full alertness. He stands, and the agony in his feet shoots up through his legs. He steadies himself. He listens. He can hear the movement of a large animal close by. It hasn't caught his scent, or else it wouldn't move so clumsily, so noisily. He feels for his dagger, in case. And then he remembers Goliath's sword. A steely confidence sheaths his nerves.

He sits again, to take stock. Best not to travel yet. The darkness is more treachery than cloak. He'll start an hour before daybreak, when the wild things return to their lairs, when a paleness hovers above the earth. It will be easy to see but hard to be seen. He'll move south, deeper into desert. He'll stay high until he becomes too visible, then move down into canyons and wadis, picking a desultory course that will slow him but make him harder to track.

Saul has three fine trackers. He'll use them all. He'll play them off against each other, exploit their thin-veiled rivalries and jealousies to heighten the urgency, to increase the odds. David has used all three men and knows what they're capable of: each could find a gnat in a bog. The smallest detail—a disturbance of sand, a thread on a thorn, a crumble of food, a burnt stick, the scent of lingering charcoal, the testimony of a nomad—is to them a scroll they can read as sure and knowing as a priest reads the law. It's as if the earth is a map that every footfall inks. It's as if he's marked his trail for them deliberately.

But this is his advantage: he'll play it against them. He knows how they work. He has watched them many times and learned their trade by proxy. He knows what throws them, too. He knows what misleads.

But this is their advantage: they know he knows this. So David must be extra careful. He must sometimes do what they think he won't do and sometimes do what they think he will. He must mix folly with shrewdness, add cunning to naivete and naivete to cunning, until they themselves get lost in the labyrinth of their own guessing and second-guessing. He must leave clues that aren't clues and conceal clues that are. He must get them arguing: he went this way, no that way, no he's hiding over there, no he's circled back behind us.

While he thinks this, he makes an unguent from the stalk of a desert plant, one he made often to rub the wounds of his sheep. He kneads it into his sores, and it kisses his feet with coolness. He works the rest of the unguent into pieces of cloth he's torn from the bundle of food. He wraps these around his feet and lays a double layer on his heels.

The time has come to move. An ashen light suffuses the sky, just enough to see a few steps ahead. He can make out the texture of shadows on the ground. He moves with surprising swiftness, given the tenderness of his feet.

He resolves not to notice the pain. Or the thirst. He must get good at that.

972 BC

Gone
MICHAL

I tried to imagine him, in the vast emptiness of the southern wilderness. I had seen it once, that wilderness, from a high distance my father took me to. I was a wisp of a girl. Twelve, I think. It was a citadel of spiry rock near the Salt Sea. The waste places stretched out from there forever, rolling away into ghostly barrenness: dust and rock and sand. The distance disappeared in a haze of boiling air. Father stood at the edge of a cliff so high that just approaching it made my stomach feel strange. He stood right at the brink, his toes over the rim. He seemed unafraid of falling. Maybe oblivious to it. I inched closer only to appear brave in his eyes. I held his robe so hard I feared I'd tear it.

"That, my dear Michal, is the Judean wilderness. It is Judah's land, and it is like those who possess it: empty, fruitless, dangerous. A place where nothing grows and only wild things live. Jackals, scorpions, adders. They all make their home there. And the accuser, the Satan, he loves that place. It is his home. All *belials* dwell there."

I looked up at him. His last words hung mid-air, so I waited. For a long time, nothing. The sound of the wind piped through gaps in the rocks. Father moved closer to the cliff. His feet were now half over the edge.

"Benjamin, now that is good land," he said. He stepped back from the cliff edge. "Bountiful. Flourishing. Green on green on green. A seed falls in its soil, it springs up a hundredfold. Plump fruit. Fat cows. Big sheep."

"Father?"

"Ah, yes? Yes, Michal?"

"Does anyone live there? Any... man?"

"In Benjamin?"

"No, in Judah. There." I pointed to the wilderness.

He laughed. It was clear and hearty, the way I sometimes heard traders or threshers or shearers laugh, men whose lives were simple. It amazed me to hear Father laugh that way.

"Michal, what man would live there? What man could? He would be a madman. He would be a *belial* himself. He would be a devil."

That wilderness is where David went. He flung himself into that place of jackals and madmen and demons.

Every night, I stood at my window. I waited for him to step into the patch of torchlight in the courtyard and call up to me from below. I waited for him to beckon me. In one imagining, he comes. I stand silently, watching from my window. And then I turn and summon the guards.

But in another imagining, when he comes, I fly down the wall, fly like a swallow, straight to him. And then I fly with him, jackal or madman or *belial*, into his wilderness, as far as he wants to take me.

He just never comes.

972 BC
Missing
DAVID

I ached for her. For my wife. Saul's daughter. Your sister. For Michal. I felt her absence physically, the way one of my mighty men once told me he felt the absence of his arm after a Philistine severed it in battle. He would reach for something—a piece of bread, his idle sword, his child—and have nothing to reach with. I spent so much time in that desert, in utter aloneness. I lay at night on hard ground, without shelter, among creatures stalking other creatures, and I sounded my emptiness like a man trying to fetch water from a well gone dry. There was nothing there. It did not help that I was so thirsty, thirsty all the time. Why had I not asked for water at Nob? Why had I not asked for a flask or a skin? A man can live without bread. I know that full well. But water, no man can endure its absence for long.

I had conversations with Michal in my head, conversations I never had with her face to face. I am embarrassed to tell you this, Jonathan, you with whom I shared such intimacies, that I never could speak my heart to a woman, any woman, not if she was right beside me. Only when I was alone in my thoughts could I speak to any of them without reserve. I always wanted to ask another man about this. My father. Your father. You. I wanted to ask if this is the way it is for all men. I once, many years on, when I myself was growing old, tried to speak of it with my wisest advisor, Ahitophel. But his voiced changed, it became solemn and deep, and he rambled on endlessly, and to no good purpose. This seems a thing most men do when speaking about women.

I told Michal so many things in my head. I told her she was beautiful, that she gave me joy. I told her—perhaps this is not a thing that you, her brother, wish to hear—that I thought of her naked body often, when I should have been thinking of other things. I promised something then: that as soon as we were back together, she and I, that I would tell her all these things. I would say all these things straight to her, to her face. I would speak my heart, the way I spoke it to you. The way I spoke it to God.

It is maybe a good thing, my brother, that you did not live to see how I broke that promise.

1024 BC
Madman

David runs to Gath, Goliath's town. The giant's sword leads him there like a dowser's stick. He comes to the city gates, the gates that Goliath's huge frame once passed beneath as he went out to taunt Israel in the valley of Elah, and then one day passed beneath to go and die. He looks down the streets that Goliath once trod—even, impossibly long ago, that he must have played in: a big lumbering boy, clumsy and slow and dim-sighted, whom other boys mocked, but not openly.

David is met by a guard.

"Who are you?"

"David."

The guard laughs derisively. But when he sees David's level stare, he stops abruptly.

"The giant-killer?"

"Yes."

"You are not welcome here."

"I want to see the king."

"Don't we all?"

"I seek refuge."

"What?"

"I need his help."

The guard looks down. He reaches a large hand behind his head and scratches. Then he looks up. "You don't look like a giant-killer."

"The giant thought that too."

* * *

Five guards come and escort David to King Achish. News of his coming spreads fast. His presence in the town causes a stir. Murmuring surges through the crowd. People openly gawk. Children run near his heels. Some of the townspeople rear back in fear of him, others stand athwart his path, openly defiant. When David looks straight at them, most lower their gaze and step back if the guards haven't already pushed them.

They bring him to the house of Achish. David waits in the vestibule, a guard on either side, one behind. Two guards go to inform the king. David hears muttering from an adjoining room. An argument, though muffled, seems to have broken out. Then Achish emerges from a side room, a courtier beside him, whispering. David can hear him. "Isn't this David, king of the land? Isn't this the one they sing about when they dance: 'Saul has killed his thousands, and David his tens of thousands'?"

Achish has a shrewdness that narrows his eyes and tightens the muscles under his jaw. David can see him toting the situation up in his mind.

"David!" Achish says. "Young, brave David. Slayer of the champion of Gath. Darling of the dancing girls. David, to what do I owe such a huge and unexpected—and may I say, undeserved—honor?"

David stares blankly.

"Will you not answer me?"

David drools down his beard.

"I have no time for this," Achish says. "Keep this idiot under guard. I will send for him if I want him."

* * *

David remembers a madman, a *meshuga*, who once lived in Bethlehem. For all David knew, the *meshuga* was still there, babbling and larruping, amusing and terrifying children. He mostly was harmless, though whenever an animal fell sick or a storm shredded rooftops or some wind blighted the crops, people openly speculated that in some vague way it had to do with the *meshuga*, that he was the harbinger of ill. Sometimes he stripped naked and smeared filth on his body and ran helter-skelter so that his privates flopped obscenely. He was nameless, his identity long lost in the rubble of his madness, but villagers called him *Balagan* and said he came from chaos and brought it with him. One leg was shorter than the other—a defect from birth, or a deformity from a childhood accident, no one could say—but it gave his step a lunging sideways quality that added to the effect.

David sought him whenever he went with his father or one of his brothers to the village, and even later when he was old enough to go alone. Not to talk with him—that wasn't possible—but to wonder at him, at the ruination of him. But there was also a strange potency about him. It was as though some other world, vast and radiant, lay veiled behind his pocked face, his spittle-flecked beard. He stank hypnotically. His eyes were variously frantic or skewering. He spoke a mix of gibberish and oracle, guttural and musical. Sometimes people openly fretted that God was speaking through him, warning them.

David remembers him because he reckons now on mimicking him.

For the next several days, David roams the town, though always with two guards beside him. He drools and gibbers. He grabs sharp stones and scores doors, cutting cryptic shapes in the wood. He flings things skyward—dirt, cabbage leaves, horse dung, roadside refuse, his own feces—and has virulent arguments with invisible hosts. He stops abruptly mid-stream and listens intently as though someone is leaning close to his ear, whispering mysteries. He fills his beard with skeins and gobs of saliva, and then shakes his head and flings them out. He mimics *Balagan*, the *meshuga*, until it almost isn't mimicry, until he feels madness scratching around inside him, looking for a place to root. Until he feels a shadow deep in himself.

And he thinks of Saul. He has watched Saul slip into the clutches of something like this, and then come up from it like a man coming out of deep water, gasping, filling his lungs with air. But Saul's madness is the madness of cunning. In his spells, he doesn't talk nonsense or fleck spittle down his beard. His mind doesn't wander: it narrows. It distills. It is as if he has been on a dangerous clandestine journey and has seen things, done things, that his soul is not large enough to hold. So his soul curls up tight and tries to hide. David's playing at madness sometimes feeds his anger toward Saul. And sometimes it does the opposite. It fills him with sadness, with deep longing for the man. It makes him sense that his own mind sits precariously near an edge over which gapes bottomless darkness.

* * *

Three days later, Achish calls for him. David stands before him and shakes his head so wildly his lips and cheeks rattle. It sounds like a wet hand slapping jowls. He scrunches his face and lets out a rumbling belch that crescendos like a thunderclap. He strings together a chant of ribaldry and shuffles and lops in a ragged circle as he sings it.

"Look at him!" Achish explodes. "He's insane! Why bring him to me? Am I lacking madmen that I need another? I have more madmen than whores. Get him out of here!"

The guards grab David beneath his arms and drag him away.

But they let him stay in Gath. He is assigned a small hut near the town's edge. Every day, food is left on his doorstep. He behaves in public unpredictably, sometimes lucid and cordial, sometimes simian and lewd. He knows Achish is having him watched, that every move he makes, every word he speaks, is reported to the king. David devises a plan around this: that his pantomime of madness will ebb and flow, but mostly ebb. He will appear to come more often into daylight and stay longer. He's seen this fluctuation with Saul enough times to have mastered its subtler cues. The calming of gesture. The straightening of posture. The regaining of poise. The slowing and clarifying of speech. The light coming back into the face, the eyes.

After several weeks, David becomes wholly himself. The neighbors grow less skittish around him. Some share vegetables or bread with him, others ask after his health. But food from the king's house comes less frequently. After a few more days, when Achish never asks for him again, he takes his leave.

But he tidies his room and leaves a small gift—a dove he's carved from acacia wood. And one of his songs, written down. He wants to depart on good terms, in case he ever needs to return.

In case Saul doesn't stop.

* * *

Saul sits beneath a tree. Light and shadow enmesh him. It makes him look as if he's caught in a poacher's net or snared in a spider's web. He cradles the bony wedge of his chin in his left hand and strokes his tightly pursed lips with one finger, over and over, like he's trying to work loose a finicky latch. In his right hand he holds his spear. He rotates it slowly, back and forth.

He is silent. His silence is a rebuke. A denunciation. Everyone is on edge, waiting for the king to say something, to give his next command. He seems to relish their anxiety. To want to prolong it. But at last he speaks.

"Listen, men of Benjamin!" A sharp sibilance hisses at the edge of each word. "Will the son of Jesse give all of you fields and vineyards? Will he make all of you commanders of thousands and commanders of hundreds?"

Son of Jesse. It has become Saul's favorite moniker for David. It reduces

David to his commoner's roots, his social nothingness. It confines him to a mere appendage in an ignoble and forgettable lineage. It makes him no more than the dried mud a farmer picks from the heels of his boot. The men have picked this up by now, that to call David by his given name is open treason, but to call him the son of Jesse is to pay homage to Saul, to pledge allegiance to the king.

Saul is on his feet now, moving among his senior officers and then out toward the lower ranks. He continues to hold his spear, to turn it. He seems momentarily jovial. Then everything about him sharpens. Even his ears prick. "Is that why you have conspired against me? Is that why no one tells me when my son makes a covenant with the son of Jesse? And none of you is concerned about me or tells me that my own son has incited my servant to lie in wait for me, as he does today. My *own son*."

A man nearly as tall as Saul, and even more gaunt, steps from amidst a knot of officers.

"I saw the son of Jesse come to Ahimelech, son of Ahijah, at Nob. Ahimelech inquired of the Lord for him. He also gave him shew bread and the sword of Goliath of the Philistines."

A thin smile crosses Saul's face.

"Ah. So there. Doeg, thank you. I had hoped there was one good man left in Israel, one man who did not plot my downfall, who had not bowed the knee to the son of Jesse. One man who has not joined the conspiracy. Just one. I thought it might be my own son, Jonathan. But no. It is you, an Edomite. Only you have kept faith with Israel's king. Well done, well done."

Saul turns to his officers.

"Now bring him to me. Bring me Ahimelech. Bring the priests of Nob. Bring them all. Bring them now."

Three of Saul's men leave and after a time return with Ahimelech. The priest walks as fast as he can, struggling beneath the ungainliness of his own flesh. He sweats profusely. A large throng of priests huddles behind him, slowed by Ahimelech's slowness. An air of anxious perplexity hangs over them all. Saul's attendants return to his side, and the priests arrange themselves in a chiasm pointing toward Saul and his officials. Ahimelech stands at the arrow point. He catches his breath, collects his nerves, wipes sweat from his face. Saul begins almost aloof.

"Son of Ahijah."

"Yes, my lord."

"Your father served me well. He was a good man. He would never betray me."

"My king and lord."

Saul sits forward, leans steeply on the shaft of his spear, eyes the priest.

"He disappeared, your father. Is he still alive?"

"No, my lord. He died many years ago."

"Ah. What a tragedy. What a shame. A good man. Loyal."

Saul stops turning his spear. He holds it in a death grip. The fierceness of his clutch turns his knuckles to white stones, embosses the back of his hand with a fan blade of bones, a skein of veins. His next words come out like steam escaping a tight lid.

"Why have you, Ahimelech, son of my loyal priest Ahijah, betrayed me? Why have you conspired against me, you and the son of Jesse? Why have you not been loyal? Hmm? You gave the son of Jesse bread—shew bread! I am not even allowed this. You gave him a sword, a sword not even I would presume to wield. You inquired of God for him. And all so that he could rebel against me and lie in wait for me. Why have you forsaken me?"

Ahimelech is visibly trembling. Confusion darkens his face. "Who of all your servants is as loyal as David? He is the king's son-in-law. The captain of your bodyguard. He is highly respected in your household. Your son Jonathan loves him."

Who is more loyal? The priest's question hangs between them. Ahimelech waits for Saul to answer, and when it's clear he will not, the priest continues. With each word he gains in confidence. His tone turns accusatory, peremptory, prophetic. It's as if Samuel himself were speaking. "Was that the first time I inquired of God for David? Of course not! He is always, as you yourself know, seeking the Lord's mind. He is a man after God's own heart. Let not the king accuse your servant or any of his father's family, for your servant knows nothing at all about this whole affair."

"Stop saying that."

"What, my lord?"

"His name."

Saul is on his feet. His eyes blink wildly as though a swarm of gnats is flying at him. He flails his spear-hand like a *meshuga* brandishing a firebrand, trying to ward off things that only he can see. He is almost shrieking.

"You shall surely die, Ahimelech, you and your father's whole family. Just as the prophecies have foretold."

He turns to his personal bodyguards. "Kill them. Kill the priests of the

Lord. They too have sided with David. Kill them all."

His speaking aloud the name of David constricts the word in his throat. He goes pale as though choking. His voice turns tragic. "For they knew he was fleeing, yet they did not tell me."

"My lord," Abner says. "You want us to kill Ahimelech? He is a friend of the king. He is loyal to my lord. He is the Lord's anointed."

"Kill… them… all!"

No one moves. His guards all look at the ground. Several fold their hands over their belts. Others let their arms hang limp. Saul's voice is deadly calm now, wintry cold. He narrows his eyes and looks at his men one by one, as though weighing their worth and finding each beneath his contempt.

Then, slow and deliberate, he turns to Doeg. He is the only man who has not looked down throughout the whole drama. Doeg meets the king's gaze steady.

"*You. You, Doeg.* My faithful Edomite. You turn and strike down the priests. *You* raise your hand against the Lord's anointed."

It's not a command: it's a simple statement, the summary of an act already accomplished. And, indeed, before the words are out of Saul's mouth, the killing has begun. Doeg strikes down Ahimelech with a single elegant slash of his sword that splits the priest shoulder to hip. A neat red seam appears on Ahimelech's rotund body, and bursts. He falls without sound. Doeg moves on, unresisted, unaided, unhesitating, cutting down all eighty-five priests. Each receive death peacefully, praying as they fall, not one raising a hand in his own defense. Their passivity is its own act of refusal, of defiance, and seems to enrage Doeg. Blood spatters him until it soaks him.

He returns to Saul, panting hard. His eyes stare out with wild hunger from a mask of darkening crimson.

Saul is pale and mute.

"I have done as you asked, my lord."

Saul seems mesmerized. Then he rouses himself to attention.

"It is to fulfill the prophecy," Saul says. "The prophecy against the house of Eli. That not one man in his line would see the prime of life. Well done, Doeg. You have been God's instrument of judgment. Righteousness has been fulfilled this day. You have avenged and vindicated the Lord, and your king, this day by raising your hand against the Lord's anointed."

Doeg's eyes darken.

"I have not finished, my lord," he says.

Doeg travels to Nob, where all the families of the priests live, and puts to death every last living thing, every flapping chicken and lowing cow and braying donkey and bleating sheep, every pleading wife and flailing son and crying daughter, everything down to the last tiniest suckling infant. He returns at nightfall, sheathed black with dried blood, none of it his own.

"They are all… dead?" Saul asks.

"All killed, my king."

"All?"

"All."

"Well done," Saul says weakly, "well done, my good and faithful servant."

But the words gall him: all those dead, but not one of them David.

* * *

The sky is on fire. It rises first as a scrim of smoke, as if a giant thumb has smudged the bottom edge of the horizon with ash. The smoke billows, writhes, darkens. And then flames appear. They dance on the ridge, gyrating as though an enemy taunting him, baiting him to come fight. David knows, from the flames' blackness, from their fierceness, that other things besides wood and stubble fuel them. David knows that Nob burns.

Later that night, a boy shows up. His skin is dark with soot. He is shaking hard. He is mute and wide-eyed. He gesticulates wildly. When he tries to speak, it is incoherent: howls, grunts, babble, a noise like choking. He collapses into fits of sobbing. He refuses food and water.

David learned as a boy how to make medicine from plants, things soothing or stinging on a wound, sweet or bitter on the tongue. They eased pain, brought relief. He brews a concoction of thick sour liquid and coaxes the boy to drink a cupful. The boy scowls at the taste but almost instantly calms and turns drowsy. Before the medicine takes over, while the boy is briefly clear, David asks him who he is, what he's seen.

"I am Abiathar. My father is Ahimelech. His father was Ahijah. Saul's servants… they came. They ordered all the priests to come. My father goes, he and the priests, they all go. Brothers, uncles, cousins, everyone. No one returns. Then a man comes. He kills…" A fresh wave of terror shatters the boy's mounting stupor. "The man kills everyone. My mother. My sisters. My baby sister. She is only a suckling. He shows no mercy. He kills everyone. Everything."

"This man, his name?"

"An Edomite."

David bows his face to the ground. He covers the crown of his head with his hands. His shoulders shake with his own crying. When he speaks, his voice is tight.

"I am responsible for this. I am the one to blame for the death of your father's whole family." And then, speaking to himself, "That day when Doeg was there at the house of God, faking his devotion, I knew he would be sure to tell Saul. I should have killed him on the spot."

He looks toward Nob. The fire's dying makes the sky glow a lurid red.

David gathers the boy in his arms, the way he imagines his father held him the time the snake bit him. The boy starts sobbing again. He slumps his whole weight against David's chest.

"Stay with me," David says. "Others will join us. You will see. Don't be afraid. The man who seeks your life seeks mine also."

David thinks of Saul seeking this boy. Saul has never been good at seeking anything. He always needs someone else to steer him or find him. He gets lost easily, turned around, disoriented. He himself must be tracked down, brought back. It's always been that way.

"You will be safe with me," David says. And he starts to sing over the boy, soft. It is a song about the wings of a dove. And the boy, all at once, succumbs to the medicine and the voice and the bruising weight of the day. He falls dead asleep in David's arms.

972 BC
Father of Plenty
ABIATHAR

My name means father of plenty. Nothing in my past explains this. I come from a cursed line. My past is desolation.

My father, Ahimelech, was a good man, though much afraid. He lived his life, each step of it, under the shadow of that curse. He was a doomed man leading doomed men. God had made an end of us.

My father's father was Ahijah. Maybe you have heard of him. He served Saul for a time, but not well. He was more necromancer than priest. My father feared him and rarely spoke of him. Some say he went to serve the Moabites or Philistines after he saw no future with Saul. I do not know. I chose long ago that my loyalties would never flag, would never veer.

Ahijah's father was Phinehas, one of the wicked sons of Eli. Neither Phinehas nor his brother Hophni were good men. They devoured widows' houses. They forced themselves on servant girls. They desecrated the shew bread. They stole the fattened portions of honest people's sacrifices. They were the reason God put a pox on our house. They were the reason God planned to destroy us.

My grandfather Ahijah sought refuge from that curse in making himself Saul's toady.

My father, Ahimelech, sought refuge from it in his own virtue.

But the curse hovered over us like a sword.

That sword, I believed, fell upon us by the hand of Saul, through the hand of Doeg. They were God's chosen instruments to exact vengeance upon our house, our family, our priestly lineage. They were the earthly fulfillment of Samuel's ancient prophecy. How else to explain it?

But David believed otherwise. He said that God would never allow a mere man to raise his hand against the Lord's anointed. God exacts his revenge in his own way. He would never use a cur like Doeg. If any man took what only God can give, David said, that man would bring a curse upon his own head.

It gave me comfort, those words. I long ago made peace with my doom. I long ago accepted that our priestly line must end, that my father and my uncles and my cousins and my brothers and I must pay for the sins of our fathers and their fathers. But I could not make peace with the bloody handiwork of Doeg. David taught me that there was no peace there to be made.

When I was a child, the son of my father, my name made no sense. Father of plenty? Where was the plenty? Where in all our emptiness was any abundance? Where in the vast desert of our lives was any stream? But a father is made by his offspring. He is defined by his future. And in David, my future opened wide.

I took refuge from the curse in him.

In time, I even came to believe that the curse upon my family had passed over me, as though David was the lamb's blood on the lintel posts of my house, telling the angel of vengeance to move on, denying the destroyer entrance.

David, I believed, would spare me my fate.

1023 BC
Adullam

When anyone in the land thinks of a prophet, they think of Samuel: the cliff of his brow, the thicket of his beard, the massive hummocks of his shoulders, his leathery skin, his depthless eyes. They think of his weather-stained robe, its collar thick as a yoke. But especially, they think of Samuel's voice, its terrible ancient deepness. His voice is more frightening than the worst earth can deliver: flood, hurricane, landslide, fire. It can break and devour you without trying.

Gad is nothing like that. He is small, and wiry, all sinew and gristle. His movements are quick and darting, like a dragonfly, and he speaks in a way that reminds David of metal striking flint rock: ringing brightly, sparking the air with light. He is almost jovial. The laughing prophet, the men call him. He speaks God's truth like he's sharing juicy gossip or swapping an inside joke. He chirrups it. Even condemnation comes off as a friendly clap on the back, an affectionate ruffling of the hair.

Like now.

"Do not stay in the stronghold," he tells David. "Go into the land of Judah."

It is so kindly, so warm, so cheerily offhand, it's as if he's simply directing David to the best market for sheep wool, or commenting on the roundness of this year's crop of melons, not giving him divine writ to spare his life.

Gad is one of the men who has gathered around David in these desperate days. How they know of him, how they find him when even Saul and all his trackers and their cunning fail, is a mystery. They just show up. They arrive at daybreak. They come at dusk. Solitary men wandering into camp like they're just returning from an errand, not utter strangers who now must submit to the rough protocols, the secret tests of loyalty, devised by David's inner circle. Or they come as a bedraggled pair, whatever patchy alliance they worked out along the way clearly reaching its limits, crumbling beneath the strain of their hunger and weariness. They stumble the last hundred yards, entranced by the aroma of roasting meat. Or, occasionally, they come as a cadre of men, a small disheveled posse, grubby and smelly, with a pecking order already established among them.

Men avoiding debt. Men dodging prison. Men fleeing brutal masters. Men escaping shady pasts. Angry men. Bitter men. Hunted men. Haunted men. Men with stories they rarely tell. Men whose histories are lost in shadows, in hearsay, in echoes, whose pasts are rumors laden with guesses, whose bloody deeds are never sung aloud, never spun as legend, but only whispered, if that.

There's Beltiel, a rogue who used to barter weapons between warring tribes. Through long handling, through deep familiarity, he learned to handle those weapons with telling precision. He's short and slight—his rib bones flute his flesh when he removes his jerkin—and one eye is squelched shut and permanently bruise-colored, but he is so blurring fast and unerringly precise that men twice his size give him wide berth. There is the nameless Moabite warrior, a sullen taciturn man who only looks at you with flat grey eyes if you speak to him, so silent most men took him for a mute until one day, in a game of bones, he grabbed a man who was cheating, pressed his face close, and said in a steady, level tone, "I will kill you tonight." No one doubted him, and only David's intervention, where he ordered the cheat to pay back double, spared the victim.

There is Baako, a happy talkative youth, trusting and generous, whose presence among them puzzled the rest—he seemed in no particular distress. They chalked him up to an adventurer, a youth out wild faring, until the word got out that he had maimed bare-handed the man to whom he was the indentured servant—maimed him so he would never walk again and could barely use his hands—and then stole his bag of coins, killed his cow for good measure, and fled.

Men like that.

And there are many men from the nations round about, nations Israel wars against. Philistines. Egyptians. Amalekites. Amorites. Jebusites. Moabites. Midianites. Cushites. Hittites. David takes them all, if they can fight, if they will pledge fealty. It surprises him that in many of these outsiders, these non-Israelites whom Saul fears with rabid intensity, he has found loyalty deeper than even among his own kin. They seem to understand each other, David and these men.

Men like Uriah the Hittite. He came to David with some unspoken sorrow. Loss hangs on him like a millstone. He speaks little, and softly, but in battle he is fierce: he can slay a hundred men by himself, cut through them like he is merely scything barley. Bodies fall before him without resistance. David trusts him with his own life. And sometimes, he trusts him with his secrets.

"Uriah, sit with me, drink with me, talk with me."

"Yes, my lord."

"Please, call me David, at least tonight. I need a friend, not a servant. I need someone I can speak openly with."

"I will be that man," Uriah says.

"I have a fear."

"My lord?"

"It's Saul."

"We all fear the mad king, my lord."

"David."

"We all fear him… David."

"But I fear him for a different reason. Not because he hunts me. Because…" and here David's voice drops several notes, "because sometimes I think like him."

"That is how it should be, my lord. David, I mean. You must think like your enemy. Otherwise, you cannot outwit him."

"Yes, true. But this is different."

"My lord?"

David hesitates. Then barely a whisper: "It feels at times he's inside me…"

"I am not sure I get your meaning now, sir,"

David says no more, and after several minutes Uriah takes his cue and leaves, unbidden.

"Oh, Uriah."

"My lord."

"This, this conversation, is to be our secret. Make no mention of this to any of the men. Thank you."

"Understood, my lord."

Among these men, though different from them all, is Gad. The laughing prophet. When Gad hears God speak, his eyelids close and twitch, and a wide array of emotions play across his sharp features: ecstasy, grief, alarm, anger, peace, expectancy, and a dozen more. But whatever God says—a dire warning of impending judgment, an urgent prompt to move camp, a tactical instruction for routing the enemy—he delivers in the same chirruping voice, a morning bird singing from a blossoming tree. David is learning to ignore the voice and attend to the words, or else he risks missing what God is saying. Else he thinks everything is good when it's not.

"Do not stay in the stronghold. Go into the land of Judah."

Deeper into desert. Further into wasteland.

He thought they were safe here. His brothers and father and mother, and all their servants, have just come down. Saul's campaign to destroy him has widened to include his family. His parents are hobbling with age now. His mother is the shadow she's always been, only dimmer, thinner. His father is a bent and withered version of his once irascible self. He looks at David with filmy watery eyes, reaches toward him with a shaking hand. His skin seems about to molt. David is startled by his decline. He once thought his father an immovable, implacable force. And now he is a dry stick. *Will I be this?* he thinks. *This husk? This ghost? This man whose hand I could crush in my own?*

David arranges a meeting with Moab's King Mesha. It is tricky—not getting the meeting, but plotting how to handle it. Deep suspicions, sometimes enmities, exist between Moab and Israel. It is a history complicated by both closeness and estrangement, by bloodline and bloodshed. Moab was Lot's son, Abraham's second nephew. So Moab was related to Jacob, to Israel. Moab's descendants were both friendly and belligerent toward the Hebrews, the sons of Jacob, in their years of desert wanderings. They traded with Israel, but they also refused to let them pass through their land. Moab's ancient King Balak employed a pagan sorcerer, Balaam, to curse Israel, and later still Moab's women seduced Hebrew men into immorality and idolatry. More recently, more critically, Saul early in his kingship fought and cruelly subdued Moab. That is the rawest of the wounds.

David needs to be shrewd.

But he has another tactic if all else fails.

* * *

King Mesha greets him effusively. David suspects it's part of an elaborate ploy but returns the greeting with equal fervor. They embrace. They kiss.

The king is uninterested in whatever David has come to speak about until they have eaten. A meal is served: roast duckling, goat cooked long over coals, sweet strips of tender lamb, stew made from gazelle and roots and field herbs, a bounty of fruits, fresh and dried, goblets of various wines. David realizes how hungry he is, how long it's been since he's eaten well, and sets into the meal with undisguised appetite.

After they finish and David wipes the juices and oils from his face and hands, King Mesha begins. "You have come to speak with me, David. Let us do so man to man. Plainly. Without hiddenness. As friends. Talk to me, my friend."

David wonders why Mesha treats him as an equal, as if he is already seated on Israel's throne, as if they are two sovereigns making treaty. Or even more: it's as if David and Mesha grew up together, two friends with shared memories, coming together now to reminisce, to swap family lore.

But is all this, he wonders, just Mesha's cleverly devised, flawlessly executed plot to get him to lower his guard, to say too much? An intuition tells him it's not. Mesha, he senses, genuinely extends friendship to him. His own experience with Saul, he realizes, has tainted him. One king cannot be trusted, so no king can be trusted. But maybe this is wrong. He himself will be king one day, if his anointing means anything. Will he not be a king others can trust?

"I have come," David says, "to put myself at your mercy."

"This is not how friends speak. Just tell me what you need."

"Your enemy has become my enemy. Saul means to harm me, me and all I love. He means to kill me. He pursues me now."

"So I have heard. I will protect you."

"No, I would not imperil you on my behalf. Saul could make war on you. I would not ask you and the people of Moab to pay a debt you do not owe. It is my debt. I alone will pay it. Your kindness is enough. But my mother and father—they are old and feeble, and Saul means them harm as well. My brothers can fight. But my father and mother, they are but sheep. If I go elsewhere, Saul will follow me and leave you unharmed. Will you protect my mother and my father? May they stay with you until I learn what God will do for me?"

At this last remark, Mesha pauses and seems to weigh the words *until I learn what God will do for me*. David can see a fierce intelligence behind the king's eyes. He is no fool. He knows the rumors. He knows what king of

Israel he must deal with next. David is considering using his last advantage here, but then Mesha smiles broadly, throws his arms wide, booms, "Yes, David. Yes, my friend. While you wait, *while you learn what God will do*, your father and mother are safe. They will be like my own father and mother."

"Thank you."

"Yes, you are welcome. But David, I have a question."

"Yes?"

"You do not find our way of life in Moab, hmm, objectionable?"

David hesitates. "I… we do not see eye to eye on many things."

"Beautifully understated. Do not your priestly books call what we do detestable?"

"My lord, Moloch is not *Yahweh*."

"Ah, your sweet *elohim* of mercy. Of loving-kindness. Your shepherd *elohim*. An *elohim* you people talk to, like a friend. This doesn't seem strange to you?"

"More than one Moabite has been drawn to our God."

Mesha laughs. "Because Chemosh, Moloch, is a demon? A *belial*? Isn't that how you see it?"

"My lord, I have known many Moabites who live better than what they believe."

"And have you known any Israelites who live worse than what they believe?"

"Perhaps all of us. King Mesha, I admit, I do not trust in your *elohim*, in Chemosh. But I trust you. Will you help me?"

"Yes, David. I have already said so. I will help you until you see what your *elohim* will do for you."

"Thank you."

David bows and turns to leave. The king calls after him.

"David?"

"Yes?"

"I do this for you, and gladly. But even if not for you, I do this for our ancestor, yours and mine. I do this for Ruth."

* * *

David sends a delegation the next morning to deliver his parents safely to King Mesha, with instructions for the men to meet them. He and the others set out for another refuge, as Gad had counseled.

His brothers, all seven, are with him. He welcomed all of them, even Eliab, when they brought their mother and father to the cave in Adullam.

He was genuinely glad to see them, even Eliab.

None of them can go back to Bethlehem, not now. All their lives are imperiled. So they have joined him and his company of fugitives and scofflaws. They must run with him, hide with him, fight with him.

Fight *for* him.

They all understand, without anyone saying anything.

David worries most about Eliab. He is sixteen years David's senior. He has always been the unquestioned leader.

David takes the lead as they set out. His young brothers—though all still older than him—crowd near him, especially Ozem and Raddai and Nethaneel. They are eager to be seen with him. Abinidab and Shammah, the second and third oldest, walk directly behind him. They are quiet. The men who formerly occupied these positions say nothing but look aggrieved.

Eliab starts a few paces behind Abinidab and Shammah, but saunters. He falls further and further back. Several times, David turns to see where he is. His face disappears and then reappears in the throng. After a while, David loses sight of him altogether.

"Abishai, lead the men."

David wanders back through the crowd. He greets and encourages his men along the way. He asks one how his leg is healing up, another if he has received any news about his ailing father. At last, he spies Eliab, alone, trailing far back. He walks up to him as naturally as possible, as though he just happened upon him.

Eliab does not look at him. David hasn't rehearsed anything to say, and for several minutes they walk alongside each other in silence, neither acknowledging the other. But the air around Eliab roils with his anger.

Eliab is the first to speak.

"I'm here for the others. For *my* father. For *my* mother. For *my* brothers."

"Then you did the right thing." David means to speak gently, but his tone is authoritative, patronizing.

"Don't tell me what to do, how to do it, when to do it. Don't tell me if what I did was right or wrong. I couldn't care less what you think. I will do what I will do, regardless of what you say."

"Then go."

"What?"

"Leave." David's heart thunders in his ears. He is afraid. Even more, he is angry.

"You can't make me," Eliab says. His voice is iron hard. "How did you become so smug and arrogant? You have no right to lord it over any of us."

"Now listen, my brother. If you are part of this," David gestures at the crowd of men walking in front of them, "then you are part of me." David's arm curls back, his finger landing on his chest. "And you are *under* me." He stretches his hand out, palm down. "And you will do what I say, and you will do it how I say, and you will do it when I say. And if none of that suits you, you will leave."

Eliab's face reddens, then darkens. David waits briefly for a reply. Eliab gives none. David is about to retake his position at the head.

"I have a request before I agree."

"A request? Or a condition?"

"A request."

"I'm listening."

"When you come into your kingdom, I sit at your right."

David thinks of Jonathan, of his vows to him, his covenant with him. Of the dream they both dream.

"Let us get to the kingdom part first," David says.

And as David walks back, he shakes most of the way.

972 BC
Scofflaws
DAVID

I don't know where they came from. Or how they knew to find me. But every day, another man, or group of men, straggled into camp. Refugees. Refuse. Scofflaws. Scavengers. Brutal men, to a man. I grew up with brothers and nephews that would pick a fight or hold a grudge or settle a score with mindless ease, but these men were beyond that. More beasts than men. They were wild donkeys, kicking at everything. They were famished boars, lunging at everything. Sometimes all I did, it seems, was break up brawls. It took all my wits to keep them from killing one another. Trying to lead them, it gave me new compassion for your father, Jonathan: holding together all those squabbling tribes, each taking grievance at the least slight, each ready to strike pledge with any rebel promising less taxes, more wine. I knew that if I could lead men like these, I could lead anyone.

But I was lonely all the time. Ahitophel once tried to explain this to me, how a man can be thick in the midst of many men and all the while feel utterly alone. He can have friends he drinks with, argues with, works with, fights alongside. But he still feels utterly alone. He said that there is a part inside each man that no one else can see, that the man himself hardly knows, but it's this part that a man most wants seen. But I am not sure. Wise men are not always wise. My loneliness felt more like the weight every leader must bear, to be for others something they need and yet resent needing.

This too gave me new compassion for your father.

It's then I started talking to you in my head, even though you were still alive. But I couldn't get to you, or you to me. So I made a place in my head, a broad cave, deep and cool and dry, and daily we met there. I would bring to you my many trials, and battles, and problems, and we would sit together over a cup of mead and we would talk together, brother to brother. I would tell you of Beltiel's latest outrage, or of Neham's treachery, or of Abnosh's attempt to rape a man's daughter, and you would always say the same thing: *Yahweh* will give you wisdom. Wait on *Yahweh*, and his voice will be like the wind in the tamarisk trees. Yes. I knew that. But somehow you telling me, even if only in my head, helped me know it again.

Jonathan, you were always a man after God's own heart.

1023 BC
En Gedi

The scouts come back with stories of paradise. A fast, cool brook gushes from a chasm in a towering rock face. The water pours down steep gorges, tumbles over boulders, white and laughing in its falling, and pools crystalline in sandstone bowls. All along the brook's edge, thick reeds cluster. Fat hyrax, smug as Amorite kings, lounge here. Lower down, on grassy banks, docile ibex graze. It is a table prepared in the wilderness.

It is En Gedi.

Near the top, a thick musculature of rock hides a deep cave. From there, the entire valley, all the way to the glassy hazy expanse of the Salt Sea, is in clear sight: no army or even scouting party can take them unawares.

"My Lord, it is like Eden. When you see it, you can well imagine Adam and Eve walking there."

"Before or after they ate the fruit?" David asks. But he is smiling. His heart thrills to the news. The desert, its relentless heat and cold, its constant taunts of hunger and thirst, has made the men sour and testy. Their mood could quickly turn violent. Some of them are churlish even when rested and well-fed. When tired and hungry, they draw into themselves ominously and are ready to draw blood with the least provocation: the wrong look, a slight jostle, a veiled insult.

Eden would be welcome relief.

"Lead us there," David says.

And then to all the men: "Tonight we dine on meat, and bathe in cool springs, and sleep on soft reeds."

A cheer swells the canyon, ricochets off its walls, booms as it grows, and falls back on them in waves. So loud, so wild, it is as if they are summoning Saul.

* * *

David reserves the top three pools for drawing water: anything below that can be used for bathing, though he insists the men remove all their clothing first.

"A single thread floats down this stream and catches on a rock or branch, Saul's trackers will find it. And though we're hidden here, we're also trapped."

David stands at the lower pools. To reach the upper pools and the cave requires traversing steep flanks, slippery with loose rock, to the south. It's dangerous—a false step would hurl you down and over the lip of the gorge, but also the route exposes you to view from the valley below, where a keen-eyed scout might see you, see the thin cloud of dust your scrambling stirs up, and run back to report to Saul. They must wait until dusk to climb it.

"Trapped," he says again, and gestures in a sweeping motion. The men turn to look at what his gesture takes in: massive brown rock walls and overhangs on every side rising hundreds of feet. Even his best climbers would struggle to find a seam to thread their way up, and the last thirty feet would be unscalable.

"If Saul finds us here, our paradise will become our *Sheol*."

He squints up at the canyon walls. They are honeycombed with small caves. "Put a man in that one, and that one, and that one. Have them flash their blades in the sun if anyone approaches."

That night they feast, gorging themselves on roasted hyrax and ibex, and wild figs they find near the canyon's entrance. The men laugh raucously. Abishai scowls at their loudness, but David lets it be. It's been too long since the men laughed. And tomorrow, who knows what awaits them?

* * *

What awaits them, standing at the cave's mouth in early dawn, is Joab. David's nephew. Abishai's brother. There is a fresh cut on his cheek. He limps. David embraces him. It is like hugging stone.

Later, he sees Joab bathing in the lower pool, cleaning a deep wound in his thigh. Blood from the wound blooms in the water, eddies around him, feathers out in the current, thins to a thread, carries downstream.

972 BC
Nowhere Else to Go?
JOAB

Believe me, it was not my idea to join my uncle and his ragtag group of brawlers. God, those men lacked discipline. Even the ones who could fight hadn't a shekel's worth of sense when it comes to warfare. It was all just rampage. They knew a few tricks with fists and swords and slings. But they knew little else. It was each man against the world. It was personal glory, nothing more.

Well, they had a fit leader in my uncle.

But Saul, he was out to kill the lot of us. My father, he was long dead. My mother, Zeruiah—that's David's sister, in case you need help sorting all that out—was not a woman any man wanted to get himself on the wrong side of. She was mean as a black adder. My God, *I* feared her. She could slaughter a pair of oxen like she was lopping off chicken heads. But she was no match against an army, and she was getting old, and more than half blind. So I took her to be with her parents in Moab. I never much trusted that King Mesha—he was sneaky as a weasel—but what could I do? I wasn't going to stuff my mother in a cave of men who hadn't washed in months—though God knows there were times I dreamed of doing worse. Anyhow, I took her to Moab and then I set out to find David, which took all of two days. Made me wonder how hard Saul's trackers were actually working. My brothers, the idiots, were already with David. Abishai, he just liked killing. And Ashael, he just liked adventure.

And me, I needed somewhere to go.

Back when my uncle first ran, I stayed with Saul's army. He fed me. He paid me. I had nowhere else to go. I never was much good at farming and such. And at first, no one said anything. Saul didn't seem to notice or care. What did I have to fear? I was just David's nephew. David was no king. He was a fugitive. A criminal. He had no following, except a bunch of losers and drifters no one else wanted. He had no child of his own. He was good in battle, yeah, but Saul had cartloads of warriors. All Saul wanted was David dead. A stray nephew here or there posed no threat to him.

But the more we stopped fighting Philistines and Midianites and such, and the more we went on long tiring marches through empty deserts looking for my uncle, things took a turn. Would I kill David with my own hands? I didn't know. We were never close. My mother couldn't get away from that household fast enough and never wanted us near it after.

But David was blood. He is blood.

Would I get his blood on my hands? I didn't know. You can't know things like that until they're on you, see?

Saul, he sensed all that. He was sly and crazy, pretty much half and half. I sensed that he sensed my, what do you call it? When you're between this and that? Divided. He sensed I was divided. The way I sensed Saul sensing it—well, another man would have missed it. Saul, he'd narrow his eyes, just the slightest, like this, like he's squinting. He'd tighten his mouth, like he was tasting something a little off. Like this. As I say, another man would miss all that. Not me.

And one day, I just knew I wasn't safe no more. Saul was aiming to do me in. He'd have his Uncle Abner, that old slayer, do the deed, or maybe Doeg. That man loved blood. Abner, probably. He was the commander over me. He could order me anytime, anywhere, to come with him, then pull me close like he was my friend, then slip his dagger through my ribs. He would hang on too, hold me upright until I fell from the weight of my own dying, smiling at me all the while. Or Abner could order any one of his men to stick me through with my own spear as I slept.

So while they all slept, I slipped out. The night watchman saw me. I clamped my hand on his mouth and held him hard. He cut me, on the hip, on the face. But I just held on until he didn't move. I woke my mother, Zeruiah, in her bed and dragged her off, bitching the whole way, to Moab, to King Mesha. He didn't seem overly pleased for another mouth to feed.

Her parents were already there. My grandfather Jesse seemed happy to see her, which told me how senile that old bastard had become.

Then I walked into the desert and found, without hardly trying, my nephew David and all the wild stinking men he kept company with.

Maybe you're wondering if I would do that now, knowing all that I know.

But I had nowhere else to go.

1023 BC
Do Not Destroy

Saul's best tracker bends close to a low bush. The soldiers know to keep well back: a single footfall can ruin a clue, one broken branch can destroy the trail. The tracker peers, sniffs, tastes, turns his angle of vision this way and that. He mutters to himself.

He looks now at dark flecks on small leaves. He snaps the branch that holds the leaves and lifts it up to the sun, turning the branch slowly between his thumb and finger. He squints to see sunlight bleed through the skin of each leaf. Whatever he sees seems to confirm something for him. He puts the leaves in his leather pouch. It now bulges with things he's collected along the way. To the men who watch him, he seems to be gathering a midden of meaningless debris: sticks, stones, twigs, leaves, ashes, bones, dirt.

But to him, they are better than divining rods.

"He's gone this way," the tracker says to Saul, and points west. All the men follow the direction of his finger: a steep gorge, falling fast, and far ahead the blurring air of the Salt Sea.

One soldier turns to another as they resume their march into the sweltering heat of the valley.

"I thought Joab would have been more careful. It's almost like he wants us to find him. It's almost like he wants to lead us to his uncle."

* * *

In early dawn, eight of David's men float in the buoyant saltiness of the Salt Sea. David stands on the flat shore watching.

"Join us," Baako calls.

"Someone must watch over you fools."

"Afraid you'll sink?" Ashael taunts.

"Afraid my presence will make you sink. And how could I go on without you?"

All the men laugh.

They return to their stronghold in En Gedi. At midday, a scrim of dust, barely visible, rises above the stark hills in the lower distance. It signals that a large company approaches. David's men clamber up the crags and take refuge in the labyrinth of caves. David and twenty men go into a cave that is deep, convoluted, tunnel bending on tunnel. They press into the shadows near the cave's mouth. Cool musty air opens at their backs. At least half a dozen corridors branch off behind them.

Saul's men, David knows, hate caves. A cave is ripe for ambushes. But their fear isn't pragmatic. It's superstitious: many believe the stories their maids told them as boys, of *golems* and *dybbuks* and monstrous behemoths skulking in the mountains' bowels, of deep chasms dropping to fathomless black lakes where Leviathan lurks, insane with hunger. One man in Saul's army used to tell tales of a cave in Lebanon, with spires and shafts hundreds of feet high, a bottom no torchlight could reach, a ceiling shrouded in blackest spectral shadow. The cavern twists for miles and miles, he said, further into darkness, and those who ventured deep never came back.

"Eaten," the man said, with fixed grim certainty.

"By what?"

"A werewolf," the man said, and all fell silent.

Someone is here. Light and dark crisscross the entrance. A shadow looms against the far wall, then diminishes. Whoever it is breathes hoarsely, through his mouth. He scuffs his feet on rocks. He clanks his belt and sword on stone. He is loud as a blacksmith. He makes no attempt at stealth. These are not the sounds and movements of a stalker, a tracker, an assassin. This is not someone on their guard. It is someone unaware of the snare he's stepped into.

David signals Abishai and Baanah to draw their daggers and move with him. They creep soundlessly forward in a shaft of inky shadow, until they are just above and behind the intruder. They are close enough to touch him.

Then all of them stifle a cry of shock: it is Saul.

He crouches on his haunches, humming to himself. His clothes are hitched up around his thighs, their hem falling around his feet. A cabbagey smell assaults the men, and their hands fly to their mouths and noses. Baanah looks like he's about to vomit. Abishai looks like he's about to laugh. Instead, both men, each with a hand still over their faces, pantomime for David a classic dagger stroke that every Israelite whose hands are trained for battle knows: a curving motion with the arm, forward and back, that thrusts the blade diagonally beneath a man's fifth rib, into his heart.

Abishai faces away from Saul and whispers into David's ear, "This is the day the Lord spoke of when he said to you, 'I will give you your enemy into your hands for you to deal with as you wish.'"

As I wish.

What David wishes overwhelms him. His throat goes dry. His eyes sting. His heart hammers so hard he's sure Saul can hear it.

As I wish...

What does he wish? He closes his eyes, in part to ease their burning. He calls up a day—how long ago? Many years. He is young, maybe five. He walks beside his father. They are silent. It is close to evening. Eliab, already an adult, descends a steep and rocky trail, bringing his father's sheep home.

"Watch," Jesse says to David.

Jesse begins to call each sheep by name. His voice is musical. It is a voice David has never heard him use before. The name of each sheep rings out on the air, hovers for a moment like a scent. With each name, a sheep looks up, alert, agile, and hastens toward Jesse. He names them all until all are gathered close to him, crowding against one another in their eagerness to press their bodies against his legs. David is up to his neck in sheep. Eliab now stands outside the circle of the flock.

"You see," Jesse says. "The sheep know my voice."

"Yes, Father."

"They trust my voice."

"Yes."

"Each sheep knows to come to me when I call its name."

"Yes."

"Learn this one thing, and it will answer many things."

"Yes."

But Jesse rarely speaks his name, and now he is such an old man, so decrepit in mind and body, is it worth even wishing for?

* * *

David creeps forward. He makes no more sound than a snake. He is so close to Saul that he could slip a dagger into the hollow of his neck without even thrusting, just easing it in like he's sounding water. He raises his blade. Then lowers it. He sees Baanah at the edge of the shadows, violently gesturing for him to do the deed. David inches closer. The smell is choking. Saul has stopped humming.

David raises his blade again, and brings it down.

* * *

He returns to Baanah and Abishai and holds up a piece of Saul's robe.

They are stunned with indignation. An argument of gestures breaks out. Baanah threatens to go kill Saul himself. David shakes his head violently and presses his hand against Baanah's chest, who pulls away and spits.

All three turn to watch Saul walk back toward daylight.

They return to where the other men wait, and the argument erupts fully, loudly. All the men side with Abishai and Baanah. This could have been the beginning of a new day, they say. You could have been king tonight, they tell him, feasting and drinking and sleeping in a soft bed rather than sleeping on stones and scrounging your next meal.

"Why not let Saul empty his bowels and die in a cave?" Abishai says. "That's a fitting tribute to the man. A perfect ending. But instead you seal our fate. Behold your kingdom," he says, and gestures to the gloom all around. And then, quiet: "You could have been sucking the breasts of your wife tonight."

"My wife Michal, you mean? Saul's daughter?" "How pleased she would be with me, distinguishing myself in this way."

No one says a thing.

"The Lord forbid," David says, and each word is its own dagger strike. "The Lord forbid that I should do such a thing to my master, the Lord's anointed, or lift my hand against him. He is the anointed of the Lord."

David utters this—*the anointed of the Lord*—in a voice ragged with fear, with love, with sorrow. "He is the father of Jonathan. He is the father of Michal. He is the anointed one. The Lord forbid…"

Anger's darkness ebbs from the men's faces. In some, shame stains their faces red.

David turns and walks out of the cave. Saul is halfway down the slope. Saul's officers stand in a loose huddle, shielding their eyes against the bright sky to watch their king descend. His troops sit in whatever scraps of shade they can find.

"My lord the king," David cries.

Saul turns sharply. He shadows his eyes with his hand, squinting up, cocking his head side to side to see where the voice is coming from. David's men crowd behind him at the cave's mouth, just out of view. He senses his other men in the other caves doing the same.

He takes several steps closer to Saul, bows deeply, kneels.

"Why do you listen when men say, 'David is bent on harming you'? This day the Lord delivered you into my hands in the cave. Some urged me to kill you, but I spared you. I said, 'I will not lay my hand on my Lord, because he is the Lord's anointed.' See, my father, look at this piece of your robe in my hand. I cut off the corner of your robe but did not kill you. See, there is nothing in my hand to indicate that I am guilty of wrongdoing or rebellion. I have not wronged you, but you are hunting me down to take my life. Against whom has the king of Israel come out? Who are you pursuing? A dead dog? A flea?"

Anger wells up in David, puts fire in his voice.

"May the Lord judge between you and me. And may the Lord avenge the wrongs you have done to me. But my hand will not touch you. As the old saying goes, 'From evildoers come evil deeds,' so my hand will not touch you. May the Lord be our judge and decide between us. May he consider my cause and uphold it. May he vindicate me by delivering me from your hand."

Everything is still. No one moves, above or below. The sky above is empty. It too seems to wait.

"Is that your voice, David my son?"

And then Saul weeps. Huge wracking sobs. His throat is so thick, David can barely make out what he says next.

"You are more righteous than I. You have treated me well, but I have treated you badly. You have just now told me about the good you did to me. The Lord delivered me into your hands, but you did not kill me. When a man finds his enemy, does he let him get away unharmed? May the Lord reward you well for the way you treated me today."

And then Saul's voice clears, and a steadiness enters it.

"I know that you will surely be king and that the kingdom of Israel will be established in your hands. Now swear to me by the Lord that you will not kill off my descendants or wipe out my name from my father's family."

David hesitates. In one swoop, Saul has both acclaimed him king and denied him a king's right: to deal swift and decisive with the most immediate threats to his reign and dynasty, the offspring of the former ruler. Undisturbed, they would wait in the wings, hover in the background, pretend fealty, bide their time. David thinks especially about Prince Ishvi, whose lust for power is revealed more than disguised by his oily charm. Would David not dispatch assassins to bring his head to him in a sack?

But then he thinks of Jonathan. Jonathan would rule with wisdom, with justice, with overflowing generosity. But he has laid it aside already, for David's sake.

"I give you my oath," David says.

With that, Saul leaves. Within minutes, the place where he and his troops stood is desolate.

There is tension over the meal that evening among David's men, a brooding sourness about how close David was to killing Saul, and then flinching. But no one says a thing.

But David thinks of it all night. He imagines the soft yieldingness of Saul's flesh, the blade falling through him swift and easy, and Saul turning around wide-eyed, bright with surprise and fear. He imagines holding the knife steady in Saul's side, holding Saul's gaze steady, looking upon the king's wild panic, feeling his life empty from him, watching until his eyes go black.

It would have been like killing a snake that had reared up to strike him.

And it would have been like killing his own father.

It would have destroyed his enemy's body but raised his ghost. He would have been rid of Saul forever. And he would have never been free of him.

* * *

They move camp, deeper into Judean wilderness. To another maze of canyons, another honeycomb of caves.

Caves are always the same temperature. They never change; summer, winter, it doesn't matter. Outside, it can be hot as a smithy's furnace, but the cave is cool. Outside, it can be cold as loneliness, but the cave is warm. A cave draws its heat from earth, not air, and so its warmth or coolness depends only on a man's condition when he enters. A sun-scorched man finds a cave refreshing as a lake. An ice-caked man finds it comforting as a bath. But a cave saves its surprises for the man who falls asleep in one. He might wake sodden with sweat, as though he has been held over a fire. Or he might wake shivering with cold, as though he has fallen in a blizzard.

David wakes burning.

He dreamed of Michal. She is beautiful. Her body is lithe and dusky. She looks up at him and smiles. Her smile is without wariness. Without shadow. Without guile. It is a smile clear as brook water. It invites him to come in. To come home. When he hesitates, she reaches out her hand. A gesture of pure trust. There is no fear in it, no threat, no hint of withdrawal. No shade of betrayal. No sense that she would ever hurt him. He reaches out his own hand and walks toward her. Their fingertips are so close he feels a shiver of heat transfer between them. And then he wakes.

His knuckles ache from reaching. And everything else is burning.

* * *

He's slept in his clothes, as always. At night he leaves everything on, except for his sword, which he lays beside him. He ties that on his back now and walks to the cave's mouth. Sunlight gilds the edge of the ridge directly above him. The way the rocks block the sun stains the sky black. It makes it hard to see. He strains his eye upward, to trace in the tinted sky any hint of Saul: a glint of armor shafting up, hazing against some bend of air, or a puff of dust from the clouds the army's feet stir, or vultures carving wide arcs in the sky.

What he sees terrifies him: just over the horizon, on the other side of the ridge, a sizable company advances.

Baako, the night watchman, has fallen asleep and left them all vulnerable.

And now it is too late. They are trapped. Their only route out is down a narrowing gorge of mountain pass that will push them straight into the arms of Saul. Their only chance now is impossible haste. They must run full out and hope to emerge a slight distance ahead of Saul's army, with enough time to scatter into the caves further down the canyon.

* * *

David knew this was coming. Several weeks ago, a messenger boy showed up, panting hard, bending in half to regain his breath. He had run a long way flat out. When his breathing steadied, he spoke. "Look, the Philistines are fighting against Keilab and are looting the threshing floors."

David pictured the mayhem of it, Philistines in a lust of plundering, grain spilling everywhere, drifting, mounding. Large men, salivating, pulling Israelite women under their hairy sweaty bodies. Hewing away at any who resisted until the ground was a slurry of blood and dirt and chaff.

A pure white anger flared in him. He called in Abiathar, his new young priest.

"I am enquiring of the Lord. Shall I go and attack the Philistines?"

Abiathar consulted the Urim and Thummim: "Yes. Go, attack the Philistines and save Keilah."

David marshalled his men, but they balked. Some openly confessed their fear at such a venture. Fighting this close to Saul's territory, they said, imperiled them terribly. David enquired again, and again the answer came: "Go, for I am going to give the Philistines into your hand."

The men were learning to trust David, to trust his strange intimacy with God. David seemed to talk with God the way some men, but few, talked with their fathers, and some talked with their friends: an easy rapport, a spoken and unspoken affection, a willingness on both sides to divulge inmost secrets, to place even the most fragile thing in the open palm of the other.

So they girded their loins and went down, and indeed the Philistines were given into their hands. It was that simple, that direct: some fever of panic drove the enemy into a delirium of fear, and they fell limp and soft before David's men, and tumbled into death.

The people of Keilah gathered around, exultant. They hailed David a hero. They sang the songs of old, of David's power to slay the tens of thousands. That night, David's men feasted, each man eating and drinking until his belly ached and his head swam. They sprawled along the warm wood of the threshing floors and slept like the slain.

But David didn't sleep, and in early morning a silhouette stood against the wide opening of the threshing shed. He recognized him as the same boy who first brought him news of Keilah's predicament.

"You are looking for me?"

"Yes, my lord."

"What?"

"One of the elders of Keilah left here before the banquet last night. He went to Saul. He reported that you are among us. Saul's army marches toward the city as we speak."

He already knew what it meant but called in Abiathar anyhow. When the priest had placed the ephod on, and the lights and the perfections, David made his inquiry: "O Lord, God of Israel, your servant has heard definitely that Saul plans to come to Keilah and destroy the town on account of me. Will the citizens of Keilah surrender me to Saul? Will Saul come down, as your servant has heard? O Lord, God of Israel, tell your servant."

"He will," Abiathar said, as though God had whispered it in his ear.

"And will the citizens of Keilah surrender me and my men to Saul?"

Again unhesitating: "They will."

The news fell on him like stone from a high tower. The future rose up as a vast bleak landscape, an endless waterless desert. When he told his men, their indignation exploded. Several wanted to do to the people of Keilah what they had prevented the Philistines from doing. But David said no.

They left at daybreak. For weeks they wandered from place to place, always hungry, always thirsty, their bodies drooping from heat and exhaustion, aching from lying in hard places, smelling like rot, smelling like death.

* * *

Then one day a man approaches the camp. He walks with steady purposefulness, making no attempt to disguise his presence. Everything about him exudes friendliness, as though he is an emissary come to welcome them to some invisible but glorious kingdom. David's bodyguards watch him, puzzled, squinting into the brightness to discern who he is. Their hands coil on their sword hilts.

At a thousand feet, David leaps up and starts running. Weariness falls off him. Laughter fountains from him. The other men look on, more puzzled.

The two men meet in a violence of embrace. The force of it sets the other reeling. By now, the others have caught up. They stand around, astonished.

"David!"

"Jonathan!"

"How did you find me?"

"I always know how to find you."

"Your father should make you his tracker."

Both laugh, grimly.

"I cannot stay long," Jonathan says. "My father will soon send out servants to look for me."

They go to the place David prays each morning. Their elation quickly burns off in the light of reality: David is still hunted, Saul's hatred is unabated. It is, in fact, growing. It has become all-consuming.

"Killing you is all my father thinks about," Jonathan says. "It is all that consoles him."

"Who sings for him now?"

"No one."

"Will he... come to his senses?"

"I can't see it."

"Jonathan, perhaps I should walk back with you. Give myself into your father's hands."

"No. Never."

"But I can't do this anymore. Look at me. Look at my men. We're pathetic. We're stray dogs. Dead dogs. We are gnats your father hunts. It seems God is with him and not with me. It is only a matter of time before he catches me. Why prolong what is inevitable?"

"Don't be afraid. My father Saul will not lay a hand on you. You will be king over all Israel, and I will be second to you. Even my father knows this."

David sees that Jonathan believes this. Conviction makes his voice ring, his own bearing kingly. David realizes, as he has many times before, that Jonathan would make a brilliant king. His bravery, his generosity, his intelligence, his skill. He is born to it. Men would happily follow him. He would rule justly, wisely.

And all Jonathan has to do, to eliminate him as a rival, is betray him. It would require the simplest guile, the subtlest half-truth. If anyone could set a snare for David that he'd wander straight into, oblivious as a quail, it is Jonathan. Is this what is happening now? But no. David also sees in Jonathan an innocence that, in truth, would make him a foolish king. And he sees that Jonathan himself knows this. He will only ever bend all his bravery, all his generosity, all his intelligence, all his skill to this one thing: ensuring David one day sits on the very throne his father Saul now sits upon.

"Why?"

"Why what?"

"Why do you protect me? Why do you care for me? Why do you believe in me?"

"You are the man Samuel spoke about. Not me. God has chosen you, David. Not me. His will be done. Now let us renew our covenant."

The two men cross arms and join hands.

"I swear to you, David, before our God, that I give you my friendship, my allegiance, and my love unto death."

David, overcome with emotion, whispers, "And me with you."

The sky pulls a shroud of dark shade around its eastern edge. A funereal blue arcs above the horizon. Jonathan and David kiss. Jonathan, without looking back, walks away. David weeps so hard the landscape takes on the appearance of flood. He raises his hand in a gesture of silent parting. Jonathan never sees it, but David knows he feels it, laid on him like a hand dressing him for burial.

* * *

Right after this, the Ziphites—his own people—betray him, just as the elders of Keliah had. They make a pact to deliver him from one of his strongholds into Saul's hands. It is once more the young messenger boy who finds him to tell him.

"What is your name?" David asks the boy.

"Josheb-Basshebeth."

"And what is your age, Josheb?"

"I am fourteen. Almost."

"You are not an Israelite, are you?"

"A Tahkemonite, my lord."

"Can you handle a sword?"

"Fair enough."

"Join me, Josheb. Fight with me."

Josheb's face shines. He stands tall and stretches out his neck so his chin, lightly tufted with soft whiskers, juts out. There is a rash of pimples along his jawline.

"My lord, I am ready to die for you. You will not be disappointed."

"Already I'm not."

* * *

Now Saul advances, fast, close.

It is almost a relief to David, this day of reckoning. This day, he thinks, that will end all their running and hiding, their dodging and scavenging. Today, it ends.

David and his men scatter down the hill, rush down the narrowing canyon. But even as they run, threading through the narrow wadi, David knows their timing's off: his men will only be halfway out before Saul and his army swing round the hump of the ridge that divides them. Saul will bear down on them with the full weight of his maniacal anger, his unslakable bloodlust. Saul has all the advantages today—superior numbers and weapons, a wide downslope from which to force David and his men into a pinched and crouching defense. His hate. His madness.

And this: Saul's torment has infected his troops. It's made devils out of otherwise good men. David saw it recently in the eyes of Cush, a Benjamite soldier he once enjoyed fellowship with, a man funny and tender. David spied Cush early one morning. David remained hidden in the cleft of a rock, but Cush came close enough for David to see the texture of his skin, the hue of his eyes, the coarseness of the hair bristling in his meaty ears and nostrils. Whatever the man once was had been extinguished by something feral and rabid. Hatred burned in his eyes. David was shaken by it.

Whatever shallow pool of kindness Saul's troops might have felt toward David and his men when this pursuit first began, the cruel sun has licked up after weeks and months of marching. Their thirst has turned to bloodthirst. David knows that any man in Saul's camp, no matter how much affection he once held for David, would happily dispatch him to *Sheol*, just so he could turn and go home.

And now those men, fevered with bloodthirst, fly toward him. David senses they are no more than a hundred yards away. In a moment, in a breath, they will round the corner and see him, catch him, crush him. Saul's vengefulness, incarnate in each man, will surge hugely. It will drive out all shred of mercy. It will triple their strength.

My father will not lay a hand on you.

It is so clear, it is like Jonathan is standing beside him.

And he knows: Saul at this very moment turns back. Somehow, by some means or the next, Saul has ended his pursuit.

David slows, and those around him do as well, puzzled but unquestioning. By the time he reaches the mouth of the wadi, he's almost sauntering. All those already in the clear have realized, without knowing how, that the peril has lifted. They wait in the shade for the others to catch up. Some eat the food they packed that morning in haste. Ashael's mouth is green with the juice of an avocado. A light-heartedness, almost frivolity, flickers among the men.

David is standing joyful in their midst when Josheb-Basshebeth walks over the hillside and straight toward him.

"Where have you been, my young warrior?" David says.

"Delivering a message to Saul."

David's brow lifts in surprise. Joab and Eliab begin to draw their swords. "What message?"

"I told him the Philistines were raiding his land. He has gone now in pursuit of them."

Six hundred men roar with laughter. But not Joab. And not Josheb-Basshebeth.

When they subside, Josheb-Basshebeth speaks again.

"But it's true, my lord. What I told Saul is true."

Only now, and slowly, do Joab and Eliab re-sheathe their swords.

David decides right then to make Josheb-Basshebeth his armor-bearer for life.

* * *

But Saul is soon at it again. David wakes and knows it in his bones. He gets up and walks to a high place where he can see the land stretch in all directions. He discerns, on the horizon, a grey smudge against the shimmer of daylight. Twenty miles back, he estimates. At least two thousand men. Here by nightfall.

He thinks of calling Abiathar, inquiring of God through his priest, but doesn't. Instead, he prostrates himself on the packed earth. It is still cool from the night's chill. He lies there until he feels its coolness bleed into him. He lays his palms flat on the ground and presses his cheek into it, into the dust's silky fineness. And then he prays, "Speak, O Lord, for your servant is listening." It is the one prayer Samuel taught him. The old man said he had prayed it daily from his earliest days. And though many times, he said, God remained silent, the prayer had never failed him. God always answered it, seldom with words, but often with deeds. Or with a vastness of silence that always hid within it an answer that no words could convey.

David stays on the ground a long time. He falls asleep. He wakes. He hears nothing. But peace holds him like ropes. The sun's warmth blankets him. It is benediction. It is promise. He arises but otherwise doesn't move.

He knows what to do. He sees it, clear. He is to stop running. He is to stop hiding. He is to go to Saul. He is to hunt the hunter. He is to catch Saul in his own snare.

He is to run the man through with his own spear. This time, he will not withdraw his hand.

* * *

But now David has another problem. All of them are starving.

At first, all the men could talk about was food. Around the fire, they would each recount famous meals they had consumed, at weddings and festivals, in harvest times: meat tender and savory, the fat crackling in the open flame, bread that plumed white with steam when you broke it, fruit whose juices drenched your mouth sticky and sweet. But later, that talk became a kind of taunting. Now they brood in silence.

There is so little to eat. Fruit that's hard and bitter, picked unripe, or soft and bruised, nearly putrid, picked too late. Nuts so dry they turn chalky in your mouth. A thin bitter broth made from bones and gristle and wild herbs. Once in a while, meat, but the portions are vanishingly meager, and so stringy it chokes you.

David dreams of manna and quail, of waking at sunrise to find sweet bread scattered at his feet, enough for the day, of catching fistfuls of fresh plump fowl straight from God's hand. But he also understands how the people in the desert tired of it, day after day after day, a thing that after a while you tried to swallow without tasting.

Moses. David thinks about him more and more: a leader tired of leading, tired of hearing men's grievances, men whose bitterness was part of them before they ever showed up but who need someone else to pin it on. These men gathered about him are eager to blame him for their misery. He sees in them a feral readiness to turn on him, tear him to pieces, and feel vindicated in doing it.

If it weren't for a few loyal men, men loyal to their bones, men like Uriah the Hittite, who would choose death over betrayal, he might just walk away.

Was Jonathan mistaken? Was Samuel? That day the prophet came to his father's farm, insisting that no one eat until all the sons of Jesse had paraded before him, was he wrong about him, about the anointing? Maybe Samuel was sore hungry himself, hungry as Esau giving up his birthright, hungry as his men are now, and he anointed David just to get the thing over with. But Samuel's dead, and the dead don't speak.

And Samuel never did eat that day.

But how else to account for these present circumstances, unless Samuel was wrong? I am no king, David thinks. I am no anointed one. I am king of rats. The emperor of cave-dwellers. Lord of the riffraff. Chieftain of scavengers. Prince of parasites. I am leader of all with nowhere to go.

My kingdom is a rabble.

A hungry, cursed rabble.

* * *

"What?"

"You heard me."

"Say it to my face."

"That's your face? Mistook it for your ass. Except probably your ass ain't that ugly."

Baako throws a punch. Baanah ducks it and hits him across the jaw. It knocks him down. Baanah picks up a stool to smash over Baako's head, but Baako spears him in the groin with a stick he's snatched from the ground. When Baanah doubles over, Baako jumps on his back and begins clubbing his ears with his fists. Baanah hurtles backward into the side of an adobe wall that partly collapses. They scuffle on the ground.

Four men pull them apart.

"Next time I'll kill you."

"With what? Your breath? That's the only thing that scares me about you. That almost killed me this time."

This growing restlessness, this rancor, this violence—for David, it is more pressing right now than Saul's pursuit. The king's madness comes and goes. His murderousness is like the moon, waning, waxing, sliding beneath clouds. But this, this hot-temperedness, this quickness to argue and brawl, this aggrieved spirit, it is with him always.

This hunger.

He tries to turn it outward, to find things for the men to do. He sends them on scouting missions. He sends them on raids. He sends them hunting. But there's too many of them with too much time on their hands and never enough food in their bellies.

And then he comes up with a plan. A simple, elegant, clever plan.

* * *

"Greetings! Blessings on you and all you love."

Eight men, all armed, stand behind David in V-formation.

The farmer looks at him sideways.

"Do not be afraid," David says. "I come in peace."

"I know who you are. You're Jesse's boy."

David smiles tightly. "Yes. But now I'm all grown up."

"I don't want no trouble."

"Nor do I. Nor do we. We all love a life without trouble—not making any, not suffering any. But not everyone has the luxury of an untroubled life, do they?"

"What do you want from me?"

"Nothing. I want to help. We, my men and I—we're going to be in the area for a little while. We want to look after things for you. Keep an eye out. Make sure nothing happens to any of your animals. Your sons. Your daughters. Your wife."

"I don't need no help."

"Oh, but you might."

"Saul's been here. Recent. Looking for you. He's going to find you, for sure." The man, clearly, is trying to sound menacing, but his words come out in a fearful rush.

"You know," David says, "that's exactly the kind of trouble I was talking about. If Saul were ever to hear about any of this, from you, or from someone you know, well, that would be a lot of trouble. For you. For people you know, people you love. You don't want that kind of trouble, do you?"

The farmer hangs his head, shakes it.

"Pardon me? Did you say something?" David says.

"I don't want that kind of trouble."

"I thought not. As I said, we come in peace."

And so David and his men protect the farmer's sheep, and the farmer keeps them fed. And keeps his own mouth shut. And then David adds another farm, and another, and another. Soon, they watch over many farms. Many sheep. Many households.

David must exercise a strong hand with his men, to keep them from poaching. He himself watched, just last week, a plump, clumsy ewe lamb wading into still waters. The remembered taste of mutton made him shake with craving. But no: these sheep are for protecting. That conviction runs in him deeper than hunger.

"You never take," he tells his men, "another man's ewe lamb. Do you understand? It is as foul a thing in the eyes of God as taking that man's wife." He says it with fierce authority, a royal fiat, and even his hardest, most scabrous fighters shrink back from the force of it.

"Do you understand?"

"Yes, my lord."

And the men have found that when he sends them to ask after a farmer's health, the farmer sends them back with the very mutton they've craved, and with bread and cheese and currants and olives and oil and wine and root vegetables and nuts and wool and leather.

It goes very well.

But soon they all are hungry again. Even a dozen farms are not enough to feed six hundred men and their families adequately. Until now, David's kept to the smaller farms. They're easier to manage. There's less likelihood of word getting back to Saul. It's harder for the farmer to mount any armed resistance. The larger farms sell their produce in the towns. In *Mizpah*. In Hebron.

In Gibeah.

But David must do more to feed these hungry bellies. Hungry bellies are mutinous.

* * *

"Abishai?"

"Uncle?"

Take some men and begin to watch over that large holding north of Hebron.

"That is a big farm, uncle. The largest in the area. You think it's... wise?"

"I think it's foolish. But you know what is idiotic? Starving. Or killing each other. Or doing Saul's work for him. Tell me what options I have."

Abishai stares at him blankly.

"Now do as I say."

It is a sprawling farm rich in land and livestock. Many hands work it. There are fields of grain, forests of orchards, rows of vines, olive groves. Huge flocks of sheep and goats come in and out daily. It has its own creamery, winery, bakery, and butchery. It has an olive press, a threshing floor, and a shearing barn. It alone could feed them, all of them, for months.

A man named Nabal owns it.

* * *

Nabal is drunk. Most days he is deep in his cups by late morning, and by evening he's sloppy and loud and rickety on his feet. He's usually harmless, and sometimes funny. But other times, the drink seems to narrow his mind and darken his mood, turning him cruel. The servants, as best they can, steer wide of him, lest he burden them with inane or impossible demands or swipe at them with whatever's in his hand. His nose in recent years has swelled bulbously. It's pocked as a termite hill, and veiny and purple. His gut has grown huge, a swaying billowing sack beneath his shirt, and sometimes its girth pulls his shirt up to expose the white hairy expanse of his belly. He is puffed up everywhere with flesh. Even his fingers look yeasty.

But he still likes to be in the thick of things. Today, it's wool-shearing. The quick rasp of shearing blades like the susurrus of locust wings. Filaments of wool like the ghosts of moths. Snowy mounds piling up on the floor. Nimble boys gathering it into bags. Each sheep freshly shorn, naked and stubbly, stunned and shivering, tottering away.

Nabal moves his girth with painstaking effort, heaving himself around, shearing the odd sheep himself, bending his shoulder toward the task as though he's stuffing himself into a rock cleft half his size.

It is work and play altogether. Nabal, despite his drunkenness, is giddy. It's been a good year. Hardly a sheep's been lost. Most years, he rages even as he resigns himself to a usual attrition: sheep poached by drifters, ravished by wild animals, ravaged by insects, lost by their own wandering folly, felled by the endless ailments that stalk them. But this year, except for a few sheep that perished from illness, the flocks came back in the same numbers they went out. Now he has mountains of wool, and a ready market. And he knows how to drive a hard bargain.

"There are men here to see you."

It's Nabal's chief steward, a man of few words.

"Huh. What?"

"There are ten men waiting to see you."

"Who?"

"David's men."

Nabal's eyes narrow. He hands his shears to a servant, gathers his bulk under his tunic, and follows the steward. David's ten men stand waiting in the yard. The steward introduces Nabal to Abishai, who steps forward. "We greet you in the name of our leader, David. Long life to you! Good health to you and to your household! And good health to all that is yours!"

Abishai waits, but all Nabal does is fix him with a withering look. He continues. "We bring greetings from our leader, David. And also a message." Abishai repeats the message from memory, but his voice alters in the speaking of it, becomes lower, more officious. "Now I hear it is sheep shearing season. When your shepherds were with us, we did not mistreat them, and the whole time they were at Carmel, nothing of theirs went missing. Ask your own servants and they will tell you. Therefore, be favorable toward my young men, since we come at a festive time. Please give your servants and your son David whatever you can find for them."

Abishai finishes, steps back with the other men, waits.

Nabal puts his thick fingers on his chin and rubs. He looks away from the men, toward the land stretching down to the river. It's late day, and the sun makes the river's surface bright and dimpled as hammered bronze. Some boys play at the water's edge, and their voices ricochet up the hill. It is a kind of music.

Nabal turns back to Abishai.

"Who is this David? This son of Jesse?" Nabal hisses this. It is obvious he knows full well who David is, that he's picked up Saul's name for him, Saul's seething contempt. "Many servants are breaking away from their masters these days." Nabal looks at all ten men, grinning sideways, almost leering, then looks away again, toward the river. He seems suddenly bored, finished. But then he turns back and fixes Abishai with a hard glare and speaks with ferocity: "Why should I take my bread and my water and the meat I have slaughtered for my shearers, and give it to men coming from who knows where?"

Nabal thrusts himself upward and forward as he speaks. His chin nearly touches the face of Abishai. His great belly almost brushes him. Abishai gives Nabal a steady gaze. All the men's fighting hands are tight on their swords. Then, without a word, Abishai turns and all ten men depart.

Nabal puts his hands on his hips and looks around dramatically, as though he's played this all to an astonished audience. His steward stands off at a distance, blank-faced, silent.

"Well," Nabal announces. "Ha. Ha ha. David, indeed. David, the king of nothing. David the fool. The little son of Jesse has learned that no one messes with Nabal."

He stumps away, laughing, cursing. His servant runs to find Abigail, and quick.

* * *

David squints toward the sky's fierce brightness. The rim of canyon above him is a dark edge against the heaven's starched expanse. He tries to make out details in the shadows. He sees a thick cloud of dust rise. He can't see yet what stirs it, but he guesses, by the cloud's denseness and its slow hovering movement, that it's a pack of animals, at least six. Not a war party. The thought disappoints and relieves him, almost in equal measure.

But it doesn't cool him. His anger is unquenchable. It's primal. He is like a seam in the earth where the deep fires break through.

He has sworn an oath: he will kill Nabal and every man in his household. It is a vow as sacred to him as betrothal or fealty. An unbreakable pledge. A king's decree. He must fulfill it, and every muscle in him bends toward it. As with all his men, especially Joab and Abishai. In each man, in all his men, breeds a dark rage only massacre can subdue. This kind only comes out by killing.

David is under oath to raise his hand against that fool.

* * *

Some nights he dreams blood.
Bright, then dark.
Hot and slippery.
Cool and sticky.
Black and crusted.
Vultures circling above.
The strange slowness of carnage.

Most times he is at a distance from it, looking on. Sadness and satisfaction split his heart. Other times he is in the middle of it. His body wheels and surges. His weapons flash. He sees blood on his own arms, his hands; feels its heat but doesn't know if it springs from his own veins or someone else's. Doesn't know if the blood presages victory or defeat. All he knows is he can't stop.

When he wakes, it is always the same: starting up suddenly, his heart like a bird inside a cage, frantic to escape. Ahinoam, beside him, wakes too.

She places a hand on his hand and brings it to her rounded belly. She spreads his palm on her naked skin and holds it there until he feels the life inside her move.

It calms him like music.

* * *

Ahinoam of Jezreel. The sister of Amhid, who joined David a month or so after he left Gath. They were both running, Ahinoam and Amhid, though from what, neither ever said. There were a few women in the entourage—sisters, daughters, wives, a few mothers, at least one aunt, three female cousins. And there were a few women who came with some man but were not bound to him by either blood or oath. These ones passed from man to man.

Amhid first claimed Ahinoam was his young brother, Arhid, and no one questioned this: she was bedraggled and scrawny, dressed in soiled and baggy clothes, and she never spoke. Few paid her any heed.

But one evening in En Gedi, David was coming back from his place of solitude. He glimpsed movement behind thick sheaves of reeds and moved stealthily, in case it was an enemy. He climbed several shelves of rock to a place where the ground flattened like a rooftop. From here he could watch without being seen.

She was naked. She had a dark lean beauty that struck him breathless. She was lifting her left arm—the skin underneath was pale, and a nest of black hair bristled from the hollow of her armpit—splashing water on her breast, rubbing its underside. Blood swelled in his groin. He could not look away. He watched until she finished and then slipped away while she dressed.

He tried to make the vision of her go away. It came to him unbidden. It crowded out his prayers, clouded his plans. His times alone were often spent battling the distraction of her. He began to time his visits to his place of solitude so that he might glimpse her again, bathing.

He lacked the courage to speak to her.

Sometimes he slaked his lust by thinking about Michal. But his memory of her was fading day by day. He struggled to remember her face, her voice, her movements. Even the memory of her body, which he thought he would never forget, dimmed. He could only recall her in fragments, as though she had been carved up into pieces: an angular hip bone, a small firm breast, the downward curve of her buttocks. And what dominated his remembering was her growing coldness, the way he touched her and she tightened and didn't soften. His desire for her withered before it even aroused.

One day David called Amhid into the inner chamber of the cave that served as his makeshift throne room.

"You lied to me."

"My lord?"

"You tried to pass your sister as your brother."

"My lord, I…"

"Why?"

"My lord, please. I thought the men would mistreat her. I thought they would molest her. It was all I could think to do, to protect her."

"I will protect her."

"Thank you, thank you. My lord, do not be offended. I am a simple man, and not wise like you. But even you—as good and strong as you are, my lord—even you cannot be everywhere. How will Ahinoam not be like these other women, passed from man to man like a gourd of wine? Like a shank of mutton?"

"Ahinoam?"

"Yes, my lord. Is that... you seem... troubled. Her name is Ahinoam. Is it... alright, my lord?"

"It is fine. It is nothing."

But it is something: Ahinoam is the name of Michal's mother. Ahinoam is the name of Saul's wife.

"How will I protect her? Amhid, you make it sound as if I am no shepherd. As if I am merely a hireling. I am the good shepherd, Amhid. Does a shepherd not know how to protect his sheep? To provide for his sheep?"

"Yes, my lord. I mean no disrespect. I just feel... I feel that my father, our father, Ahinoam's father, would require this of me. That I must care for her."

"I will tell you, Amhid, how I will protect your sister. I will marry her."

Amhid falls back as though struck.

"Oh my lord, you are truly my king. Oh, thank you. Thank you."

And so David took Ahinoam to be his wife. And her belly, five months later, now swells with his child. His first. At night he places his hand on her naked belly. Then he places his ear there. Then he puts his mouth close.

"My son," he says. "May you never go hungry. May no one ever seek to harm you. I will call you Amnon. May you always be blessed, my son. May you want for nothing."

* * *

David stops, and four hundred men behind him lurch to a halt. He turns and speaks to them. "It's been useless—all my watching over this fool's, this Nabal's, property in the desert so that he loses nothing. I have blessed him and he has repaid me evil. May God deal with David, be it ever so severely, if by morning I leave alive one of his who pisses against the wall. Every man will be laid in his own blood."

This is the second time he's made this oath. The men all roar. Bloodlust, David thinks, is stronger than drink. It is stronger than the other kind of lust. Once awakened, only one thing can abate it.

From an eyelet of rock, a mule's head appears. Another appears, and another. There are three altogether, all heavy laden, each led by a man himself riding a mule.

And then a woman appears, riding a mule without packs. She maneuvers her beast in front of the other animals and begins down the steep trail. She rides, he sees, expertly.

She is veiled. He cannot see her face. But he sees her body, the way it sways with the motion of the animal's descent, the way her breasts move beneath her shift, the way her wide hips roll.

She stops on flat open ground, twenty feet in front of David. She dismounts and bows low. She gets on her knees, then on her hands. She crawls toward him until her head is over his feet. She pulls her veil back but does not look up.

Something about her, kneeling in the dust, kneeling at his feet, quiets him. She is like a finger pressed to his lips. She is like music.

When she speaks, her face is still bent to the ground.

* * *

This morning, David sent ten men on an errand, led by Abishai. They were to collect the debt owed them by Nabal, for protecting his holdings. Many times David's men had begged and argued with him to poach a few of the rich man's sheep.

"That fat oaf can spare a few. He's not like those other farmers. Their sheep are like their family. Little Hannah. Little Naomi. But this man, he throws himself around like a king. He doesn't even know a one of his sheep by name. They are just shekels to him, coin in his pocket."

"No. We use the same rules with Nabal that we do with any of the farmers. Same."

It galled his men, but also, in a bitter way, amused them.

"Our leader hasn't seen a sheep he doesn't think's his own daughter," one said to another.

"Agreed. I think he'd rather roast us on a spit than blame some rich man's little ewe."

"Ach," said another. "What I wouldn't do just to suck the bones of even one of those gristly smug rams that strut about like Goliath. Maybe if we killed it with a slingshot, David might see the point and forgive us."

They all laughed, but without mirth.

But now that David's goodwill had come due, his men were pleased with his decision. They saw its wisdom. They fully anticipated Nabal's gratitude, his generosity. Nabal would have heard from other farmers the cost of refusal. He would know it was in his best interest to do as David wished.

And so a festive mood buoyed them all. They laughed at the least little thing, found the smallest flippancy or wisecrack a thing of outrageous comedy. Tonight they would feast, and fill their bellies with meat and grain. Tonight they would down strong drink until their heads spun, their legs wobbled. They'd eat cheese until their breaths reeked. They'd devour fattened ewes and smear the grease on their faces until their faces shone.

Only hours away.

But Abishai and the others returned empty handed. Everyone could tell by their grim faces that Nabal had done more than refused David. He had insulted him. He had mocked him. He had cursed him.

Every man was aggrieved and sore bent on vengeance.

* * *

But now David feels this woman's forehead touch his feet. He feels a wetness on them. He feels her hair lightly brush them.

"My lord," she says. "Please let your servant speak to you; hear what your servant has to say. Let the blame fall on me alone. May my Lord pay no attention to that wicked man Nabal. He is just like his name—his name is Fool, and folly goes with him. But as for me, your servant, I did not see the men my master sent. And let this gift, which your servant has brought to my Lord, be given to the men who follow you."

The servants' mules are laden with twice the food David had hoped for.

"And now, my lord, as surely as the Lord your God lives and as you live, since the Lord has kept you from bloodshed and from avenging yourself with your own hands, may your enemies and all who are intent on harming my lord be like Nabal."

David kneels beside her and lifts her head. When he sees her face, he starts. It is Nabal's wife. Abigail. He has only ever seen her at a distance. She is ravishing. Her eyes are pure black lustre, deeply knowing, and her skin creamy as ewe milk. David swallows hard. His mouth goes dry. A dizziness comes over him. He tries to speak but can't.

She leans her face so close to his he can smell her, her heady scent of spices and oils and some deep womanly muskiness.

"Please forgive your servant's presumption," she whispers. She looks into his eyes. "The Lord your God will certainly make a lasting dynasty for my lord, because you fight the Lord's battles. No wrongdoing will be found in you as long as you live. Even though someone is pursuing you to take your life, the life of my Lord will be bound securely in the bundle of the living by the Lord your God, but the lives of your enemies he will hurl away as from the pocket of a sling. When the Lord has fulfilled for my Lord every good thing he promised concerning him and has appointed him ruler over Israel, my Lord will not have on his conscience the staggering burden of needless bloodshed or of having avenged himself. And when the Lord your God has brought my Lord success, remember your servant."

This last—*Remember your servant*—she says with distinct emphasis. It is not a plea. It is an invitation.

David leaps up with antic haste. The words he couldn't form a moment ago now torrent out of him: "Praise be to the Lord, the God of Israel, who has sent you today to meet me. May you be blessed for your good judgment and for keeping me from bloodshed this day and from avenging myself with my own hands. Otherwise, as surely as the Lord, the God of Israel, lives, who has kept me from harming you, if you had not come quickly to meet me, not one male belonging to Nabal would have been left alive by daybreak."

He reaches down to Abigail and bids her rise, helps her to her feet. The touch of her hand jolts him. It momentarily numbs him, then leaves his insides tingling. It is the same sensation he once had when, coming in at day's end from war, he trod one of Saul's carpets and a shock shot through him.

He can barely repress braying or whooping, gambolling like a colt testing its legs.

Then he turns solemn and accepts her gift to him as fitting tribute, as due recompense. And when next he speaks, he is kingly.

"Go home in peace. I have heard your words and granted your request."

She bows, and with slow dignity mounts and rides away. David watches her until her figure disappears over the lip of the canyon rim, watches the way her body sways. She never looks back. But he's sure she wants to.

* * *

The voices of the men and their families all around him are happy. Sated. Ira, son of Ikkeh, from Tekoa, stumbles by, leaning hard on the shoulders of his stick-boned wife. His mouth is dark with wine stain, shiny with mutton grease. He greets David and staggers on, his wife almost lugging him like a wooden beam.

David hopes this is not a night one of those pesky nomadic clans, the Amorites or Ammonites or such, chooses to raid. His mighty men would be as helpless as Joshua's circumcised army. Then Uriah the Hittite walks by, sober and steady. He greets David with just a nod.

"Ah," David says to himself. "I have not to worry with men like that in my camp. And when he fights, he is worth a dozen of my men."

*　*　*

David looks up into the night sky. Stars pulse and zip in the blackness. He reaches toward them. They look close enough to touch, to pinch in his fingertips, to juggle in his palms. He could flip their icy coldness or scorching hotness from hand to hand.

How close is God? Is he hiding in the stars? Is he just beyond them? Are they the backside of his garment? Or is God closer, much closer, moving with lion stealth at the edge of firelight, seeing without being seen, hearing without being heard? There are times he's sure God traces a finger across the nape of his neck, rests a hand on his shoulder, puts his lips to his ear and speaks, or just breathes. But there are other times God flees him, hides from all his seeking, sees him pleading and says nothing, does nothing. Just lets him twist in the snare of his own tangled heart and bind himself deeper.

My God, my God, why are you so far from the words of my groaning?

But wasn't Abigail God's voice in his ear, God's finger on his skin, God's hand on his shoulder? She was like an angel the old men talk about, showing up disguised as mortal and only later unveiling a fierce and terrible beauty.

But thinking of Abigail, he thinks of Nabal, that fat sweaty oaf. Indignation strikes him with fresh urgency. Anger rises. The urge to kill rushes back.

But thinking of Nabal, he thinks again of Abigail, her lithe and delicate loveliness. The darkness of her eyes.

Joy surges, anger abates.

That night, Ahinoam's body, its boniness, all its ridges and hollows, leaves him unsatisfied.

*　*　*

And soon, everyone is hungry again.

One morning, a servant of Nabal, grazing sheep on tableland, waves Abishai over. Under David's orders, against much protest from his men, David has resumed his watch over Nabal's sheep and servants. For Abigail's sake.

Abishai walks over to meet the man. The servant gives his message with frantic breathlessness: "My master is dead. When my mistress Abigail returned from her encounter with your master, she found Nabal terribly drunk. So she waited to speak to him until morning. When she told him all that had taken place, my master turned white. He went rigid. He was a stone, neither speaking nor seeing nor hearing. For ten days he stayed this way. And then last evening, he fell straight over, not one part of him bending as he fell. And he died."

Abishai runs back to camp.

"What message is so urgent that you have left your post until relieved, Abishai?" David asks.

"Uncle, I have come straight from a servant of the late Nabal."

It takes David not even a heartbeat to catch this.

"Late?"

"He died last evening, after ten days of living death. A great terror befell Nabal the day after Abigail left here."

Elation sweeps over David, like a man about to eat after long emptiness.

"Praise be to the Lord, who has upheld my cause against Nabal for treating me with contempt. He has kept his servant from doing wrong and has brought Nabal's wrongdoing down on his own head."

He pauses, measuring his next words. A word he's never used before forms in his mouth, seems to hum on his tongue. He looks directly at Abishai.

"Take ten men and go to Abigail with this word: 'David has sent us to you to take you to become his wife.'"

Take. That's the word. Speaking it, he feels a surge of power. It's what kings speak. It's what kings do. With men. With plunder. With captives. With cities. With wives.

They take.

By nightfall Abigail comes to him, and he takes her. He is giddy. His desire is huge, and almost better, his sense of vindication. He doesn't notice Ahinoam's grief. Or he does and doesn't care.

972 BC
Damn Fool
JOAB

I wasn't there the first time David had a clean shot to kill Saul, that time in the cave. But when brother Abishai told me, I could have run David through with my own blade. I told him so, to his face. I told him what a damn fool thing he did. He was always talking God this, God that, God will save me, God will vindicate me, but when God himself put his enemy right into his hands—when God himself led Saul like a lamb to the slaughter—David goes soft.

I wanted a real bed, not these stones we slept on. I wanted real meat, cooked proper, not this bony stringy vermin we gnawed on. And he threw it all away. In the name of mercy. What about mercy for us? What about mercy for me?

Damn him. It still gets my blood hot.

So I told him what to do. I knew how to kill a king. I'd killed one once, an Ammonite king. He died like other men. Eyes wide, mouth open. He bled. His blood took a while to show up on the ground. But once it did, it was red like any man's.

So I told him. I told him how to kill Saul. I told him how deep Saul sleeps. I'd seen it myself. Lots.

"Listen," I said, "that man sleeps like a dead dog. You could kick him, you could stomp him, and he wouldn't even turn over. You could pull an ox out of a well easier than you could get that man to wake up."

"And so?"

"And so? Don't you hear me? I once saw Abner trying to rouse the man. He had to shake him until his teeth rattled."

"And so?"

"And so? You are… I'm saying that you could find him dead asleep right in his own camp, walk right up to him, run him through clean. He wouldn't even wake to thank you."

Well, I told David all that. And the way I saw it turning in his head, the way it made his eyes all wolfish, I knew I had him thinking.

Spear

They live well that fall and winter. David inherits all Nabal's land, and all his servants, and all his animals, and all his buildings. The winter rains come early, and fall hard and cold, but the men are warm and their bellies full.

Saul retreats to Gibeah to wait out the winter. David's men relax and build houses near Hebron. They settle into slow easy rhythms. Even Ahinoam and Abigail work out an uneasy truce. They share the work of the household with few words, kind or cruel.

Everyone seems to forget Saul.

Except David.

He thinks about him daily. He remembers Saul's times of darkness, when he lay on the floor curled in on himself, moaning. And he remembers Saul's times of lightness, of clear-mindedness, of big-heartedness, when he spoke kindly, when he spread his long arms wide.

"My son."

"My king."

"You know what I love?"

"Please tell me, my king."

"I love that you fight my battles so that my kingdom might enjoy peace. That I might enjoy peace."

"It is my honor, my king."

"And I love that you love my daughter Michal. She is precious to me. She too is worth fighting for."

* * *

That spring, when kings go out to war, king Saul goes out too. But it is not to fight Israel's enemies. It's not to fight Moabites, or Amorites, or Amalekites. It's not to fight Philistines. Saul marshals every warrior in Israel, all the armies of the Lord of hosts, to fight one man.

Saul goes out once more to kill David.

But this time, David plays it differently. He sends deliberate signals, leaves obvious clues. He makes it so easy for Saul to find him that a man more cautious would hesitate, become wary, suspect a trap.

But Saul, he knows, has lost all caution. He is not a man on a mission. He is a man in the grip of an obsession, without a shred of wisdom. If David baits, Saul will take the bait.

* * *

And now David stands over him. Saul is recumbent. Asleep. He looks small, looks harmless. His eyelids twitch slightly. His breath whistles faintly. But these are his only movement, his only sounds. Unlike some of the men sleeping around him, unlike his general and chief bodyguard, Abner, whose slumber is a wrestling match with himself, Saul is a weaned child at his mother's breast. His long limbs fold over his chest as if someone carefully tied him in an elegant slipknot.

David knows full well the risk he's taking. One mistake—tripping, sneezing, coughing—will cost David and Abishai their lives. Or if one soldier wakes, jolted from sleep by an owl's screech or a vivid dream or the shock of premonition, they are dead men. He could have sent others. But he needed to come himself, to see Saul close-up, to look on his face and see if madness found him even in sleep, or if this was his one last refuge from himself.

His face is childlike. It is as if he has seen a great wonder, a flaming seraphim or frolicking Leviathan, a thing of unearthly beauty or hideousness, and the sight has returned him to some mute and primal state. This, David thinks, must be how he looked the day Samuel anointed him. It is how he have must looked when the Spirit fell on him and he uttered strange speech, his mouth full of music and oracle.

This is how he must have looked the first day he lifted his newborn son Jonathan into his arms.

David's wife Ahinoam gave birth two weeks ago to their first child. Amnon. He came out of the womb purple and tiny and wizened and mute. David thought he was stillborn. But the infant let out a weak cry, and then a lusty howl, and everyone laughed and clapped. David held him, and Amnon stared at both of them with large, dark searching eyes.

"I am a father," David said. "My son. My son. O my son. I will give you all I have lacked. I will be the father I wish I had."

* * *

Saul's spear stands rigid above the king's head. Its bronze-tipped iron point is thrust inches deep into the earth. David recognizes it: it's the same spear Saul tried to kill him with. David closes his eyes and sees it all again. The whirr of the spear's shaft cutting air, hitting the wall, falling. Saul leaping up in an ecstasy of rage, grabbing it, thrusting it, running straight at him with it. It seemed a thing both attached to Saul and apart from him.

And now here it is, inches away.

David stands over Saul for a dangerously long time. At last Abishai steps close to him and whispers, "Today God has given your enemy into your hands. Just like in the cave. Now let me pin him to the ground with one thrust of my spear. I won't strike him twice."

The sons of Zeruiah are beginning to wear on him. Their eagerness to kill is bottomless. Their appetite for mayhem is unfillable. If ever wars were to cease to the ends of the earth, the sons of Zeruiah would perish. Sometimes David watches Joab and Abishai when someone new comes into their camp. He watches the shifting and narrowing of their eyes, the flexing and coiling of their muscles, the way their hands close on their weapons. He knows exactly what they're doing: mentally rehearsing the havoc they would love to unleash. They see everything in opposition. Everyone is an enemy to destroy. Every man, until proven otherwise, is a rival to thrust their weapon through.

But he cannot fault them for lack of bravery. When David asked Abishai and Uriah the Hittite which one would join him to go down to Saul's camp—David intentionally asked them when Joab was not around—Uriah hesitated, and even dared to challenge him.

"Is not Saul as you are, my lord? Is he not the Lord's anointed?"

Abishai, however, jumped at the chance.

"I will go, my lord. I will raise my hand against Saul. He is just another man to me."

* * *

David looks around Saul's camp. All his men lay sprawled like the slain. Abner snores and mutters, lost to the world.

This is a day Saul's men will all regret. This is their day of infamy, when they did not protect their king.

And for more than a few, David thinks, this will be their day of freedom, when finally they crawl out from under the thrall of the king's madness. David envisions many of them, one day, thanking him.

Abishai lifts his spear two feet above Saul's heart.

David's heart leaps, with joy.

But then he almost throws himself atop Saul, to catch the thrust of Abishai's spear.

"What the hell?" Abishai hisses. "What are you doing?"

"Do not destroy him. He is my father. My king."

Abishai looks at him with disbelief. His brow V's sharply. His mouth twists hard.

"You damn fool! This is the second time the Lord has given this man into your hands. If you have an ounce of wisdom, a shred of pride, you will strike him now."

"You know so little, Abishai. This man is the Lord's anointed. Who can lay a hand on the Lord's anointed and be guiltless? As surely as the Lord lives, the Lord himself will strike him. Either his time will come and he will die, or he will go into battle and perish. But the Lord forbid that I should lay a hand on the Lord's anointed."

"My lord," Abishai says, and now his voice is cold with threat. "You don't know what you're doing. Your own men will raise their hands against you for this. What will you tell them this time?"

"The Lord forbids it," David says with equal coldness. "Now get Saul's spear and water jug, and let's go."

Abishai, ramrod and bristling, takes the items. He hands the spear to David.

The weight of it surprises him. It seeks the earth.

They half walk, half run from the camp, weaving nimble between bodies sodden with sleep. A few of the men snort and rattle their cheeks as though about to wake. They keep their pace steady. Abishai suggests slitting the throats of every third soldier—a soundless, quick, efficient way to kill a man, that will cause panic in the camp when the others wake. David does not dignify this even with a rebuke.

* * *

Daylight seeps into the edge of the sky by the time they reach the far side of the gulch and climb to the ridge overlooking Saul's camp. They take a moment to catch their breaths. Then David yells across the distance.

"Aren't you going to answer me, Abner?"

Voices of alarm and confusion burst from Saul's camp.

Then a voice, gravelly with sleep, calls back. "Who are you who calls to the king?"

David's voice, spiky with sarcasm, calls back. "You're a man, Abner, aren't you? And who is like you in Israel? Why didn't you guard your lord the king? Someone came to destroy your lord the king. What you have done, it's not good. As surely as the Lord lives, you and your men deserve to die, because you did not guard your master, the Lord's anointed. Look around you. Where are the king's spear and water jug that were near his head?"

Voices of surprise and accusation surge.

Then the voice of Saul, almost mournful, slips through the din.

"Is that your voice, David, my son?"

David feels lightness in his head, thickness in his throat. He has to fight down the urge to run to Saul. He has to fight down tears. His mind tells him that this is just Saul's serpent cunning, to speak the one word that undoes him, to hold out the one promise he cannot resist. *My son.*

He forces his mind to rule over him and pushes a coldness and aloofness into his voice. "It is I, my lord the king."

"My son."

"Your servant. But tell me, why is my lord pursuing his servant? What have I done, and what wrong am I guilty of? The king of Israel has come out to look for a flea. Why? Now listen to me, my lord the king, please listen to your servant. If the Lord has incited you against me, then may he accept an offering. But if men have done this, may the Lord curse them. These men have driven me from my share of the Lord's inheritance. They want me to serve other gods. I beg you, my king, do not let my blood fall to the ground far from the presence of the Lord."

David finishes almost gasping. A great silence hangs between him and Saul. There is enough daylight now to see Saul's tall willowy figure. Saul sways, sways the way a cobra does, side to side, rhythmic, when it tries to mesmerize a sheep or cow, to daze it before striking.

"I have sinned," Saul says. His voice now is so strong and clear, it is as though he stands next to David. "I have sinned. Come back, David, my son. Because you considered my life precious today, I will not harm you again. Surely I have acted like a fool, a *nabal*. I have erred greatly."

David steps into a shaft of daylight that falls like water from the steep rocks above him. He holds up Saul's belongings.

"Here is the king's spear. Let one of your young men come over and get it. The Lord gave you into my hands today, but I would not lay a hand on the Lord's anointed. As surely as I valued your life today, so may the Lord value my life and deliver me from all trouble."

"May you be blessed, my son David. You will do great things. You will surely triumph."

David cannot tell whether this is confession or accusation. Saul was once among the prophets: the Spirit, the *ruach*, would rush upon him, whirl him dizzy until he fell in a heap of his own limbs, his eyes bright with ecstasy, babble on his lips. Did he long ago see David's rise? Is his whole life, then until now, a knowing of this, a fighting of this, an accepting of this, only to fight it again?

A few moments later, a young man climbs up to David to retrieve the spear and water jug. David has seen the boy before. He smiles at him, and the boy smiles back.

"What is your name, son?"

"Elhanan, son of Jaare-oregim, the Bethlehemite."

"That is my town. Our town. You will serve one day, Elhanan. You will fight for me. Perhaps you will kill a giant. One day I will be your king."

"Yes, my lord."

As David climbs back up the hillside, he sees Joab watching him. Joab shakes his head, slow and heavy, like a great animal mortally wounded. His look is more weariness than disgust.

972 BC
Mercy
MICHAL

Anyone who tells you anything about woman—that she is willful, or capricious, or cruel-minded—simply forgets the lineage of that trait. Our fathers make me. I spent my girlhood wanting something from my father, exactly what I cannot say, and then I spent my early womanhood giving all that wanting to David. I despised my father then. I was embarrassed by him—his sour breath, his pale skin, his thin voice, his spidery hands. His fits and piques.

I swore never to be like him.

And now I mirror him, inside and out. Except for the madness. Unless bitterness is that.

I am not much inclined to advice—giving it, taking it. But note this: oaths are dangerous things. They often come back to mock you. I swore never to be like my father, and it circled back on me like a jackal on a lion's prey.

But David, he never circled back. He just kept running. I think I knew this before he left. What I didn't know at first was what he stole from me. He fled with every hope I carried not to be my father's daughter. He scattered that hope like a wind scatters a thistle's seeds.

I once hid an idol beneath my bedsheets to protect David. I covered the top with goat hair. It was to dupe my father's guards. My father had sent them to my chambers to fetch David, summon him to his own death like you might summon a man to a banquet. I told the guards he was sick in bed. Look, I said, there he is. They looked, and there he was: a lump beneath the covers, a clump of hair splayed on the pillow.

But he was long gone, escaped out the window.

Now I think it's all I ever had of him: an idol, a dead statue tucked away in the folds of my own desire. I thought I had him, while all the time he was gone.

Do you know when it happened, when I finally fully hated him? When he didn't kill my father. He had two clear chances and turned both down flat, like my father was an old whore he was too prim to touch.

Virtue looks ugly to its victims.

David's mercy did not exalt him in my eyes. I did not see it as valor or honor. For one, it further reduced my father. It unveiled even more his piteousness. It almost seemed David did it for that reason, to spite my father, to expose his feebleness. And to spite me.

But I hated him, because back then my father was the single obstacle to David returning. When David spared him—twice—well you see, don't you? It's a message only a fool could miss. David kept my father alive to keep me away, to keep away from me. Love for me would have made him plunge the knife, thrust the spear. Staying his hand could only mean the opposite.

Twice he had this chance. Both times he failed.

He took mementoes, though. The first time, a piece of my father's robe. The second, his water pot and spear. He knew what he was doing. His mercy was cruel. Beneath all his pretense of innocence, he chose his touchstones well. These were things that mattered to my father. They were his royal symbols. His insignia.

The seamless robe of his kingly authority that until that moment was perfectly intact.

The spear that, waking, never left my father's grip. I believe that Father believed that spear warded things off, hexes and curses and the evil eye, that it was more shield than weapon.

The water pot, which had become my father's image of himself. In a land where a man sooner survives without arms than a water pot, it had become my father's promise that in him, from him, flowed rivers of living water.

David knew. These things he took, just to show he could.

Both times afterward he called my father. The first time they were close enough to touch, if they had wanted. The second time they met across a good distance. Both times, David showed him what he'd taken: robe, spear, water pot. And my father fell into his trap. He was smitten by David all over again, as people were wont to do. David this and David that. My son. He begged him to return. He begged him for mercy. He called himself a *nabal*. I was surprised he didn't break out in song, heralding David's exploits against the tens of thousands.

"Come back," my father said to him. "Come home."

But David didn't come. This wasn't his home. He returned my father's relics, revealing them for what they were: cloth, clay, wood, iron. And then he bundled up his own virtue like a rescued lamb, plucked from thornbushes at a cliff edge, and walked back into his desolate kingdom. Lord of barren wastes.

And bereft of me. Free of me.

But my father made his grievous prophecy, for indeed my father was among the prophets: one day David would be king. God himself would establish the kingdom of Israel in his hands. In that moment of terrible clarity, he asked David for the one thing he knew he would need most on that day: mercy. Mercy for his descendants. A promise that he would not be cut off, that his family's name would not be wiped out.

So here I am. Saul's daughter. Saul's daughter, alive, spared, not wiped out, not cut off, but barren as was David's land of exile. Barren as his waterless desert.

I ask you, is this mercy?

1011 BC
Ziklag

Hebron is now too dangerous. Though Saul searches for him less and less, he occasionally roars back to the task with fierce energy. David and his men and all their families must scatter each time into wilderness, often for months.

It exhausts them. So after many seasons, David returns to King Achish in Gath.

"You're back?"

"My king."

"Your king? So you're a Philistine now?"

"You are my king."

"This is novel. This is precious. You must be more mad than when last we met. How can the King of Israel and the fighter of the Lord's battles and the slayer of Goliath turn from his chosen path?"

"I am no king. Saul has driven me from the land. I have no inheritance among those people. Saul has turned me from them. And from my God. I am loyal to you alone."

"And your..." Achish points at his own head, rolls back his eyes, lolls out his tongue, "...your own little spell of madness, that went away? For good?"

"Yes, my king. It was more fear than madness."

"And you are not afraid anymore?"

"I am, my king. But it is different now."

"How?"

"It gives me courage."

"Fear gives you courage? This makes no sense."

"It is hard to explain…"

"You mean it is hard to explain to me, an uncircumcised pagan?"

"My king, I mean no disrespect."

"What do you mean?"

"It is about my God?"

"Try… try to explain, even to an uncircumcised pagan."

"When I am afraid, there are times I turn only to myself. I try to find the courage in myself. It only makes me more afraid. It makes me… mad. But there are times I turn to my God. To *Yahweh*. He never lacks for courage, or comfort, or wisdom, or anything. The Lord is… my shepherd. My shield. My rock. My salvation. He walks beside me even when death and enemies are all around me. I want for nothing."

Achish listens with a look of, what? David cannot tell. Curiosity? Bewilderment? Hope?

"So you are still mad?"

"No, my king."

"But you speak of your *elohim* like—like it is a friend. Dagon, the *elohim* of Philistia, he is no friend. We do not think of Dagon or speak of Dagon this way. We do not speak *to* Dagon. No one goes to Dagon to find… strength. Courage. To get any of the things you go to your *Elohim* for. We go to him… we go to him to give him things. Things he demands. And to get from him things, things we need. Rain. Sun. Crops."

"*Yahweh* gives to me things I need as well. I don't have anything to give him. Just myself. And my uprightness."

"I see. Why are you coming to me, then? Asking me for things? Why not your *elohim*? Why doesn't he give you back your inheritance?"

David is silent.

"Well?"

"He gives me other things besides this. Other things he does in me. The man I was—the man, the boy, who killed your champion Goliath—he would not have been a good king. He would… he would be a Saul. Or a Nabal."

Achish studies David for a long time.

"Come live in Gath, David. Be my guest. I actually miss you, crazy or not."

"No, my king. We are many, and women and children as well. Assign us a place near your borders. We can protect your people and not be a burden to you."

Achish's eyes take on a look of feral intelligence.

"I have," he says, "just the thing."

* * *

Achish forces out the fifty-eight men and their families living in Ziklag, further toward the coast, and gives the village to David and his men and their families.

They establish themselves quickly. Soon their lives attain the rhythms of the ordinary. They grow crops. The land is surprisingly giving, with thin but rich loam that produces plump sweet cucumbers, stalky leeks whose heads when cut release an eye-stinging pungency, thick-tasseled barley that grinds down to silky flour. Groves of fig and olive and pomegranate trees flourish. They build their own smithy and hammer out tools and weapons. They build a shed for shearing and cleaning and carding wool, and many households have their own spinners and looms. They build a tannery, a butchery, an oil press, a winepress.

They build a place where the men train the boys' hands for war. They teach them the art of swordplay and javelin throwing and slinging. They show them how to use a shield as both defense and weapon. They show them all the soft places on a body that open to vital places, the body's hatches to its hidden life and sudden death.

The priest Abiathar grows fat, like his father, like his grandfather, like his great-grandfather. He marries a stick of a girl who is surprisingly fertile: she always, it seems, bulges with another child on the way, with one swaddled and bundled on her back, while her growing brood flits among her skirts. When any of his boys turns three, Abiathar begins to train him in priest craft. He joins his brothers in memorizing the law. In learning how to mix sacred oils and incenses. In learning about—though not yet touching—the Urim and Thummim.

David asks Abiathar also to train another man for priestly duty. Zadok. A skillful warrior who lacks the appetite for killing.

"Zadock," David says to Abiathar, "would make a good priest."

"My lord?"

"He is better suited to priest craft than to warfare."

"I have my sons. And Zadok—he is not from a priestly line."

"There is a rumor he descends from Aaron himself."

"My lord, it is mere rumor. There is no…"

"Abiathar, I am not asking your permission."

"Yes, my lord."

For the most part, the men and their families are happy. But there is always a group, shifting in its composition and allegiances, who tries to stir dissent. They murmur. They complain. The worst of them David presents with an ultimatum: change, or leave. Most choose to change, but some only mimic it. Beneath the skin their resentment remains, and grows.

David never knows where Joab stands. He never joins the grumblers. But he holds aloof. He keeps to himself. He scowls and curses sometimes, but mostly he is a stone with eyes. He watches everything.

But most of them are content. They work the land, build and repair their homes, draw water, hew wood, stitch garments. Their sons and daughters play together and fight each other, and some of the older ones fall in love. They cook meals and wash clothes and graze sheep. They make songs and sing songs. They reminisce about life before this, often remembering it as better than it was, but sometimes as worse.

"These are not leeks," one man says to another. "These are weeds. The leeks we used to grow in Hazor, now those were leeks. A one of them could feed a whole family for two days, even three, and you'd have to give the rest to the animals."

"Well, go back then."

But there is nowhere else to go.

* * *

Every five or seven days, David and his men gird up and march out. The women and children gather around as they leave. The children are excited, their faces flushed. The women are anxious, their faces pale. A newly married couple holds hands and looks at each other for a long time, and they part wordless.

David leads them into sprawling desert south of Ziklag. They raid small villages, populated with Geshurites, Girzites, Amalekites. It is a grim business. They leave none alive, no one to tell the story. They leave only blood and ashes.

Sometimes on the evening of the day they've left, but more often a day or two later, they straggle back to Ziklag carrying plunder. They arrive, not exultant, but weary, solemn, silent. Their clothing and skin are dark with blood and grime. Always, a few don't return, and in the night a keening goes up from those households.

Two men, usually Joab and Uriah, stay behind to burn the village and its fields. They are good at it, at burning. They know just where to set the torch, up in the roof thatch, down low in the grain. They find the place where wind caresses the flame. Once a fire catches in a roof, the roofs and fire collapse into the room and consume everything. Once it catches in a field, it climbs the stalks, leaps from tassel to tassel, runs until it runs out.

Everything burns until everything's gone.

Uriah often stands so close to the fire that the skin on his face is turning red. Joab usually finds a high place and watches, to make sure they destroy it all.

David usually does not return to Ziklag right away. He takes a few men, usually Abishai and Baanah among them, and more and more Joab and Uriah, though they are loathe to trust the burning to others, and they ride to Gath, to report to Achish.

* * *

The king's servants greet David and his men with crisp efficiency. These meetings have become routine. The once lavish rites of hospitality have been shorn down to a few abbreviated gestures: a kiss, a dab of oil on the forehead, a cool sweet drink. A servant is dispatched while the other servants stand watchful, as still as men sleeping upright. David knows otherwise. Their hands would fly to their weapons at the least rumor of peril, and even he and his men, instinctual and habitual killers that they now are, would have no easy time of it.

In a few moments, Achish enters. His robe, gilded and intricate, flows from his arms like the pinions of some fabled sky bird. His smile is a shock of whiteness. His eyes are a shock of blackness. His dark hair and beard are redolent and brilliant with oil.

"David!"

"My lord."

"You are well?"

"I am alive."

"And I see you have been… visiting our neighbors. You wear the garment of vengeance. Where did my servant go today?"

David knows not to hesitate, that the words must roll off his tongue unhitched.

"Against the Negev of Judah."

"Your own people!"

"Not my people. I have no inheritance among them."

Achish's brow tightens, darkens.

"It is a terrible thing, to have no inheritance."

"It is indeed, my lord."

"You know you have an inheritance here? Think of me as your god's gift to you."

"I do, my lord. I am in your debt."

"And I in yours."

* * *

David and his men leave Gath and set out for Ziklag. He lets them travel the last mile without him. He intends to linger in the wilderness before returning. Let the others go back to their wives, their children, their livestock. He has another need.

He goes through a knot of forest, down a slope of scrub brush, out unto a small grassy clearing. Here, a stream rushes fast and white around a tight bend, then pools calm and dark. It eddies in smooth rings before easing back out into the swift current. He stands on a rock ledge and leans over the still water. His sees his reflection. The image is sharp and exact.

His flesh is growing loose and creased. It's like leather that's been stretched too hard. He gets down on his knees and presses his face closer, closer. A lock of hair falls from his forehead and twitches the water's surface. His image shatters, then recomposes. He waits until the surface is like burnished metal, until it mirrors the pocks on his cheeks, the rivulets of sweat on his brow, the splinters of whisker on his chin, the cracked dryness of his lips. And his eyes. He wants to see his eyes.

They are flat. They are dark. They are empty.

He closes them.

The image of a young girl floods him. They had found her near the end of the raid. She was hiding beneath a threshing floor. She was maybe fourteen. One of the men dragged her out, stood her up. She looked straight at David. Not a look of fear or pleading. Contempt. Loathing. Defiance. She knew who he was, and she was rejecting him.

"This one would make a good wife," the soldier said. "Or a good lay."

"Kill her," David said. "No one left alive."

David falls into deep waters. His arms and legs spread wide. He sinks. He settles on the cold stony bottom. He feels rather than sees a cloud of sediment bloom. It is blackness all around him. He lies there until all breath is gone. Until he feels his life press against the thin wall of death.

When the Lord has fulfilled for my lord every good thing he promised concerning him and has appointed him ruler over Israel, my lord will not have on his conscience the staggering burden of needless bloodshed...

He drives upward toward the light. His head breaks the surface. He drinks air in huge gulps.

He walks home, his skin shining with newness. He sees Ahinoam in the haze of twilight, and then Abigail. It is Abigail, not Ahinoam, who holds Amnon: the child has knit his two wives together. The child has brought them peace.

Amnon jumps down from her arms and runs toward him. David hitches his tunic and runs toward his son. His arms are flung wide to the horizons. The kisses he will lavish on his boy already grow sweet in his mouth.

"My son, O my son," he says.

But when he closes his eyes that night, trying to find sleep, trying to find his own peace, he sees the girl in the village. He sees himself through her eyes.

He is indistinguishable from Saul.

* * *

King Achish gives David a sideways glance. It may be affection, or suspicion. David cannot quite tell. Achish's eyes slit down to glittering blades. They flash with wry intelligence. A tremor of mirth or disdain works the corners of his mouth but never breaks it into either smile or sneer. David feels that he is a riddle to Achish, a riddle the king puzzles over without ever solving, a maze the king tries to find a path through but gets lost in every time.

Achish, he thinks, must have many names for him. He imagines Achish arranging and re-arranging these names, trying to fit them all together, work them into a single pattern: Israel's Champion, Israel's Bane, Israel's King, Saul's Favorite, Saul's Nemesis, Madman, Giant-Killer, Philistia's Champion, Philistia's Bane, Achish's Favorite.

Traitor.

"We are fighting your people tomorrow," Achish says. It is almost a question.

"No," David says. "Not my people. They were my people. They are no longer my people. You are now my people."

"Philistia is not your enemy?"

"Israel is my enemy. Saul is my enemy. I fight for Philistia. Gladly. Proudly. I have become a stench in Israel's nostrils. I have no inheritance among them. I am one with you. I am one of you. My king, why do you doubt this? Have I not proven myself to you over and over?"

"You must understand," Achish says, and David sees his eyes sharpen again, "that there are rumors about you. About your men. About your raids on the Negev."

"Rumors?"

"That you have left Israel unmolested in your time among us. That it is other people you harm."

"My king, it is true that your enemies are my enemies, and we destroy those who would destroy you. Amalekites, for instance. Midianites. These are no friends of my king."

"Yes. I understand. I expect this of you. I am thankful for your faithful service. But the rumor isn't that you destroy Amalekites and suchlike. The rumor is that these other enemies are your *only* enemies. The rumor is that you leave Israel unmolested. After all, Amalekites and suchlike, neither are they the friends of Israel. Neither are they the friends of King Saul—or any king who might come after him."

"My king, why do you think Saul hates me more than ever?"

"Because of the other rumor. The one that you are the king who will come after him."

"That is how his hatred began, yes. But he hates me now because I have made myself a stench in Israel's nostrils. He hates me because I attack Israel. He hates me for being faithful to you, my king."

"You understand, David, that you and your men will accompany me in the army tomorrow when we fight Israel? When we fight Saul? That you will protect me and will fight for Philistia? That you will kill without mercy your fellow Israelites? That you will raise your hand against your god's army and his anointed king?"

David has prepared for months for this testing of his loyalty, this plumbing for his deepest allegiance. Tomorrow, all eyes will be on him. His years of fiery words, of seditious boasts, of murderous claims, must be rendered as unflinching action. Before all the rulers of Philistia, he must fall on the armies of the Lord. He must fall on Saul, king of Israel. He must raise his hand against the Lord's anointed. And Jonathan. He must break his covenant with Jonathan. He must slay without hesitancy, without mercy. His sword and spear must sink into the flesh of those who are flesh of his flesh, break the bones of those who are bone of his bone. He must battle men he once led in battle, men he ate and drank with, men he worshipped alongside.

He must cut a swath of destruction through all he has loved.

His answer to Achish is instant and forceful: "Then you will see for yourself what your servant can do."

Achish smiles. "Very well, I will make you my bodyguard for life."

Bodyguard for life. That was what Saul commissioned him to be. How long ago that seems, when Saul trusted him so completely, so unreservedly, that he appointed him captain of his bodyguard: to hold Saul's life in his hands, to be the barrier between the king and his enemies. To be willing, without qualm, to give his life for the sake of saving Saul's—to drink any poison, absorb any blow, devour any sword, catch in his own heart any spear so that his king could evade it. *My life for yours,* David often thought, and meant it, and relished it. Guarding Saul was his highest honor, above marrying the king's daughter, above befriending the king's son, above leading the king's armies. To protect the king himself surpassed all that. To be shelter for the Lord's anointed, a rock wall surrounding him. When Saul went into battle, David and the men under him made it their chief duty to hedge Saul about on all sides, running at carefully measured distances so that all angles of attack were cut off. Making their king unassailable. Being his shield and his defender. If an Amalekite or Jebusite or Philistine made least headway toward the king—looked with evil intent at him, raised a weapon against him, took a step in his direction—David and his men saw it, intercepted it, destroyed its source.

David almost failed once. He and his men ran in a wide V in front of Saul, to shield any spear or arrow aimed at him. Two of the men on the left flank were quickly taken out, and David, at the helm, gave the signal to compensate for the losses, to reconfigure in a pattern the men had learned over and over until they knew it by instinct: tighten the V, close it around Saul like a sheath, and then David moves in close, a mere foot from Saul's side. But as David drew in, Saul did a strange thing: he thrust his spear into David's legs. David faltered and fell back. The man behind David was stalled by David's staggering, and the man in front had not seen what had happened.

Saul was suddenly widely exposed. Some keen-eyed Philistine archer, seeing his advantage, sent an arrow flying straight at him. It whistled above the fray and hit the king broadside, glancing his back. David had by then regained his balance. He veered sharply and drove toward the archer, who was concentrating on a second shot. David was on him just as the arrow released. It grazed Saul's neck.

Afterward, back in camp, David weighed whether to ask Saul about the spear. Did he mean to do that? But Saul was jovial, drinking wine—he rarely did this—full of congratulations and bravado, retelling the day's exploits, all the men laughing harder than was natural. David had learned not to spoil these moments, they came so seldom, they lasted so briefly.

And now this other king makes of David the same thing, his bodyguard for life.

"Yes," David says, bowing. "Thank you, my king. As I said, you will see for yourself what your servant can do."

Achish looks at him straight, but David is already looking down.

* * *

Saul's voice is strangled. When he speaks, it is like he is trying to pry hands loose from his own throat. He rarely eats. His skin is sallow and wilted. It droops from his bones. His hair is so threadbare his skull shines through. It falls from his head in long grey strands. The wind often catches these strands and banners them out. It makes him look like a bent shaft from which flies a tattered ensign, like the last remnant of a routed army.

Saul has been looking across ravines and valleys at Philistine armies all his life. He has seen this same scene a hundred times. More. The ranks of foot soldiers, solid and massed shoulder-to-shoulder, bristling with spears and rancor. The ranks of bowmen, spaced more loosely, taut as bowstrings themselves. The line of charioteers, smug in their knowledge of superiority. Behind all, the rulers of Philistia sitting astride horses, all of them, rulers and horses alike, decked out in bright regalia.

There were days when the sight of it made Saul laugh, huge with confidence. He put on his armor as if he was taking it off. There were other days it caused him some unnamed worry, as though the Philistines were his least concern but evoked for him his worst. His brow would darken. He'd stall with endless consulting. There were still other days it filled him with grim resolve, his eyes like eclipsed suns, black and burning at the edges. He'd issue orders in a clipped, blunt manner.

But today the sight of the Philistine army is like seeing the face of a ghost.

He cannot stop shaking. His arms flail. His eyes are wild. No one, none of his generals or advisers, can say anything or do anything to collect the king's shattered nerves. No one can coax a word of command from him.

"God must tell us what to do," Saul shouts, or tries to: the words garble from a constriction in his throat.

But God is silent. His court prophets have nothing. None dream any portents, hear any words. Even the Urim and Thummim turn up only darkness and blankness. Long ago Saul killed off Ahimelech and his family by the hand of Doeg. The rumor is that one got away, Abiathar, son of Ahimelech. And that now he is David's priest, giving light to David.

But all Saul is left with is darkness and blankness.

He summons Abner.

"Do you think he will be there?'

"Who, my lord?"

"*Him.* The Son of Jesse."

"Why would he, my lord?"

"Do not, Abner, mistake my present confusion for stupidity. I know he serves Achish."

"Yes, my lord. He does."

"Will he ride out against me this day? Will he ride against the armies of Israel?"

"It is possible, my lord."

Saul orders Abner away and calls several attendants close. He whispers.

"Find me a ghostwife."

"My lord?"

"Now! Find me a medium. I need some assurance, and all these fools are useless."

The attendants exchange furtive glances. Could this be a test? Saul, in one of his extravagant acts of public piety, purged the land of all such people. Or perhaps he was trying to win back the favor of Samuel before he died. Or perhaps it was from true conviction. But he issued a decree banning them all—mediums, spiritists, necromancers, witches, sorcerers, ghostwives. He attached the death penalty to anyone found practicing these dark arts, or anyone aiding in them.

It caused a frenzy of accusation. Neighbors avenged themselves on one another for old grievances and jealousies. Saul rounded each of the accused up, withered old men and women for the most part, but some who were at their prime of life—lithe and nubile virgins who inflamed men with lusts so raw they cried out in their sleep, shepherd boys whose prowess and charm seemed supernatural. He subjected each to a hasty trial and killed most, flaying them in public squares, gibbeting their naked bodies from walls and palisades. He knew that most were innocent, knew that the true occultists outwitted him, eluded him, shape shifted their way out of his grasp.

Does he really want a ghostwife?

He looks so woebegone, so tortured, so beggarly, that he must.

"There is one in En Dor," one servant says. Saul doesn't ask how the man knows this. Everyone seems to know things that to him are opaque.

Relief washes over him. His throat opens. His tongue unsticks.

"Very good," he says. "We will go to her. Tonight."

* * *

"He is the next king of Israel, once Saul is out of the way," Nasib says. Nasib is commander of the Philistine archers.

The other rulers of Philistia nod agreement.

"All the more reason for David to kill Saul," Achish says.

"All the more reason for David to win Saul back by killing us," Nasib says.

"Or letting us kill Saul," Mitinti, ruler of Ashkelon, says. "And then David—the new king—summons the armies of Israel and turns on us. You know the song well, Achish. It is sung to gall us: 'Saul has slain his thousands, but David his tens of thousands.' Tomorrow, David would love nothing more than to add to those numbers, at our expense."

The argument goes on at some length, and with no small amount of heat. But it is Achish against all the rest.

At last he calls for David.

"I am sorry, my friend. You have been as pleasing in my eyes as an angel of God. Blameless. Faultless. But the other rulers, and the army commanders, they do not approve of you.

"What have I done?"

"Nothing, my friend. You have only ever served me. I am sorry. But I cannot afford a division in my ranks. You must leave. Please be gone by morning."

* * *

As they near Ziklag, they see a scrawl of smoke above the hill where the village is. It is dark smoke, the kind grease makes. All the men run.

What they find destroys them. Their buildings burned. Their homes plundered. Their wives and children gone. It has all the marks of an Amalekite raid. That they took the women and children captive is more terrifying to the men than if they had killed them outright, and left their severed and bludgeoned bodies heaped upon the ground. The Amalekites have dark appetites. They will kill, the men know, most of the children, and all the older women, but only after they've slaked their lust with them. And what they will do with the younger ones is unthinkable.

They must have known which was David's house: they have added desecration to destruction, strewing pig entrails on the one patch of unburnt ground, defecating in great steaming mounds atop this.

The men weep until they cannot stand. Then they weep until they cannot weep. And then they groan.

And then, so quiet it could be the wind, a murmuring. And then a whispering. And then a grumbling.

And then Joash speaks aloud.

"You," he says to David. "You and your foul wars. Not a one of us would be here today if not for you, you and your greedy ambition. You're always having to prove yourself. Carrying on your battles for the Lord, or whoever. You're a fine right noble king, Lord David. King of nothing. King of dunghills. King of smoke. King of death."

And that starts it. Every man heaps insult on accusation, louder and louder, until they are no longer talking to him or even at him, or even to one another; they are screaming at the wind, cursing the heavens. Their voices are the wings of swarming locusts, the hooves of a thousand beasts stampeding.

"Let's kill him," someone says.

All roar.

Only the sons of Zeruiah, Joab and Abishai and Asahel, and Abiathar, the priest, and Uriah the Hittite, do not join in. Joab looks on with disgust. But against who, David doesn't know.

David walks away.

His feet are heavy as millstones. The curses of his men are like a beam of timber laid across his shoulders. He collapses to his knees. His sweat falls like blood.

"My God, my God, why have you abandoned me?"

Silence.

"I have carried these men now for ten years. More. What do you want from me? What are you asking of me? I cannot give it. I cannot do this another day. I cannot carry these debtors and scoffers one more step. And look…" David holds his hands out, palms upward. "There is so much blood on my hands."

And then he hears the Voice. It speaks one word. *Dance.*

"My God?"

And it is there again. *Dance.*

He rises to his feet. He strips off his clothes. He stands naked in the wind. And then David dances. He leaps. He flails. He twirls. He tumbles.

And all the weight falls off him.

* * *

Saul waits until night. He takes off his king's garments and dresses as a wayfarer, dusty and weary, bent with some old grief, fleeing some fresh trouble. He hides his face in the cave of his hood. Two of his officials travel with him, dressed similarly, and lead him unerringly to a small mud hut at the edge of the tiny village of En Dor. A wattle fence encloses a small yard where a goat and a hen mill about. They knock on the door. A thickset woman opens it a few inches, peers at them through the crack. Her face is a ruin of rumpled, mottled, whiskered flesh, blackened teeth, thornbush hair.

"I'm a poor woman. I am all alone. I have nothing to give you."

Saul pushes his way in the door with gruff impatience. "We don't care about that, woman. We will give you something. Much coin. But first consult a spirit for me. Bring up for me the one I name."

The woman recoils. "Surely you know what Saul has done. He has cut off the mediums and spiritists from the land. Why have you set a trap for my life to bring about my death?"

Saul pulls himself to his full height and swears to her, "As surely as *Yahweh* lives, you will not be punished for this. And I will pay you well."

"How much?"

"Very well."

Her voice turns silky. "Whom shall I bring up for you?"

"Bring up Samuel."

Saul has only seen him once since that day he tore Samuel's robe and Samuel tore the kingdom from him. After that, they each avoided the other. For years after, Saul wrestled with his thoughts toward Samuel, his anger at him, his longing for him, his terror of him. Wanting to kill him. Wanting to forgive him. Wanting to be forgiven by him, and blessed. Sometimes even now he dreams that they are reconciled. They sit and eat together, and Samuel discloses to him the hidden things of God.

He remembers the day, long ago, when he first met Samuel. He was looking for his father's asses and was hopelessly lost. The prophet met him, knew what he sought, and much more besides. Samuel seemed to love him. He splayed his huge hands on his head. He spoke in a voice terrible and beautiful. He told Saul things about himself that seemed impossible. Then he poured oil on Saul. It flowed onto his head like a well-fitted crown, light and warm. It oozed down the nape of his neck, gentler than the hand of his mother caressing him.

And then the Spirit came on him, one of the seemingly impossible things Samuel told him would happen. His whole body jolted with the force of it. The *ruach* picked him up and tossed him. He was like a dry leaf to a mighty wind, a small stick to surging wave. His heart swelled until he thought it would split. Strange words, wild and full of thunder, tumbled from his lips. He arose a changed man. He felt it in every sinew. Strength, and also joy, and above all courage, brimmed in him. His body seemed made of air but also weighty and solid as oak.

For the first years of his kingship he knew this feeling often, the Spirit pouring down on him, lifting him, cleansing him, emboldening him, pouring out from him vision and prophecy. Laying him flat in ecstasy, then standing him upright with courage.

But then Samuel, covered in King Agag's blood, spoke his terrible doom over Saul. *The Lord has torn the kingdom of Israel and has given it to a neighbor of yours, who is better than you.*

And right then the Spirit left him. In its place another spirit came, a *dybbuk*, hideous and devious, full of cunning and treachery, twisting into him, rioting through him. Or it moved through him like a black river, roiling and bottomless, and he a dead weight falling into it.

But he experienced the other Spirit one last time. It was also the last time he ever saw Samuel alive, the day he sent his servants to capture David, one delegation, then another, then another. Finally he himself had to go. He went burning with anger. David had dared to go whining to the prophet in Naioth of Ramah, to seek Samuel's sympathy and stir up his antipathy, to turn him against Saul more than he was already turned. David had gone to the very man who anointed him, Saul, as king, and who, on some prophetic whim, deposed him. The insult of it was beyond bearing.

Saul meant to kill them both.

But the Spirit fell on him one last time. A power beyond him pulled him until he stood right in front of Samuel. David was there beside him. Neither man looked surprised or afraid. In a spasm of ecstasy, Saul tore off his king's robes. As the weight of them fell from him, the weight of the Spirit pressed down, heavy as a hundred robes, heavy as a thousand. He knelt, and then fell back. His limbs jittered. His body gyrated. An intricate melody of words gushed from him. He was unable to move. He saw David's and Samuel's backs recede until they were only flecks against the melting air of desert heat.

The Spirit had undone him.

Samuel died last month. An old man whose fierce dark eyes, Saul's spies tell him, turned soft and grey in his last years. Perhaps it was with sadness. Samuel's sons, like the sons of Eli before him, were sore disappointments.

Saul went to Samuel's burial. The prophet in death appeared almost mirthful, a hint of a smile pressed into the stony gauntness of his flesh. His chest was still massive, but the rest of him was whittled thin. Saul stood for a long time before Samuel's corpse, aware that all eyes of Israel were on him, and all of them wondering what had estranged each from the other. He searched himself for a feeling, any feeling—vindication, hatred, bitterness, sadness, anything. He found nothing. And then, as he reached out to place the myrtle branch on Samuel's chest and then turned to walk away, one feeling, just the thinnest edge of it, caught him: envy. He wanted what Samuel now had, the endless solitude of death, the everlasting dreamless sleep.

"Bring up Samuel from *Sheol*."

The woman eyes him, tries to look beneath his hood to see him clearly. Saul pulls further into his shadows.

"Bring him. Now."

She goes to work, with potions and spells and chants. She mutters in a language Saul has never heard, a thick jumble of gutturals and sibilants, like she's choking and hissing all at once. She looses a noise like the clatter of stones in a pail, and then another like the susurrus of wind in dead leaves. She belches. Her voice rises and falls, whispers and hollers, one moment throaty and the next nasally, deep as a dying man then high as a keening widow. Her body sways and jerks and heaves. Her eyes roll up into her head, and her sockets glow with veiny whiteness. She moves in and out of trances. Just when even Saul is thinking it is all foolish connivery, the woman shrieks in her own voice. She is in cold terror.

She leaps in one motion toward Saul, her face bearing down on his. "Why have you deceived me? You are Saul!"

Saul doesn't flinch. He pulls his hood off. His eyes open with hungry astonishment. "Don't be afraid. Tell me what you see."

"I see a spirit coming up out of the ground."

"A *dybbuk*?"

"No, a *ruach*."

"What does he look like?"

"An old man heavily robed." She says this with a tone of slyness.

Saul stands and then kneels, and then splays his large angular body across the tiny space of dirt floor of the witch's hut. His face presses against the packed coolness of the earth. His nostrils fill with smells of footfall and soot and something acrid that burns his eyes.

"Why have you disturbed me by bringing me up?" The voice is so like Samuel's, ominous as a war drum, that Saul raises his head to make sure it's still the woman speaking, channeling Samuel, and not the prophet himself in all his glowering smoldering wrath. Seeing it is only her, Saul lowers his face back to the ground. When Saul speaks, his voice is thin. It is almost as if he is speaking to himself.

"I am in great distress. The Philistines are fighting against me, and God has turned away from me. He no longer answers me, either by prophets or by dreams. So I have called on you to tell me what to do."

The voice rushes back at him, wild and fierce, so tangible and immediate that Saul stands up to make sure again that Samuel himself is not in the room, come to hand-deliver the message. But it's only the old woman, except now towering and huge, her eyes catching fire and hurling it around the room, her body whirling and thrashing so that the voice emerges from her in whooping gusts. Her head and her hair whip the air. In Samuel's voice, she speaks, "Why do you consult me, now that the Lord has turned against away from you and become your enemy? The Lord has done what he predicted through me. The Lord has torn the kingdom out of your hands and given it to one of your neighbors—to David."

Samuel, or the woman, has more to say. Death and destruction, a mere day away, await Saul, his sons, his army, all Israel. But at the sound of David's name, Saul plummets, not even laying his arms in front of himself to break his fall. His body hits the ground with blunt force. A cloud of dust and soot spume around him.

The woman, as quickly as she'd loomed up, shrivels. She looks half her former size. She insists on feeding Saul and his men. She rushes around, fusses about, makes the meal, all the while muttering. "I only did what I was asked to do, only did what the king wanted. I'm bound by the king in all he says. If he bans witches or consults witches, it's all the same to me. The king is like an angel. What the king wants is what God wants."

It's wasted breath. Saul sits and stares as though he's now the one in a trance. When one of his officials speaks, he doesn't answer, doesn't appear to hear. The men, but not Saul, eat, and then they all leave wordlessly.

Without paying.

* * *

"I know what we must do," David says.

All the men look up.

"You dare come back?" Joash says. "I will kill you."

"Shut up," Joab says. "Or I will kill you."

"I know what we must do," David says again. "God has shown me. I have talked with Abiathar. He has consulted the ephod. He has confirmed what God has shown me."

The men wait.

"They are not far, the Amalekites. At most a day's journey. We will pursue them and overtake them. We will take back what is ours. We will take our vengeance."

A look, almost a fume, of poisonous contempt passes between the men.

Bikri steps forward. "Why didn't your god and your little pasty-faced priest tell us about the raid on our village? That flabby priest might have suited up with his pretty little chest plate and muttered his strange speech several days gone now, and kept us out of this trouble to begin with. Why not?" Most of the men murmur aggrieved assent.

Joab pulls his knife and steps toward Bikri. David halts him with a gesture.

"You ask me why," David says. "I don't know why. God's *ruach* is as much a mystery to me as to any man. All I know is I am usually desperate before I hear it. I am usually desperate before I seek it, want it, trust it. I wish it were otherwise. I wish the *ruach* was my greatest thirst. But it is often my least. I long for it only after I have gone to many other fountains first and come away empty.

"My men, like you I have wept myself dry. Like you, I have lost all. I have fallen to the bottom of myself. But there the *ruach* waits. This is what I know."

"I am with you," Joab says.

And with that, six hundred men are as one man again. They set out immediately. By late afternoon they reach the treacherous and precipitous Besor Ravine. Some of the men complain that are too exhausted to continue.

"My lord, we have been on our feet for days. We cannot navigate those trails in our condition. We will stumble. We will fall to our death. We must rest."

"Stay here then. Who is still with me?"

Four hundred men.

On the far side of the ravine, the land slopes and levels.

Abishai points to an object in the distance. It seems to move in circles. As they come near, they see it is a man, haggard, bewildered. Dried saliva crusts the corners of his mouth.

One of the men gives him water. He drinks it with greed. They give him food. He devours it.

He belches.

"Who are you?" David says. "Where are you from?"

"I am an Egyptian. I am the slave of an Amalekite. My master abandoned me when I became ill three days ago. We raided the Negev of the Kerethites, some territory belonging to Judah and the Negev of Caleb. And we burned Ziklag."

Abishai turns to David. "I thought you said the raiders were no more than a day's journey?"

"Closer than that," the Egyptian says. "They're not more than three or four miles from here. Drunk. Taking their pleasure."

"Can you lead us down to them?"

"You are the one they call David?" the Egyptian asks.

"I am."

"You are the one they say will be king of Israel."

"I... am."

"Swear to me before God that you will not kill me or hand me over to my master, and I will take you down to them."

"I swear. Before God."

The Egyptian leads them down a long slope, over a hill, down another slope, over another hill, and there, sprawled in the valley, drinking and eating, a thousand men debauch themselves. David feels the heat of violence rise in him and in his men.

"Steady," Joab says.

Joab arranges the four hundred men into four parties, a hundred each, and positions them strategically: one party will drive the Amalekites into the arms—into the swords—of the other three.

It begins at dusk. It is fierce. The Amalekites are many, and even in their drunkenness—or maybe because of it—fight like *dybbuks*. When evening comes the next day, though, six hundred Amalekites lie, scattered or heaped, dead, and four hundred flee on camels.

Ahinoam and Abigail, and his son Amnon, run to him. Abigail holds their newborn son, Keliab. David folds Amnon under one arm, lifts Keliab in the other. The warmth of his children against him, the way their bodies relax into his, the way they trust his love for them, gives him joy and fear in equal measure.

"Are you… unharmed?" he asks the women.

"We are fine. They were sparing us for their chieftain's pleasure. Some of the others are… they have suffered."

David looks down at a dead Amalekite. He stands on his neck.

The men take everything back with them—all that belongs to them, all they had lost, and all the rest of the plunder. It is great abundance. As they climb back up the Besor Ravine, the two hundred men who stayed behind cheer.

"David has slain his ten thousand," they begin to sing.

David laughs.

Then Bikri speaks, apparently for many. "These men abandoned us. They left us to do the bloody work. The dangerous work. They have no share in this plunder. They can take what belongs to them and leave."

Joab again pulls his knife. David walks over to Bikri. He looks around, at everyone. Then he looks hard into Bikri's eyes, his face inches away. David is shorter, slighter, but Bikri visibly wilts.

"No, my brother," David says, quiet. Every man, all six hundred, holds his breath to try to hear him. "You must not do that with what the Lord has given us. He, not I, not anyone here, has protected us and delivered into our hands those who came against us. Who listens to what you have to say? The share of the man who stayed with the supplies is to be the same as that of him who went down to the battle. All will share alike. This is how we will live from now on. This is how it will be in my kingdom. All will share alike."

"My lord," Bikri says. He steps back, head bowed. "I apologize. Forgive me. I was wrong. I will never challenge your authority again."

"Shalom, my brother," David says.

* * *

That night in Ziklag, even among their burnt homes, they feast and dance and rejoice.

In the morning, David sends all his plunder to the elders in Judea, all the places where he and his men had roamed in their early days. To all the places they had taken provisions from, where the farmers lived who had given them stock and, as important, held their silence.

"What are you doing?" Ahinoam asks him. "We need that plunder. We need to rebuild our home. We need to rebuild Ziklag."

"No," David says. "I don't think we do."

972 BC
Man of Sorrows
DAVID

I have heard men sing of the desert rapturously, as though lavishing blandishments on a lover. I have heard men curse it bitterly, as they might a *belial*. For me, the desert was taskmaster and teacher, in equal measure. It was brutal cruel, and bountiful wise. It wasted me. It tested me. It made me. I went into the desert one thing. I came out another.

You must remember, my brother, that time you found me in the desert, in the caves of Adullam, hidden in the radiant haze of the waste places. Even then, early in my flight, hunger had whittled me thin. Even then, danger, everywhere, had taught me to hold still as stone, stay sharp as thorn. I was watchful that way hawks are, wary the way conies are.

This was the quality King Achish saw in me, I think, liked in me, used in me. My usefulness to him was my wiliness. My treachery, my capacity to be more than one thing. The desert taught me that. And, strangely, the desert taught me also how to be only one thing. First it added shadows to me. Then it burned them all away.

That time you found me in Adullam, I wanted to tell you about the first time I went to Gath, to Achish. But we had such little time then, you and I, and everything was urgent. I regret now not telling you. It would have made you laugh, even then. I could have used that, your laughter. I could use it now.

When I went to Achish, fresh from Nob, fresh from your father's court,

I dragged there with me the sword of Goliath. If you asked me now what I was thinking, I would fall silent at the folly of it. Yet at the time it seemed destined. As though the sword dragged me, a stray mule I was harnessed to that was set on finding its way back to its master.

But soon enough I realized my peril. I looked for a way of escape. Then I saw it, clear as a dove descending. Maybe this was the way our forefathers saw angels, bright and huge, stepping from nowhere into daylight. I saw, clearly, that I was to play the *meshuga*. To dance wild. To slaver, and gibber, and scrabble, and grunt, to fling myself this way and that. Powerful warriors leapt from me as though fleeing a lunging cobra.

Only years later did I find why my behavior brought such deep and immediate change over Achish. His wife and his daughter both suffered the madness. They descended to their own realm of shades, and there roamed and howled. Achish beheld madness daily, intimately. My playing at it sprung on him a trap whose noose already gripped him tight, and not riches or armies or spells could loose it, day or night. He was a man of sorrows, familiar with suffering.

Jonathan, perhaps my antics would not have made you laugh. Maybe they would have made you weep. I thought for years that I was the only one who suffered at the hands of your father's madness. I know now that you beheld it daily, intimately. I know now that you too were a man of sorrows. That your suffering was its own desert. Its own exile.

Much later, I returned to Achish. Your father, your father's madness, drove me into his arms. Without a word, he trusted me. He knew I knew.

We shared in the fellowship of his suffering.

At the end, your father's madness, his suffering, drove him to a ghostwife. Did you know? I heard about it long after, from one of Saul's servants who became one of mine. Your father was ghostly pale himself, and gaunt as bones, his voice like winter wind on dead leaves. *Yahweh* would speak to him no longer, not through priest, nor oracle, nor the heavens, nor any earthly thing. The silence was living death. So he sought a witch in En-dor—my servant says she was piteous as a wounded bird—to conjure the old *se'er* Samuel from his dusty grave. Whether trick or no, she did it. Your father believed it, anyhow, speaking to the shadows the way any man speaks to another, though sheer cold terror had come over him. He departed more bereft than he came.

I am not sure why I am telling you this. Only, it is a grief beyond measure, the silence of God.

972 BC
Waiting
MICHAL

Darkness was my only companion.

But still I waited. I know I told you otherwise, that I had stopped waiting. But you cannot understand the hold he has on people. Or perhaps you can. Isn't that why you're here?

Despite myself, I waited. Everything in me was taken captive by him. Anger, sorrow, self-pity—all fueled it equally. The slightest thing—a scent, a snatch of song, a voice at a certain timbre, the rhythm of someone's footfall in the outer court, the movement of a shadow across the gap beneath my door—anything pulled me sudden and sharp to a place I resolved many times not to go. I would be having a good day of forgetting, and then some memory would fling me headlong into a wilderness of loneliness, and everything in me was plundered all over again.

David, he was good at plundering.

Perhaps since our mother Eve, women have loved men to their own ruin. Our desire is for them, but they rule over us.

I forgot to tell you, my brother Jonathan saw him once in the desert. This was early on in David's exile, when he was still in the Judean wilderness. Jonathan found him in that wasteland—he was always good at finding David. They spent an entire evening together. He told me in confidence not long after it happened.

"How is he? How does he look? What did you talk about?"

"He is tired, Michal. He is thin. But he will be fine. He asks about our father. He asks about Israel's troops. He speaks mostly about God. He prays like a child and a sage and a lunatic all at once. It astounds me. God almost seems to stand in the room when he prays. He will be fine."

"But what did he say?"

"I think I told you, Michal."

I did not ask if he asked of me. He did not, that was clear enough, but I feared knowing it for certain. And what would it mean, if he hadn't? I like to think that we hold in silence the thoughts we hold closest.

But this is utter nonsense. He never spoke of me because he never thought of me.

I resolved never to speak of him again. It was all I could do to spite him. But it didn't help. He was always crowding me. If I spoke of textile, I pictured what he wore. If I spoke of war, I pictured him in battle. If I spoke of weather, I saw him soaked in rain or radiant in daybreak. He was like a broken tip of knife blade closed in my flesh, aching with every shift in weather.

My father gave me to another man, Paltiel. A good man. But he was no David. For which I thanked God and cursed him. I pitied my good husband, my dear stupid Paltiel: to have a wife he loved who waited for another, and then, done with waiting, replaced it with something that love could never grow in.

Darkness was my only companion.

1011 BC

Lament

After their evening of revelry in Ziklag, deep silence falls. They clean the mess of the Amalekite raid with funereal slowness. They speak only in whispers and nods.

Everyone knows what it means that Achish sent David away. They know that if Philistia triumphs against Israel in the battle that rages on Mount Gilboa, the other rulers of Philistia and the commanders of their armies will come for David and his men. And if Israel triumphs, the Philistines will take out their vengeance on David and his men. And if that doesn't happen, Saul will be emboldened to cross the border and come for David, and all who follow him.

So it is a death watch.

On the evening of the third day, a man approaches the village. He comes slow to the top of the hill. He stops, he wavers. And then he runs toward them in a lopsided gait. A wound in his leg bends him forward at the waist, and to compensate he flails and jerks his right arm, wings and bobs his head. He looks like a chicken trying to outrun a fox. Some of the men laugh, some make cruel remarks. They compare him to the effigies on the walls of Jebus, compare him to Saul in one of his fits of torment.

David raises a hand to silence them.

The man arrives panting like a dog and throws himself at David's feet. The whole village presses near to watch, to listen.

"Where have you come from?" David asks.

"I have escaped from the Israelite camp."

"What happened?"

"The men fled from the battle. Many of them fell and died. And Saul and his son Jonathan are dead."

David turns cold.

"Stand up, man," he says to the messenger.

The man stands quickly, nimbly. There is a jauntiness now in his movements.

"How do you know that Saul and his son Jonathan are dead?"

"I happened to be on Mount Gilboa, and there was Saul, leaning on his spear, with the chariots and their drivers in hot pursuit. When he turned around and saw me, he called out to me, and I said, 'What can I do?' He asked me, 'Who are you?' 'An Amalekite,' I answered. Then he said to me, 'Stand here by me and kill me! I'm in the throes of death, but I'm still alive.' So I stood beside him and I killed him, because I knew that after he had fallen he could not survive. And I took the crown that was on his head and the band on his arm and have brought them here to my lord."

David looks down at these. Unmistakably Saul's. David grabs his own shirt, and in one wrenching motion, tears it hem to collar. He throws his head back and looses a wail. All his men, stunned for a moment, do likewise.

David remembers the last time he saw Saul. The Lord's anointed looked small and old, standing at the foot of a mountain, squinting up into the sunlight. *Come back, David my son,* he called out, plaintive, his voice strained with grief. He must have believed himself what he said. Everything in David yearned to go back. To be the son. But he wrestled down the yearning, pummeled it with cynicism, throttled it with all the ruthlessness the desert had taught him.

"Here is the king's spear," David said, holding it aloft.

Saul's gasp was like a crack opening in the earth. David knew he was bereft without his spear.

But now here is the king's crown, plucked from his greying dying head. His spear had not saved him.

David now thinks of the last time he saw Jonathan. His face was drawn and sad. He spoke of the future, of their future together. But the way he spoke, the way he looked, he must have known that David's future did not include him.

The Amalekite looks bored, amused, impatient.

"You are an Amalekite?" David says.

"As I said."

"Why were you not afraid to lift your hand to destroy the Lord's anointed?"

The man's hint of a smile, almost a smirk, disappears.

"My Lord, that man was a clear goner. There was no getting out of his situation in a single piece. And you know yourself what kinda people them Philistines is, what they do to the likes of a king like your Saul. I was only doing what mercy called for. What the king his very self insisted on. Who am I to defy a king? The king?"

David calls Uriah.

"Your blood be on your own head. Your own mouth testified against you when you said, 'I killed the Lord's anointed.' Uriah, strike him down!"

The Amalekite's eyes flash with hatred. He reaches for his own sword. But Uriah lays him out with a single blow, hews him open sternum to belly.

Two men drag this body away, leaving a shallow gouge in the dust. The lamenting for Saul and Jonathan starts with fresh force. David calls for Ahinoam to bring his harp. In a soft tentative voice, he sings:

A gazelle lies slain on your heights, Israel.
     How the mighty have fallen!
Tell it not in Gath,
     proclaim it not in the streets of Ashkelon,
lest the daughters of the Philistines be glad,
     lest the daughters of the uncircumcised rejoice.
Mountains of Gilboa,
     may you have neither dew nor rain,
     may no showers fall on your terraced fields.
For there the shield of the mighty was despised,
     the shield of Saul—no longer rubbed with oil.
From the blood of the slain,
     from the flesh of the mighty,
the bow of Jonathan did not turn back,
     the sword of Saul did not return unsatisfied.
Saul and Jonathan—
     in life they were loved and admired,
     and in death they were not parted.
They were swifter than eagles,
     they were stronger than lions.

Daughters of Israel,
    weep for Saul,
who clothed you in scarlet and finery,
    who adorned your garments with ornaments of gold.
How the mighty have fallen in battle!
    Jonathan lies slain on your heights.
I grieve for you, Jonathan my brother;
    you were very dear to me.
Your love for me was wonderful,
    more wonderful than that of women.
How the mighty have fallen!
    The weapons of war have perished!

* * *

Later, David approaches Joab.

"Joab."

"David."

"The men call me *my lord*."

Joab meets this blank-faced.

"I will be king soon."

"Well, congratulations. Good for you."

"And perhaps good for you. You have served a king before. And well. The Lord's anointed. You know the cost of that, the weight of that. The honor of that. You know what is required of you."

"I do."

"I am going to make you my general. You will be commander over my armies. And you will be my chief bodyguard."

"My lord," Joab says.

For the first time ever, he bows.

972 BC
My King
MICHAL

The news reached me in a dream before any messenger confirmed it: my father was dead, cut down at Gilboa. And also my beautiful brother Jonathan. I saw my father fall, more vivid than if I stood there watching. He rose to his old greatness, his imperious height his best weapon and worst weakness. His voice was stern and regal. His eyes were fire. He hewed Philistines with ruthless economy, never using two thrusts if one would do, never wasting a stroke. He was implacable. And then one, and then two, and then a volley of Philistine arrows flew into him. Even then, he staggered on, taking down many before he himself, seeing the inevitable, fell on his own sword.

Those barbarians took his body, and Jonathan's, and did grisly things to them, and hung them on the wall of Gath, until the men of Jabesh-Gilead, whom my father had rescued many years before, defied all danger and travelled far and took their bodies down, and kept their bones like sacred relics, wrapped tenderly in soft cloth, hidden in a cool dry place.

In my mind, I slipped into the cool tomb and tended their broken bodies. I anointed my father, my brother, with oils and spices. I gazed on their faces in the stillness of death. They held a majesty still. They radiated beauty. I traced their faces with my fingers. I lifted their hands into mine and pressed the backs of their hands to my cheek. I spoke soft words of devotion.

Death is magic. It changes everything. My father's madness now was nothing. His kingliness, everything. He had gone into the great shades but had stepped out free of shadow, shook it off like loose dirt, and stood before me all light, all wisdom, all beauty. Flawless. Often, sleeping or waking, I saw him now, beckoning me with arms spread wide, his smile hiding nothing, revealing everything.

I knew it was not so. I am no fool. But it comforted me. It still does. My father was always my king. He would always only ever be my king, death or life, world without end.

David, never.

972 BC

My King
JOAB

Just like that, no fancy nothing, it was done. All those bloody years of scrounging and plundering and extorting, toadying up to this pagan king, shaking down that Judean farmer. All done. Not that I mind that kind of work. I get bored with too much lolling about, dancing, singing, feasting, listening to priests drone on, all that. But we were all getting on in age. We were a bit long in the tooth for that kind of hard living. David, he was thirty already, no boy anymore. A couple wives, a couple kids. Not a great father, if you ask me, not that I'm no expert. But he pampered those boys something terrible, and yet never had much time for them. That was some trouble brewing, see?

It was my job to get things ready, political-wise, for his crowning. There were a lot of smoothing over to do. David had enemies everywhere, not least among Judah's elders. He tried to soften them up with plunder, and that worked pretty good. It was harder to get all those farmers, the ones whose sheep and olives and such kept us half-alive, to go along with the plan. David had, what's the way people say it? Ruffled feathers. He'd ruffled a lot of feathers. It was my job to unruffle them. I was damn good at it, if no one else tells you so. And old dead Saul didn't hurt things. No one in Judah was especially fond of him. So it didn't take a lot of coaxing, to get the elders to get the farmers to swing behind David. The whole prize wasn't much anyhow, being king of Judah. A lot of desert in Judah. A lot of dust and stone. A lot of nothing.

It was funny, watching my uncle. He was still young enough that the earth had no great pull on him. He could still run like a fox, fight like a badger, sneak like a cat. He could still leap over a wall. I would see him from a distance, or coming around a corner, and think he was just a boy. But less and less would anyone make that mistake when he was near. Before, it was like there was something soft inside him that he was trying his best to make hard. Now, it was like there was something hard inside him that he was trying his best to make soft. Sometimes he put me in mind of old Saul, David did, the way he seemed to always be wrestling with himself.

It was hard calling him my king. Calling my uncle, my short uncle, sixteen years my junior, my king. Not that he hadn't showed himself. He was starting to impress me, and that takes some doing. But maybe I was a bit like Eliab. I found it no easy thing to see that skinny kid, that kid no one paid any mind to when he was tending sheep way back when, to see that kid rise to this.

Well, I said to myself, could be worse. Could have been we lost.

972 BC
My King
ABIATHAR

My king. My king and my lord. That was my happiest day on earth, saying those words, pouring as I said them, the oil of anointing on his head. The oil glowed like honey and then soaked in, darkening his already dark hair. To me, it was crown enough. It bespoke God's choosing. The crown later laid on him, that was just man saying yes to what God had already decided.

He smiled at me when I poured the oil and spoke those words. It was exactly the smile he smiled that night we first met, more than a dozen years before, when he held me and let me weep myself empty in his arms. He was then no more than I was, a mere boy, afraid, full of heartache. But in my eyes, he was already this, already the king. My king. Even then I would have followed him anywhere.

He sang that day. None of us had heard him sing for many years. It stopped sometime in Ziklag. But he took his harp, and stood, and his voice cracked a little, and then grew sweet and clear. All the people opened to it as if to rain after long dryness:

The righteous cry out, and the Lord hears them;
    he delivers them from all their troubles.
The Lord is close to the brokenhearted
    and saves those who are crushed in spirit.

Lord, the Lord Almighty,
    may those who hope in you
    not be disgraced because of me;
God of Israel,
    may those who seek you
    not be put to shame because of me.

And then, without bidding, all the people rose and shouted one thing altogether: *My king.*

972 BC
My King
DAVID

Some say I never grieved your father. Some say I never grieved you. They say I was pretending sorrow before others the way I pretended madness before Achish. It was, they say, part of my cunning, my trickery to win Israel's approval and to prove my innocence in the events that ended his life, your life, your family's dynasty. It was, they say, the way I hid the blood on my hands. It was how I disguised my joy that all my rivals had perished from the earth.

I am old enough to have seen such things, not least in myself. I have tasted, and I have practiced, the wiles of men bent on getting things, sometimes for no higher reason than to get them. If you are not careful, you can end up finding no pleasure in having a thing—a kingdom, a throne, a queen—but only in taking it. I have had my fill of all that. So I do not despise what others say, the stories they weave from the threads I've cast off.

But I will tell you, my brother, that my heart was rent in two that day, and ever since. For you. For your father. Some part of me died with both of you, though in different ways. I grieved for you, I still grieve, for what might have been. So many days I have wished for your companionship, sometimes simply for the joy of the thing itself, but often for the wisdom and courage you would have given me. I have heard God's voice before, pure and simple. It is a whisper at times, a thunder at others. It is a wind shaking the leaves. It is a wind shaking the lintel posts. It is comfort and sternness all together. But I have also heard God's voice through the voice of others: Samuel, Gad, Ahitophel, Nathan, Abigail. Even Shimei, only once, strange as that may sound. But many times, I heard God's voice through you. It was a *ruach* that gave me breath when all my breath was emptied. I miss it. I miss you.

And I did grieve for your father. I grieved for what might have been. But it was different. Will you think me proud, my dear Jonathan, if I tell you that many times I was the voice of God to your father? I would hardly dare to say that, except I saw it: I sang, and he rose. I sang and my breath became the breath of God, falling, filling, lifting. I remember the first time I beheld it, the miracle of it: your father folded up like one of those bodies that farmers sometimes dig up from the bog, like a sack of shriveled leather. I had him for a dead man. Then I sang. I was unsure of myself, trembling. Before that day, I had only ever sung for sheep. And for my mother. I tried once to sing for my father and brothers, but they mocked me. So I began afraid. But as I sang, I felt the *ruach* in me, so full it spilled out of me. And I watched your father rise, rise to life, rise to joy, rise to beauty, rise to the fullness of his greatness. Rise to the fullness of being the Lord's anointed.

In all that happened after, whenever I wanted to hate your father, the two times I had a free hand to kill him, I saw him as I saw him that day. I saw him rise.

I chose, I keep choosing, not to be a man after your father's own heart. But still I choose to love him. I saw him fall and fall. But still I see his greatness. I know his death cleared my path. I know his grave became the ground that raised me up.

But still.

Do you think me false, my dear Jonathan, that I should want nothing to do with your father, that I should want to be the opposite of him, and yet still I call him my king?

1011 BC
King of Judah

David moves his family to Hebron. He settles his men and their families in various places in Judah. He gives his brothers land around Hebron. He appoints his brother Ozem chief steward of his own holdings there.

He travels to Moab to bring back his parents and sister.

Jesse is ancient. The sight of him startles David. The man who once was a whirlwind of brusque motion now inches across the room, his feet rasping the stone floor. He holds onto the wall. Walking toward David, he misjudges a step and starts to fall. David catches him, grabs him by his frail ribs, lifts him. He expects his father to react in anger. He is a man who never wanted anyone's help and then resented when no one offered it. But Jesse leans forward and kisses him on the side of his mouth. His lips are dry as cracking gossamer. To David, they are like an angel's touch.

"Where is Mother?"

"Huh?" Jesse says.

His sister, Zeruiah, is standing there. She is nearly blind. But she still looks fierce, like she could rout a whole army of Philistines with just a broom handle.

"Zeruiah, where is our mother?"

It is King Mesha who speaks. "My friend, I am truly sorry. Nitzevet was beautiful. Like Ruth. So good. So gentle. We buried her in the Hebrew way, I promise you that."

"Thank you," David says, and weeps.

"And now, my friend," Mesha says, "now that you have seen what your god will do for you, now that you will come into your kingdom, please remember me."

* * *

Joab travels throughout Judah, building support for David's kingship. He also makes inquiries among the northern tribes, testing for their support.

Most of the elders from the north send him packing. "You think we don't know who killed Saul?" they say. "He even killed Jonathan. In cold blood. He kills his only friend. What kind of man does that?"

"David is innocent of these charges," Joab says.

"You are his blood. What else are you going to say?"

"You think Saul's only remaining son will serve you well as king? Ishvi is a weak man and a fool. He fears his own shadow. He has no mind of his own, and no courage to act if he did. He will be controlled by Abner. You crown him, you crown Abner."

"And now you come to insult us. And who are you to talk? Are not you to David what Abner is to Ishvi? Are you not the real leader?"

Joab laughs bitterly. "Clearly you do not know David."

* * *

David returns to Bethlehem. He goes there to reclaim his father's land and to hire men to restore it.

He loves to sit outside in the evening, under starlight, with his hirelings. Some nights he even beds down in the shepherd's hut outside the sheep pen. The night is full of noises, alive with earth music: the yipping of coyotes, the baying of wolves, the swooshing of bat wings, the persistent scratching of hyrax, the cawing of crows, the bleating of sheep, the shrieking of wind bearing down with sudden fury on dry branches. His bed is lumpy and itchy, just straw piled up and thrashed down in a corner, but he sleeps better here than anywhere. Air enters his lungs deeply. The sounds and smells and textures and rhythms of the shepherd's life soothe him like his mother's hand once did, the few times she stroked his brow or his hair. He grows light of heart. Sleep comes swift, runs deep.

But sometimes he keeps the men up late, far past the time they'd normally turn in. They talk, and laugh, and drink, and sing. The first time he did this, they were all stiff and tight-lipped, stammering when they did speak. But he belched out loud and laughed, and they laughed, and after that they relaxed around him.

"Is that large wolf pack still around?" he asks.

"Aye, the one with the big she-wolf leading it?"

"Right. She was cunning as a Philistine."

"Still is. We call her the Amalekite. Sneaky and heartless. That bitch has grown stiff and slow with age, but it's made her more devious. One of her whelps leads the attacks now. He's smaller than the rest but has her evil ways. And she's still there, at the edge of things, giving orders like old Saul." The man catches himself, looks afraid, glances slantwise at David, braces for a rebuke. But David doesn't seem to notice. The man carries on. "Yes, she's still in charge. When the pack takes down an animal, not a one takes a bite until she comes and sniffs it out. They all back off and give her space. Then she more times than not walks away without so much as a taste. The pack takes this as their signal and falls on the carcass with terrible speed and hunger."

"I could never trap or catch her," David says.

"Who can? She's a witch. She's a *dybbuk*. She's no ordinary wolf. We've killed a few of her whelps, but they're young and stupid. But she, she grows more treacherous with age. Her body slows, but it almost makes her mind quicker."

There is silence. Then David asks, "Which ram is breeding the best lambs? Is it that big one with the crooked horn?"

"Yes, to a degree. But he's ornery, bad tempered. And smug as a Moabite. Struts around like he should get some prize for screwing all day. The one we're preferring is that sleek one, light on his feet. He's unassuming, but if you watch him, he's got some wild potency in him that's not to be meddled with. The lambs the big one makes are bullies like him. But that small ram, he's breeding princes and princesses."

David misses this, this roughhewn talk, this earthy shrewdness, the vulgarity and honesty and camaraderie of it. It wakes something vital in him. It makes him feel young, free, unhindered. Alive. Naked before the wind.

* * *

One evening David asks, "Have you ever seen a miracle?"

"Come again?"

"You know, God act in some obvious way. Fire from heaven. Water parting. An angel speaking. Manna falling."

"My lord, I can't say I have," Eala said, "you?"

"Not me. I saw a woman once I reckoned for a miracle. She had a top story that I couldn't believe didn't make her fall over. But then she paid me no heed, so I figured it otherwise, a curse or a devil, sent to trouble my sleep."

They laugh.

"I haven't either," David says. "Just once I'd like to see one."

The other men are silent. David continues.

"I used to sit out here as a boy, talking to God. I'd ask him to show me a sign. I wasn't picky. It could be anything, anything of his choosing. An angel would have done, some huge creature, wild, holy, terrible, telling me what to do. Like in the old stories. But it didn't happen. But then I realized, it is happening. Always."

David stops.

Then whispers: "*I can hear him.* All around me. Inside me. He speaks. It is as clear as you speaking. He shows me things, things I can see as plain as I see a tree or a bend in the brook. I saw the giant falling, falling forward instead of backward like he should have, falling forward like he was shoved from behind. Falling like Dagon fell before the Ark. I saw the giant falling before I even saw the giant. No voice, just the picture in my head. But it summoned me as clearly as God summoned Samuel. It called me by name."

David stops again.

"You think I'm crazy. That I hear voices."

"No, my lord. It's why we trust you."

Then a voice, sweet but strong, speaks from the shadows. "My lord, if I may be bold to venture a word."

"Come forward," David says, "where I can see you."

A shepherd boy steps into the circle of firelight. He is ruddy, slight, dark-haired, dark-eyed, maybe fourteen. David has not noticed him before.

"I was born the day you felled that giant, my lord. My father and mother, my grandmother and grandfather, they said it was a sign. They told me the story of you and the giant since the day I was born, long before I understood it. And when I did, I played that story in my mind over and over, again and again. I lived it, in valleys and hillsides, pretending I was you. The man after God's heart, the man sent to save us all. My mother said that in former days, people had the Ark of the Lord for God to go with them wherever they went. But now, we have you."

David's throat is dry as a potsherd.

"My lord, the miracle I have seen is you. You are the man. You rise, my lord. You rise, and we rise with you. Where you go, we will go. Every last one of us."

David cannot speak for weeping.

* * *

On the day Judah makes David king, his father, Jesse, presents him with a gift. A crown. It is simple and beautiful, with thin woven bands of gold and an ivy of silver leaves rising into the point of the diadem. There are five smooth stones, ordinary stones though each distinct in color, embedded along its circumference.

"Father, you made this?"

"Yes."

"When?"

His father looks as if he is trying to rummage something up from a scrap heap. But then he speaks in a clear strong voice. "The day the *se'er* came. I began it then. I finished it much later. In Moab."

"You made this over these twelve long years?"

"Yes."

"Father…"

"David, my son. I have waited many days for today."

He lays the crown on David's head, wet with oil, and presses it down with surprising force.

The metal bites like thorns.

To Be Continued

Watch for

David: Reign

* * *

If you enjoyed this book
please consider leaving an honest review
where you purchased it.

* * *

Mark Buchanan leads writers retreats in various locations.
For more information, go to the WordCraft page
on www.markbuchanan.net
or email: mb@markbuchanan.net

Selective Bibliography

I used multiple secondary sources to help me understand and enter the life and times of David. The following titles, though not all represent my own view of David, are a selective list of such books:

Robert, Alter
The David Story: A Translation with Commentary on 1 and 2 Samuel
New York, NY: WW Norton, 2000
This in my view is the single best commentary on 1 & 2 Samuel.

Borgman, Paul
David, Saul & God: Rediscovering an Ancient Story
Oxford, US: Oxford University Press, 2008

Brueggemann, Walter
David and His Theologian: Literary, Social, and Theological Investigations of the Early Monarchy
Pittsburgh, PA: Wipf & Stock Pub, 2011

David's Truth: In Israel's Imagination & Memory
Philadelphia, PA: Fortress Press, 1985

First & Second Samuel: Interpretation: A Bible Commentary for Preaching & Teaching.
Louisville, KY: Westminster John Knox Press, 1990

The Message of the Psalms
Philadelphia, PA: Fortress Press, 1985

Edwards, Gene
A Tale of Three Kings
Nashville, TN: Tyndale Publishers, 1992

Gide, André
Bathsheba. A drama in 1 Act. 1912

Saul. A drama in 5 Acts. 1898

Ginzberg, Louis
"David," Legends of the Bible
Philadelphia, PA: The Jewish Publication of America, 1956

Gladwell, Malcolm
David and Goliath: Underdogs, Misfits & the Art of Battling Giants
Boston, MA: Little, Brown & Co., 2013

Goldingay, John
First & Second Samuel for Everyone
Louisville, KT: John Knox Press, 2011

Men Behaving Badly
STL Distribution, 2003

Heller, Joseph
God Knows: A Novel
New York, NY: Simon & Schuster, 1984

Kirsch, Jonathan
King David: The Real Life of the Man Who Ruled Israel
New York, NY: Ballantine Books, 2001

Laniak, Timothy S.
While Shepherds Watch Their Flocks: Recovering Biblical Leadership
Higher Life Publishing, 2009

L'Engle, Madeleine
Certain Women
San Francisco, CA: HarperOne, 1993

McKenzie, Stephen L
King David: A Biography
New York: Oxford University Press, 2000

Peterson, Eugene
Answering God: The Psalms as Tools for Prayer
San Francisco, CA: HarperOne, 1991.

Leap Over a Wall: Earthy Spirituality for Everyday Christians
San Francisco, CA: Harper, 1997
This in my view is the single best devotional reflection on David.

Pinsky, Robert
The Life of David
Schocken, 2005. Prague, 2005

Rosenberg, David
The Book of David: A New Story of the Spiritual Warrior & Leader Who Shaped Our Inner Consciousness
New York: Harmony Books, 1997

Wolpe, David
David: The Divided Heart (Jewish Lives)
New Haven, CT: Yale University Press, 2014
This in my view is the single best biography of David

Acknowledgements

Of all the books I've written, this is my least personal, and my most. My least, because it's about someone else's life and times, stretching back 3000 years from the world I inhabit, spanning 10,000 kilometers from the town I live in. But also my most, because it's involved a long dwelling and walking with this man, David. I feel as though I have sat with him in caves, run with him in deserts, grieved and raged with him in times of betrayal, rejoiced with him over God's steadfastness amidst life's twists and upheavals, wondered at him in his affections and disaffections. I have pondered much on his virtues, moreso on his flaws. And doing so, I have reflected much on my own life.

He has become a good companion.

But I needed many other good companions to bring this work to completion.

Thank you to those who read some version of this work, in whole or in part, and who offered insights and comments. All of you helped it find its final form, and yet none of you bear any blame for its remaining flaws. Thank you (in alphabetical order) Tina-Marie Axenty, Eric Benner, Joy Brewster, Jared Brock, Adam Buchanan, Sarah Buchanan, Randy Christie, Brian Doerksen, Lee Eclov, Jessica Gladwell, Gary Guardacosta, Rob Filgate, Scott Koop, Steve Macchia, Tim Pippus, Alex Sanderson, Ken Shigematsu, Beth Stovell, Ann Spangler, and Alison Straface. My apologies if I have forgotten anyone.

A special thanks to my wife, Cheryl, who slogged through every iteration of this manuscript, from the first sprawling 500-plus pages to this, what you now hold, and still stayed married to me. Indeed, she provided generous encouragement and showed unflagging support through it all.

Thank you to my cover designers at Gearbox, David Carlson and Chris Gilbert (who also did the cover for my book *God Speed*, released in the same year as this book). They were a delight to work with – efficient, excellent, and professional in every way.

Thank you to my editor Becky Philpott (and thank you to my non-fiction editor, Carolyn McCready, for introducing us). She provided keen-eyed editing throughout, both as my concept editor and then as my copyeditor. Her many wise suggestions have made this book stronger, and her many timely interventions have spared me much embarrassment.

Thank you to my internal book designer, Randy Christie, who is also my brother-in-law and good friend. He brought his many years of professional design expertise to bear on this book — maps, charts, doodads, curlicues, and such, and the overall layout. He has created something beautiful in its own right.

Thank you to the God who loved David, despite the man's many flaws. Thank you to the God who loves me this way. Thank you to the God who, simply and deeply, is love.

February, 2020
Cochrane, Alberta

Other Books by Mark Buchanan

Your God is Too Safe
Rediscovering the Wonder of a God You Can't Control

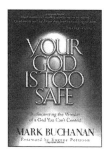

Here's a thoughtful, probing exploration of why Christians get stuck in the place of complacency, dryness, and tedium — and how to move on to new levels of spiritual passion. Buchanan shows how the majority of Christians begin their spiritual journey with excitement and enthusiasm — only to get bogged down in a "borderland" — an in-between space beyond the "old life" but short of the abundant, adventurous existence promised by Jesus. Citing Jonah, he examines the problem of "borderland living" — where doubt, disappointment, guilt, and wonderlessness keep people in a quagmire of mediocrity — then offers solutions... effective ways to get unstuck and move into a bold, unpredictable, exhilarating walk with Christ. Inspired writing.

Things Unseen
Living with Eternity in Your Heart

Blending pastoral warmth, philosophical depth, storytelling skill, and literary craft, Mark Buchanan encourages Christians to make heaven, literally, our "fixation"—filling our vision, gripping our heart, and anchoring our hope. Only then, says Buchanan, can we become truly fearless on this earth, free from the fear of losing our life, property, status, title, or comfort; free from the threat of tyrants, the power of armies, and the day of trouble. Buchanan reawakens the instinctive yearning for things above, showing that only the heavenly minded are of much earthly good.

The Holy Wild
Trusting in the Character of God

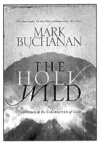

Our perception of God makes a difference in every crevice of our character, from our inner anxieties to our public conversations. It determines whether we're trusting or suspicious, whether we're happy or discontent—and whether or not we can rely on God matters mightily on the day of our death. Mark Buchanan continues his penetrating exploration of the God we worship. Bravely and honestly, he poses the direst question of human existence: Can God be trusted?

It's life drunk deeply, lived to the hilt—where we walk with the God who is surprising, dangerous, and mysterious. It's the terrain where God doesn't make sense out of our disasters and our boredom, but keeps meeting us in the thick of them.

But unless we trust in His character, we'll never venture in. We will sit at the stream all day, dying of thirst, but not daring to drink. To follow God is to drink and drink from the stream, even if it means—especially if it means—getting swallowed up.

Let Mark Buchanan show you the entrance to the *Holy Wild*, where you can live face-to-face with the beautiful, dangerous God of creation.

The Rest of God
Restoring Your Soul by Restoring Sabbath

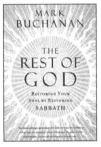

Widely-acclaimed author Mark Buchanan states that what we've really lost is "the rest of God-the rest God bestows and, with it, that part of Himself we can know only through stillness." Stillness as a virtue is a foreign concept in our society, but there is wisdom in God's own rhythm of work and rest. Jesus practiced Sabbath among those who had turned it into a dismal thing, a day for murmuring and finger-wagging, and He reminded them of the day's true purpose: liberation-to heal, to feed, to rescue, to celebrate, to lavish and relish life abundant.

With this book, Buchanan reminds us of this and gives practical advice for restoring the sabbath in our lives.

Hidden in Plain Sight
The Secret of More

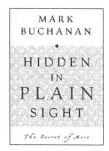

Even for the religious, life is full of questions: What is faith? Can my life be more satisfying? How can I deepen my walk with Christ? What does it mean to be happy? These bubble and boil underneath the surface of our everyday life. And though we ignore them, we know they point us to realms of wisdom or even mystery-to something more.

Author Mark Buchanan asked these same questions. "I want more, God," he prayed-and the answer was more than he was looking for. It was right there, hidden in plain sight among the syllables and syntax of a few words of advice from the apostle Peter. With time and experience, Buchanan learned to tease it out, this secret of more, and he wrote a book about it: *Hidden in Plain Sight*. The answer, he discovered, is an investigation of the cross. The answer is an excavation of the virtues. The answer urges us passionately to "make every effort." And, Buchanan tells us, the answer is worth it.

Spiritual Rhythm
Being with Jesus Every Season of Your Soul

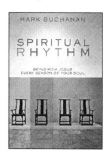

"Abide in me," Jesus tells us, "and you will bear much fruit." Yet too often we forget that fruit needs different seasons in order to grow. We measure our spiritual maturity by how much we do rather than how we are responding to our current spiritual season. In Spiritual Rhythm, Mark Buchanan replaces our spirituality of busyness with a spirituality of abiding. Sometimes we are busy, sometimes still, sometimes pushing with all we've got, sometimes waiting. This model of the spiritual life measures and produces growth by asking: Are we living in rhythm with the season we are in? With the lyrical writing for which he is known, Mark invites us to respond to every season of the heart, whether we are flourishing and fruitful, stark and dismal, or cool and windy. In comparing spiritual rhythms to the seasons of the year, he shows us what to expect from each season and how embracing the seasons causes our spiritual lives to prosper.

As he draws on the powerful words of Scripture, Mark explores what activities are suitable or necessary in each season—and what activities are useless or even harmful in that season. Throughout the book, Mark weaves together stories of young and old, men and women, families, couples, and individuals who are in or have been through a particular season of the heart. As Mark writes, "I pray that this book meets you in whatever season you're in, and prepares you for whatever seasons await. I pray that it helps you find your voice, your stride, your rhythm, in season or out. Mostly, I pray that you, with or without my help, find Christ wherever you are. And that, even more, you discover that wherever you are, he's found you."

Your Church Is Too Safe
Why Following Christ Turns the World Upside-Down

"These men who have turned the world upside down have come here also." – Acts 17:6. That was the startled cry, circa 50 AD, from a hastily assembled mob in Thessalonica. Paul and Silas had been arrested for preaching the gospel. They were viewed as revolutionaries, dangerous men who were upsetting the status quo and inciting riots. But they were just two ordinary men, walking in the power of God, sharing a simple message of his love and grace. It's been a while since we've seen the likes of this.

If you ever find church boring or you believe something is missing from our churches today, you aren't alone. Mark Buchanan believes there is a visible gap between the life Jesus offered to us and the life we're living, between the church Jesus envisioned and the church we see today. When Jesus announced that the Kingdom was at hand, this can't be what he meant. Instead of counting everything loss to be found in Christ, we've made it our priority to be safe instead of dangerous, nice instead of holy. Author and pastor Mark Buchanan believes that we need to recover a simple idea: that God meant his church to be both good news and bad news, an aroma and a stench—a disruptive force to whoever or whatever opposes the Kingdom of God and a healing, liberating power to those who seek it.

God Speed
Walking as a Spiritual Practice

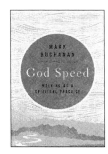

What happens when we literally walk out our Christian life? We discover the joy of traveling at the speed of our soul. We often act as if faith is only about the mind. But what about our bodies? What does our physical being have to do with our spiritual life? When the Bible exhorts us to walk in the light, or walk by faith, or walk in truth, it means these things literally as much as figuratively. The Christian faith always involves walking out, as again and again we find the holy in the ordinary.

"Come, follow me," Jesus said, and then he was off. The most obvious thing about Jesus's method of discipleship, in fact, is that he walked and invited others to walk with him. Jesus is always "on the way," "arriving," "leaving," "approaching," "coming upon." It's in the walking that his disciples are taught, formed, tested, empowered, and released.

Part theology, part history, part field guide, *God Speed* explores walking as spiritual formation, walking as healing, walking as exercise, walking as prayer, walking as pilgrimage, suffering, friendship, and attentiveness. It is a book about being alongside the God who, incarnate in Jesus, turns to us as he passes by—always on foot—and says simply, "Come, follow me."

With practical insight and biblical reflections told in his distinct voice, Buchanan provides specific walking exercises so you can immediately implement the practice of going "God speed." Whether you are walking around the neighborhood or hiking in the mountains, walking offers the potential to awaken your life with Christ as it revives body and soul.

The Four Best Places to Live
Discovering Worship, Prayer, Expectancy and Love

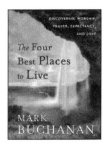

Of all the places to live on Earth, what are the best? Every year, the United Nations determines which countries answer this question. Money magazine asks the same question about cities across the United States. Forbes magazine completed a similar assessment on a global scale.

In *The Four Best Places to Live*, Mark Buchanan evaluates the four best places to live—not according to the United Nations, Money, or Forbes—but according to God and Scripture. Where do we find the greatest joy, peace, and wisdom? Where can we go to experience the deepest sense of belonging? Is there a place that abounds with adventure where we can also feel safe, refreshed, and joyful? With compelling insight, Buchanan explores what God has revealed in His Word about where we become most alive, become most fully ourselves, and can dwell most closely with Him.

Made in the USA
San Bernardino, CA
21 June 2020